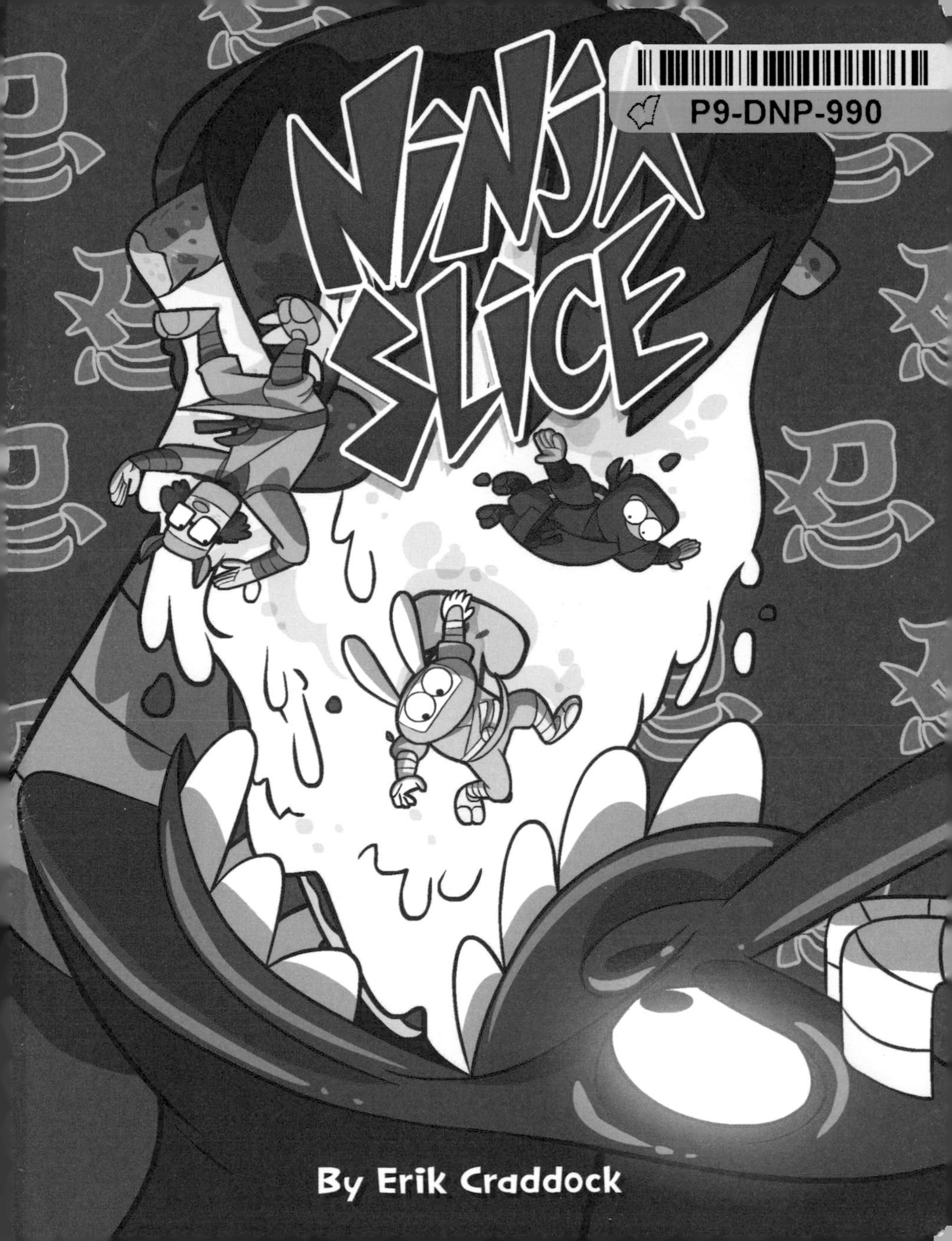
NINJA SLICE
By Erik Craddock

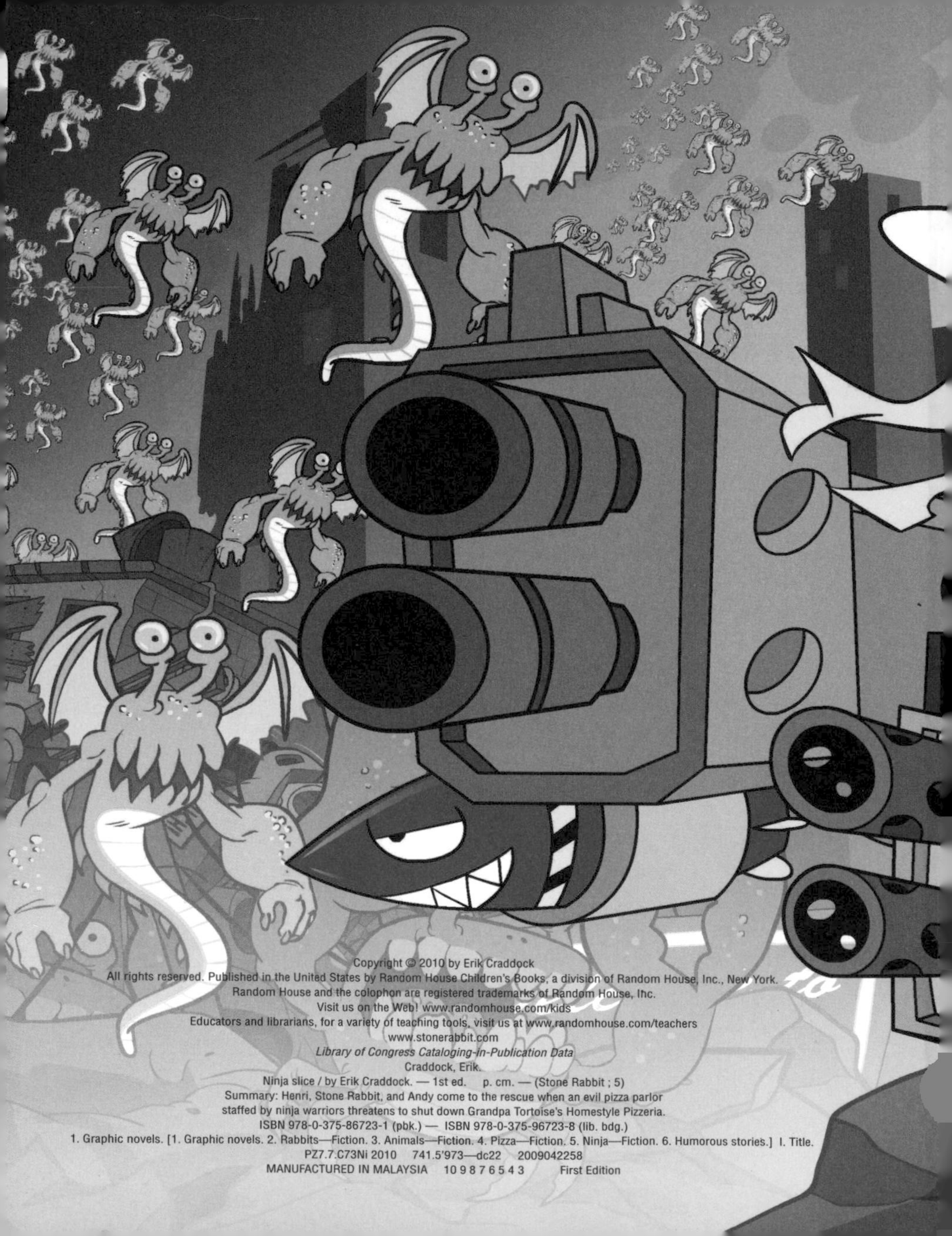

Visit us on the Web! www.randomhouse.com/kids
Educators and librarians, for a variety of teaching tools, visit us at www.randomhouse.com/teachers
www.stonerabbit.com
Library of Congress Cataloging-in-Publication Data
Craddock, Erik.
Ninja slice / by Erik Craddock. — 1st ed. p. cm. — (Stone Rabbit ; 5)
Summary: Henri, Stone Rabbit, and Andy come to the rescue when an evil pizza parlor staffed by ninja warriors threatens to shut down Grandpa Tortoise's Homestyle Pizzeria.
ISBN 978-0-375-86723-1 (pbk.) — ISBN 978-0-375-96723-8 (lib. bdg.)
1. Graphic novels. [1. Graphic novels. 2. Rabbits—Fiction. 3. Animals—Fiction. 4. Pizza—Fiction. 5. Ninja—Fiction. 6. Humorous stories.] I. Title.
PZ7.7.C73Ni 2010 741.5'973—dc22 2009042258
MANUFACTURED IN MALAYSIA 10 9 8 7 6 5 4 3 First Edition

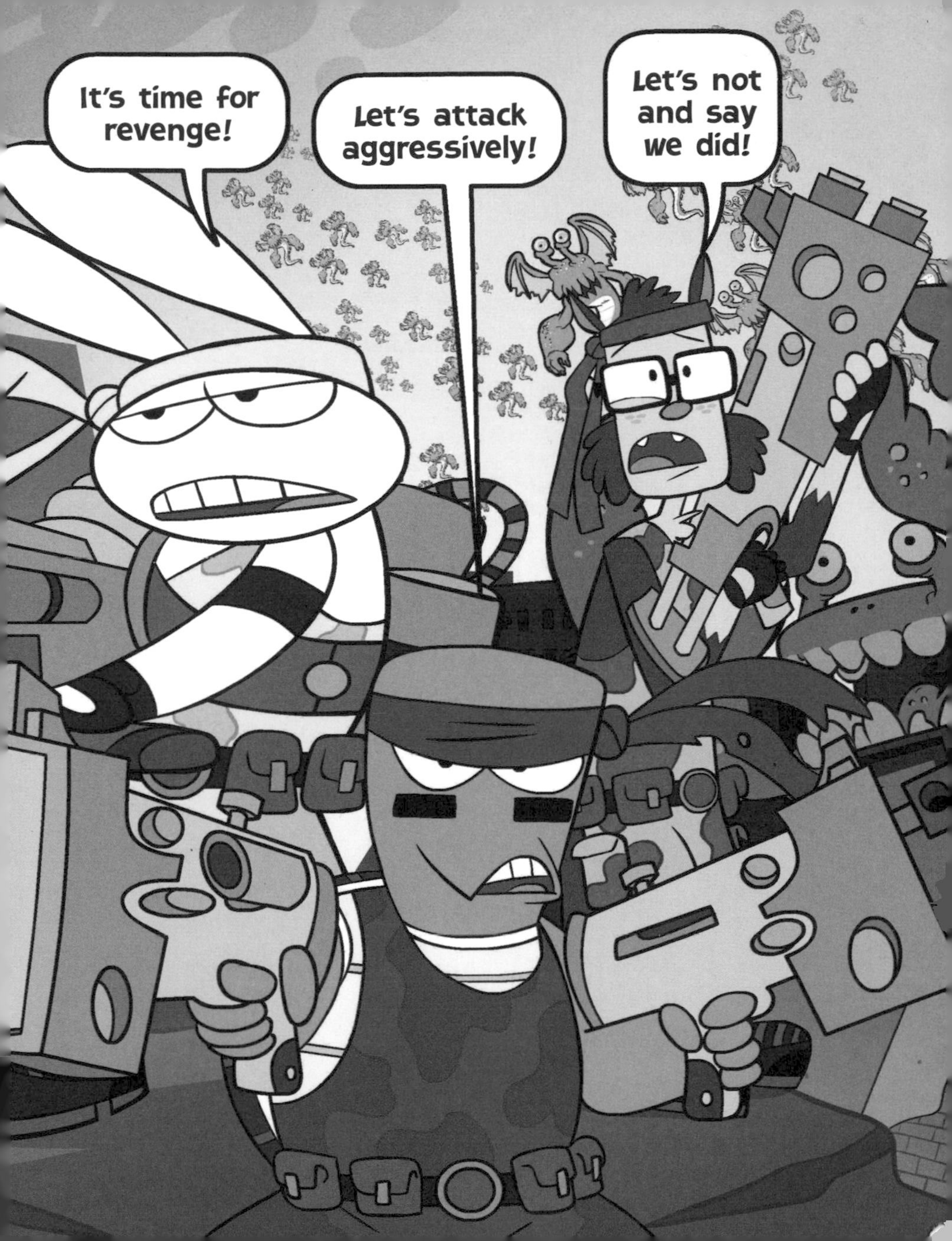
It's time for revenge!
Let's attack aggressively!
Let's not and say we did!

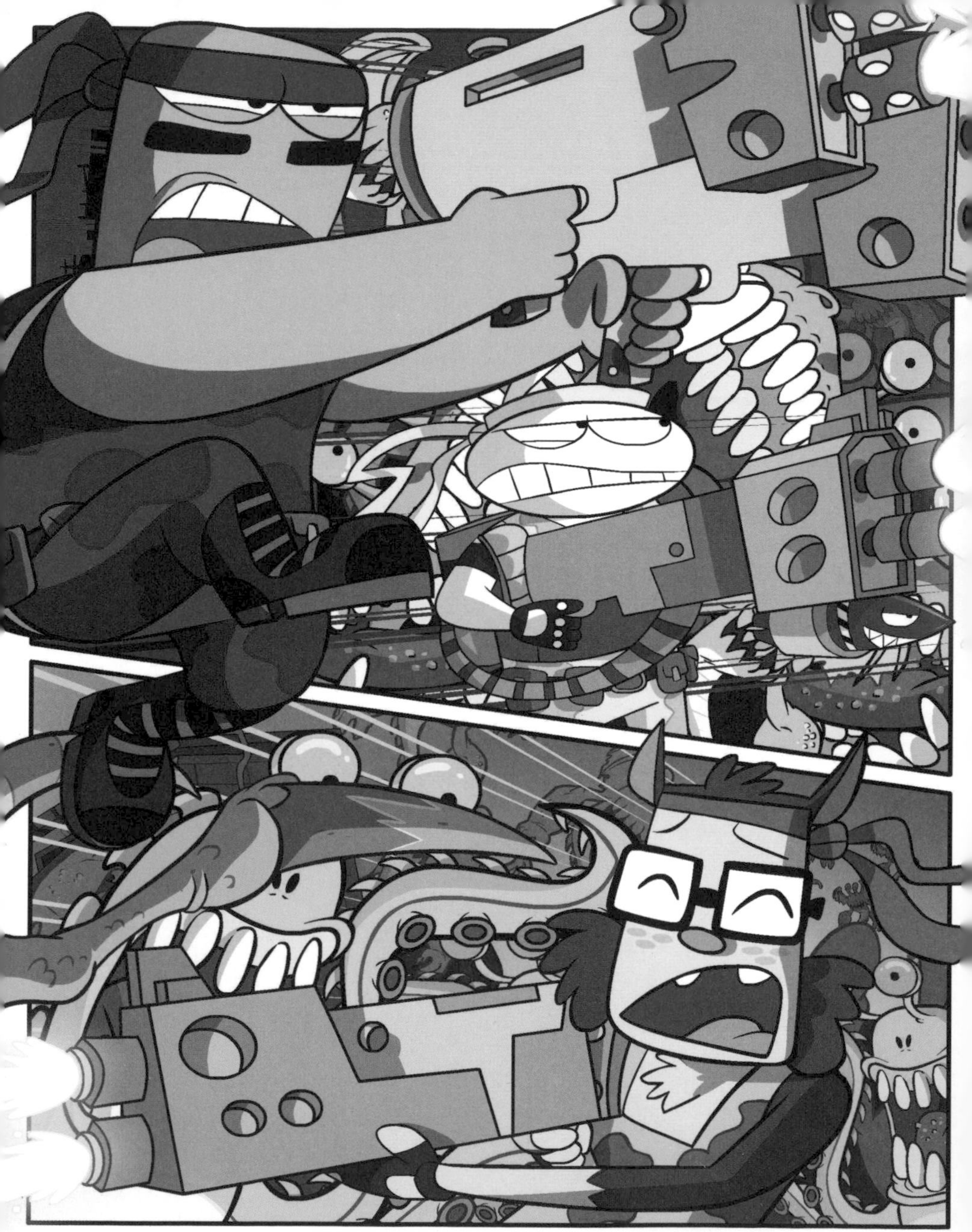

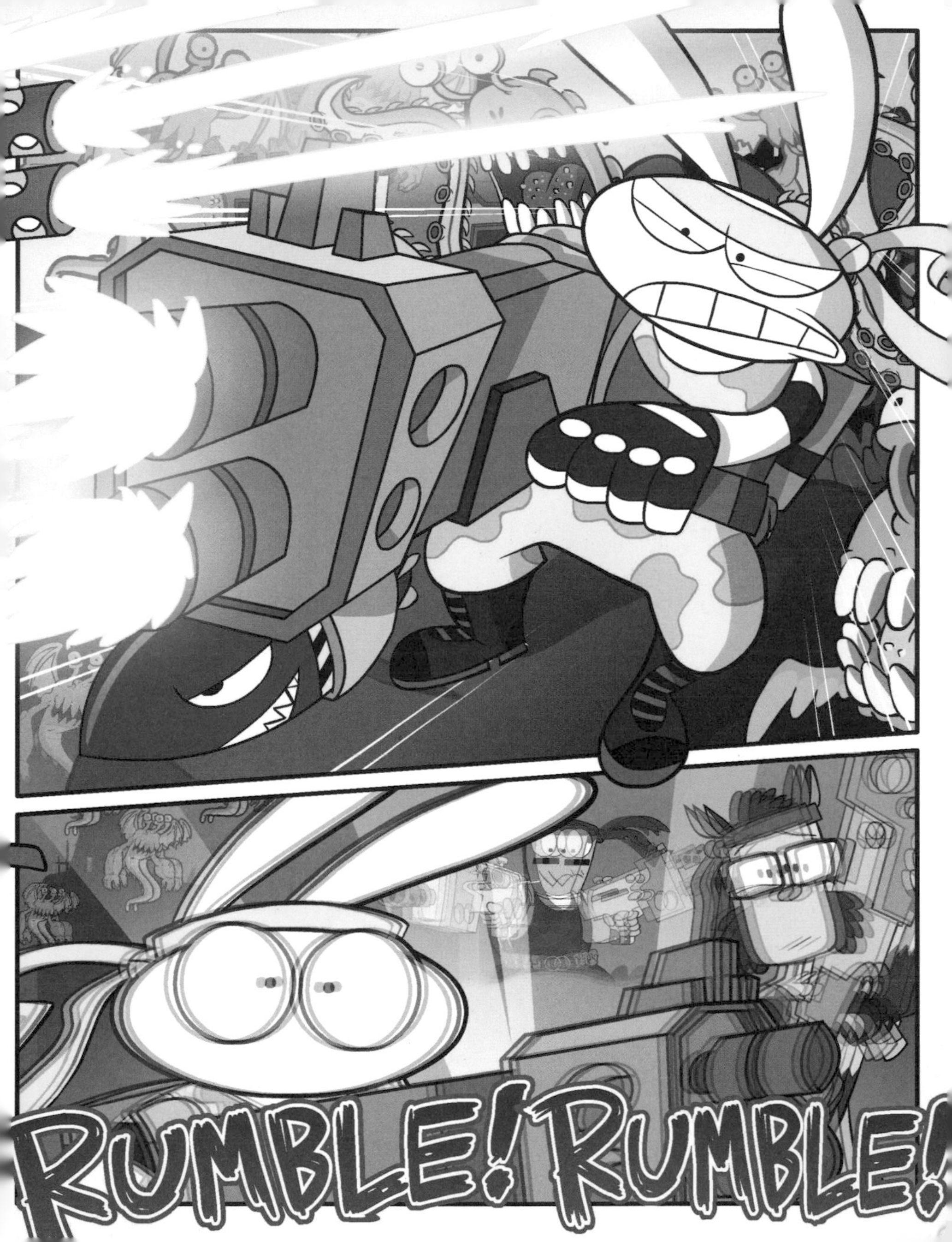
RUMBLE! RUMBLE!

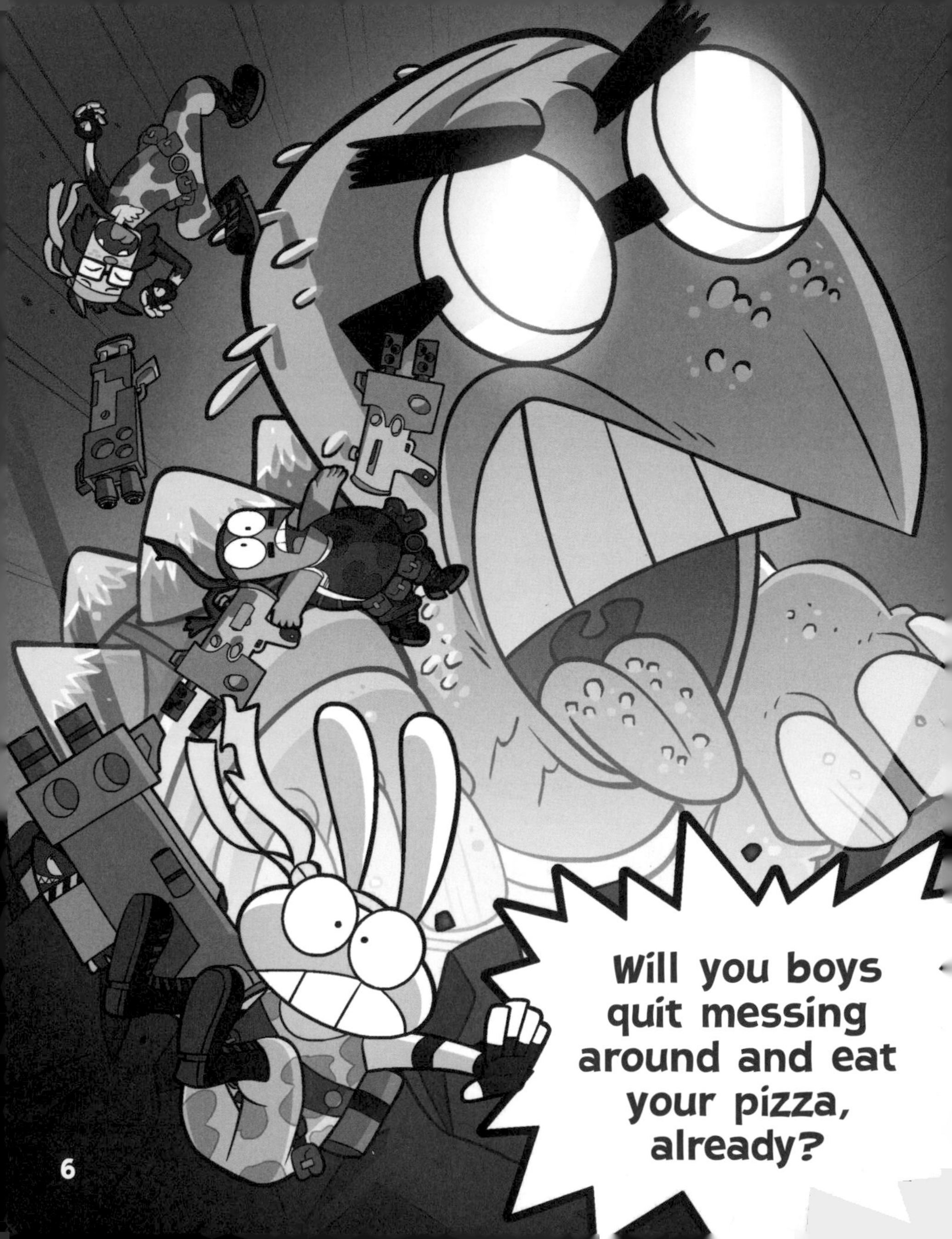
Will you boys quit messing around and eat your pizza, already?

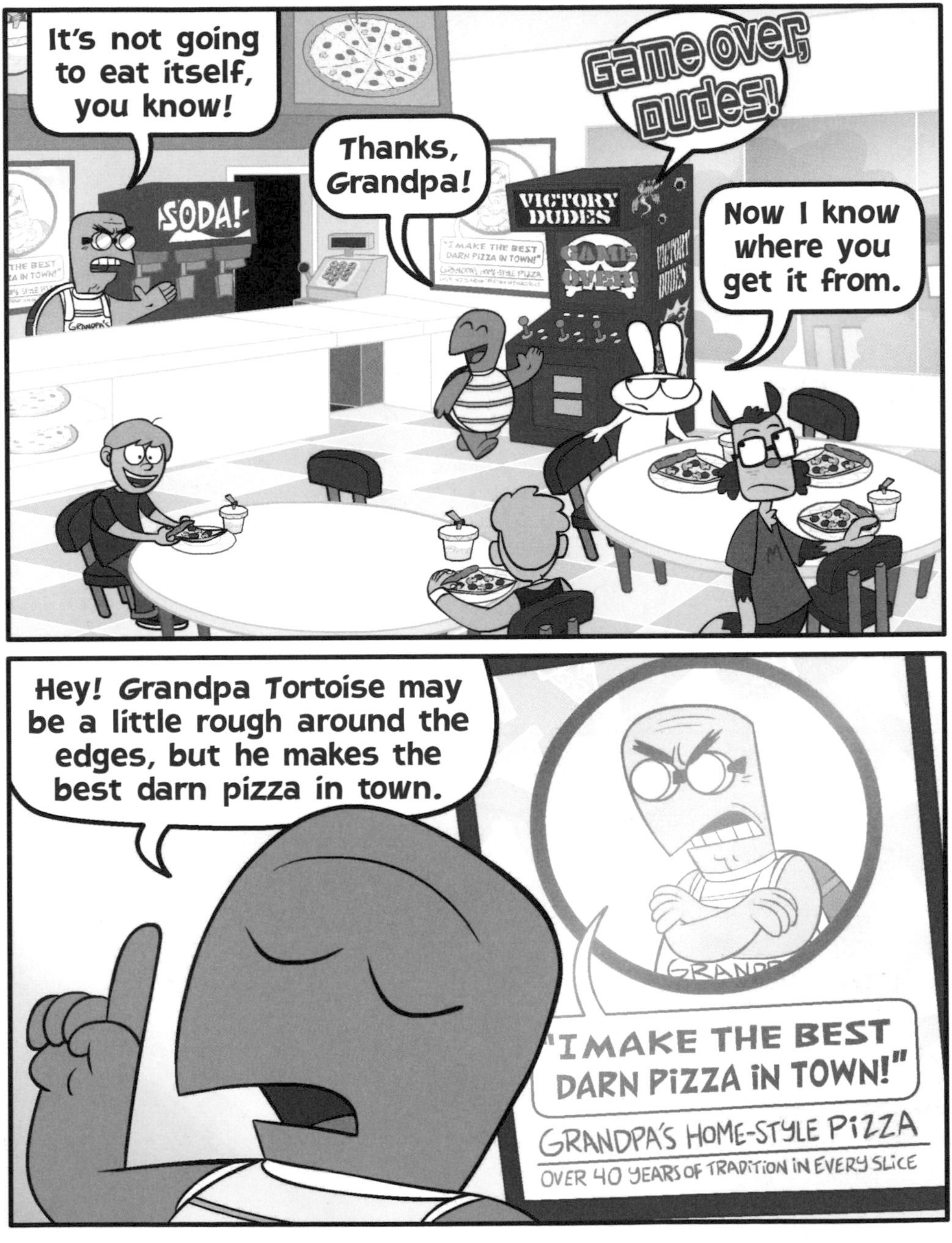

It's not going to eat itself, you know!
SODA!
Thanks, Grandpa!
VICTORY DUDES
Game over, dudes!
Now I know where you get it from.
Hey! *Grandpa Tortoise* may be a little rough around the edges, but he makes the best darn pizza in town.
"I MAKE THE BEST DARN PIZZA IN TOWN!"
GRANDPA'S HOME-STYLE PIZZA
OVER 40 YEARS OF TRADITION IN EVERY SLICE

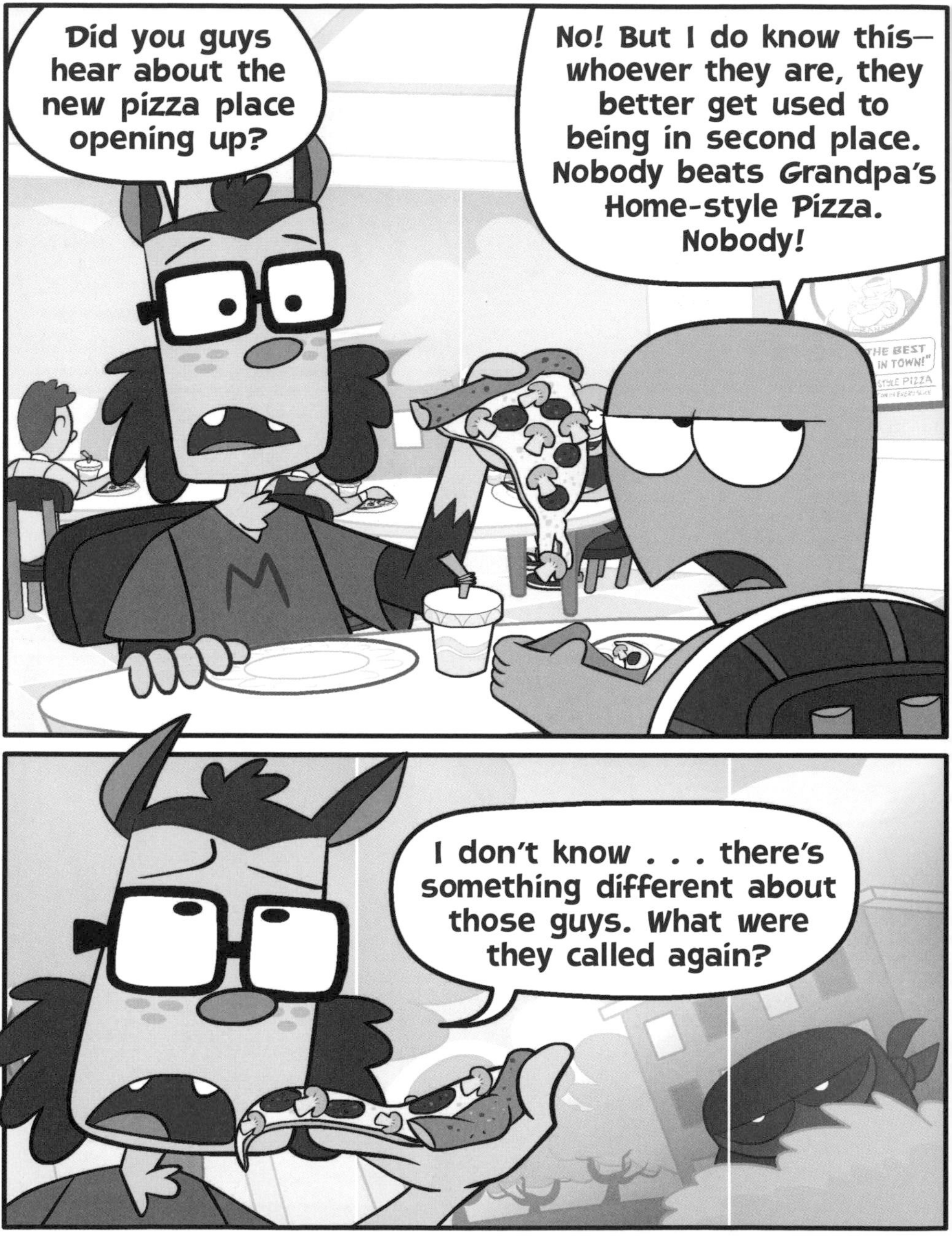
Did you guys hear about the new pizza place opening up?
No! But I do know this—whoever they are, they better get used to being in second place. Nobody beats Grandpa's Home-style Pizza. Nobody!
I don't know . . . there's something different about those guys. What were they called again?

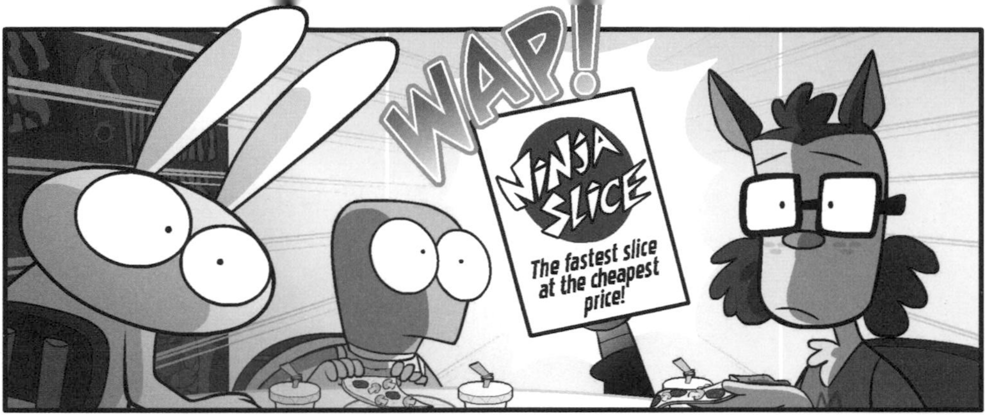
WAP!
NINJA SLICE
The fastest slice at the cheapest price!

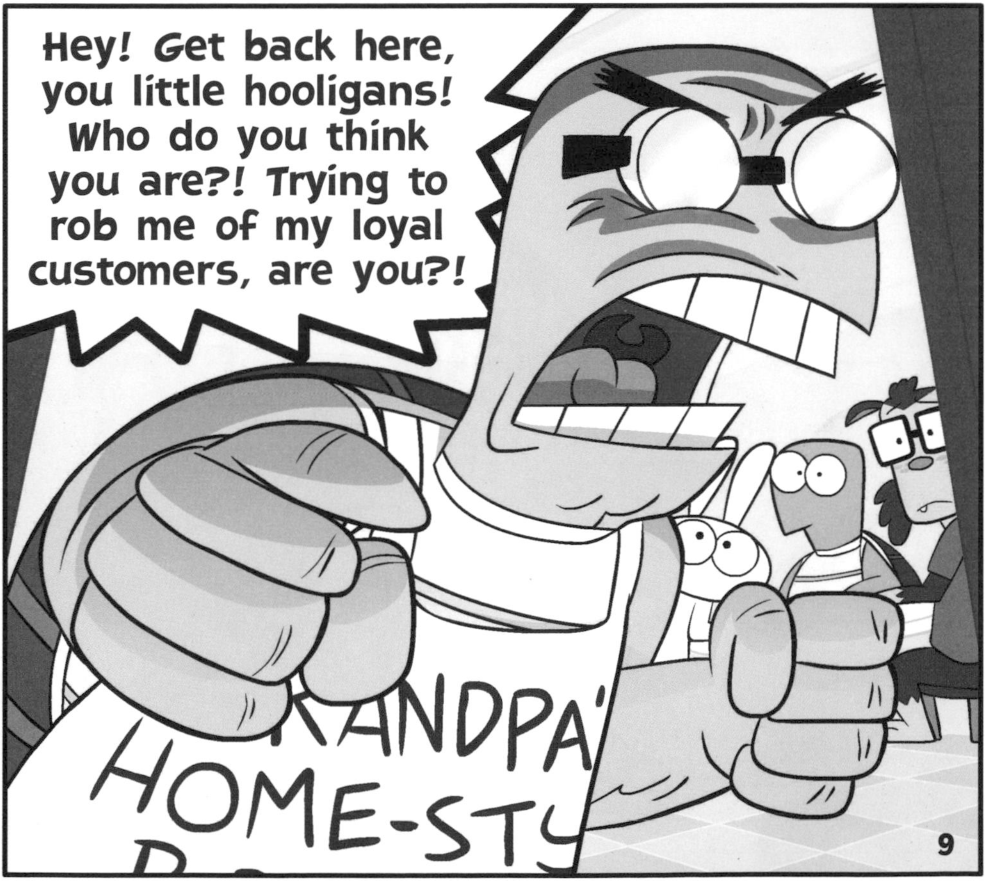
Hey! Get back here, you little hooligans! Who do you think you are?! Trying to rob me of my loyal customers, are you?!
RANDPA'
HOME-ST

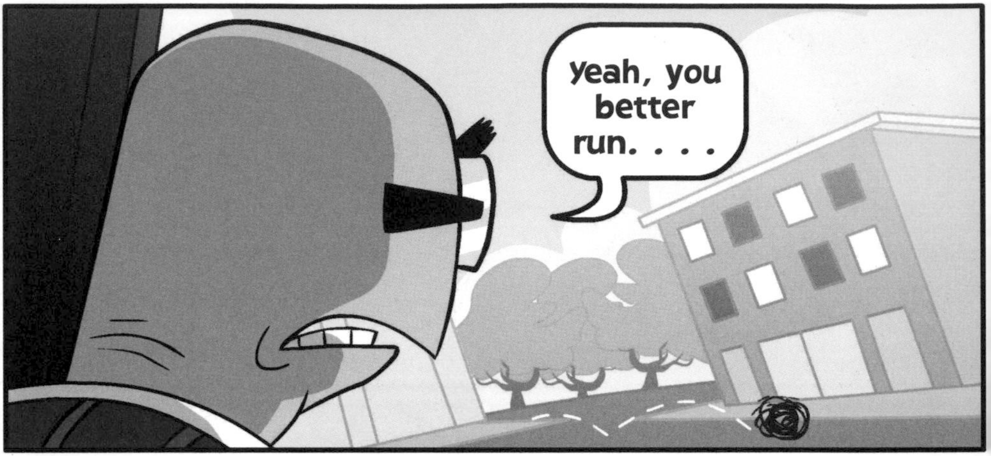
Yeah, you better run. . . .

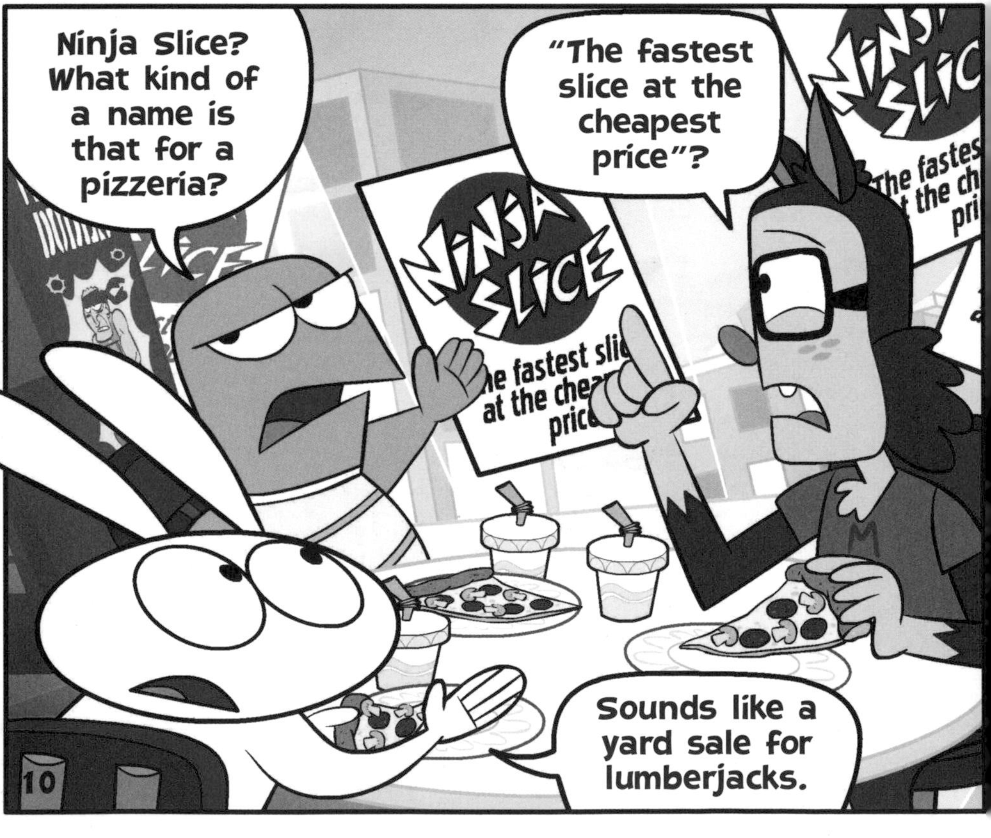
Ninja Slice? What kind of a name is that for a pizzeria?
"The fastest slice at the cheapest price"?
NINJA SLICE
Sounds like a yard sale for lumberjacks.

So you boys want to eat at that Ninja Schlop place, huh? Well, let me tell you something!
SLAM!
You won't find a single knead of love in their dough, nor a shred of cheese spread with joy over their pies! No sir! Those fellows care not for craft nor tradition.
GRANDPA
HOME-STYL
But it's only pizza, Grandpa. Take it easy.
!
PLOP!

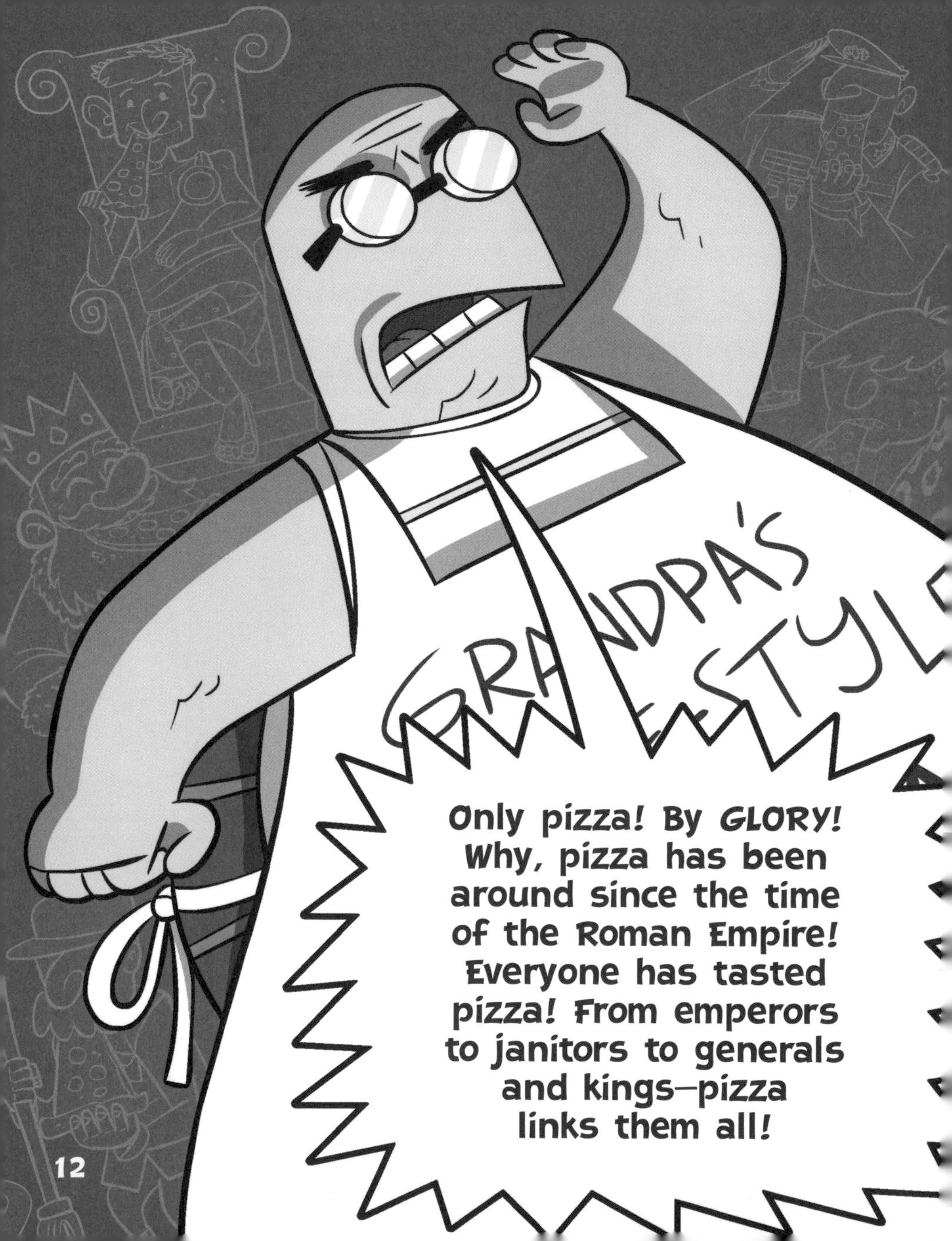
GRANDPA'S STYLE
Only pizza! By GLORY! Why, pizza has been around since the time of the Roman Empire! Everyone has tasted pizza! From emperors to janitors to generals and kings—pizza links them all!

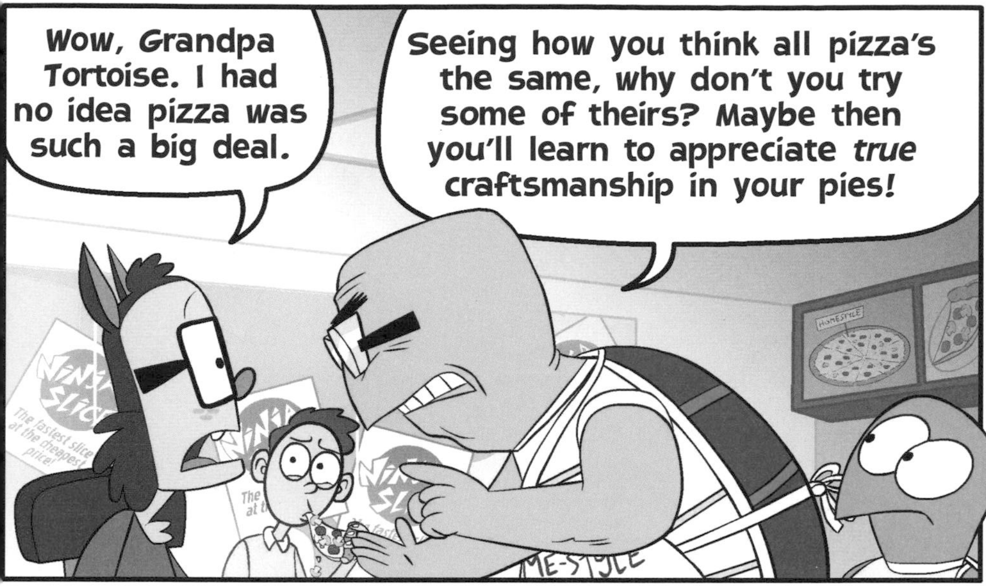
Wow, Grandpa Tortoise. I had no idea pizza was such a big deal.
Seeing how you think all pizza's the same, why don't you try some of theirs? Maybe then you'll learn to appreciate *true* craftsmanship in your pies!
HOMESTYLE
The fastest slice at the cheapest price!
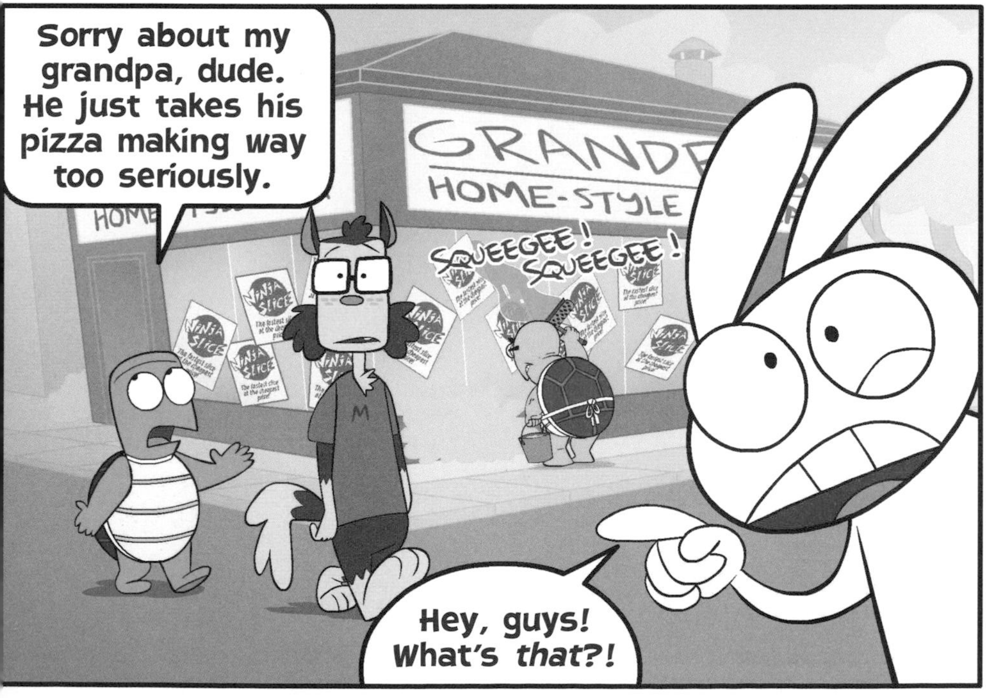
Sorry about my grandpa, dude. He just takes his pizza making way too seriously.
GRAND
HOME-STYLE
SQUEEGEE! SQUEEGEE!
Hey, guys! What's *that*?!

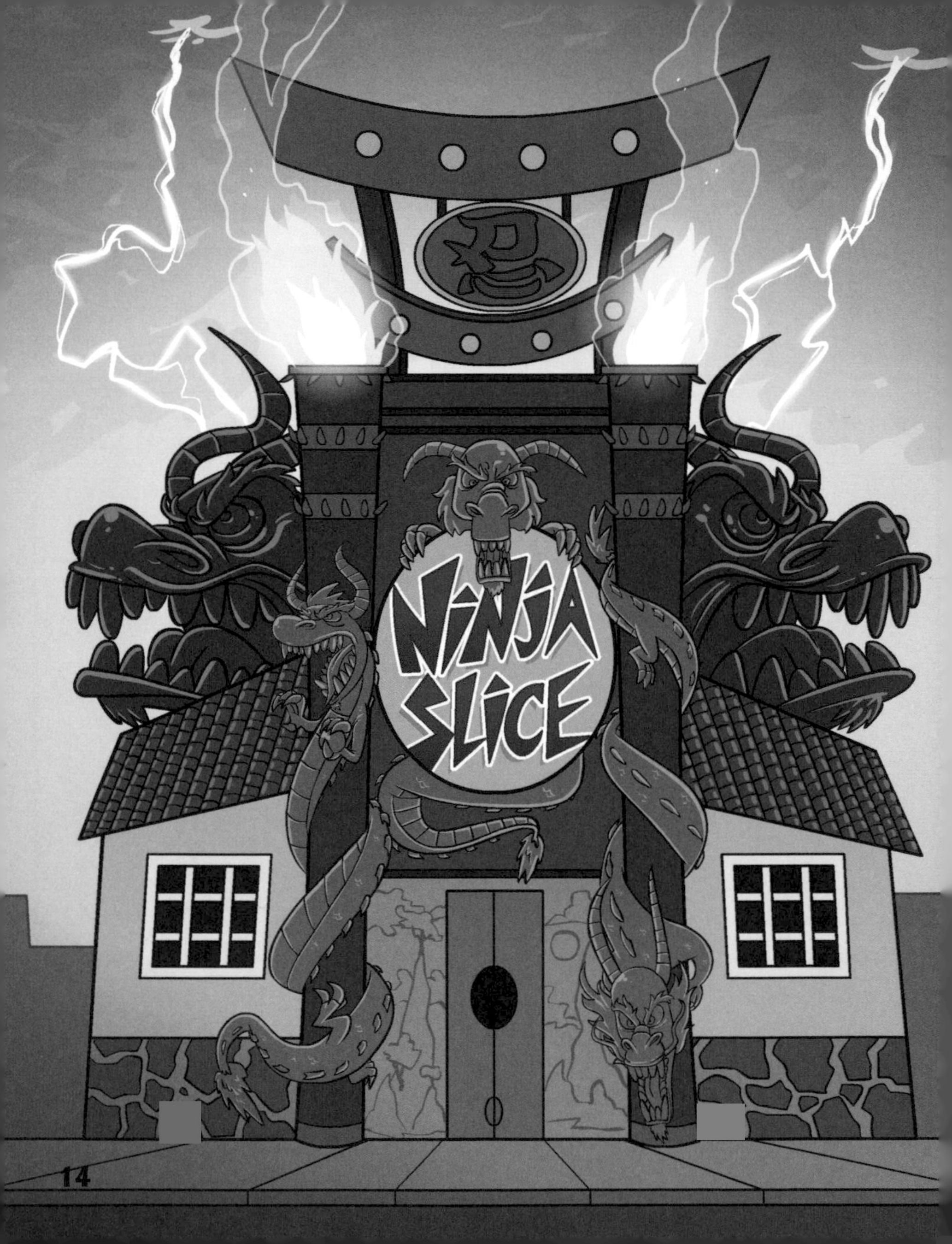
NINJA SLICE

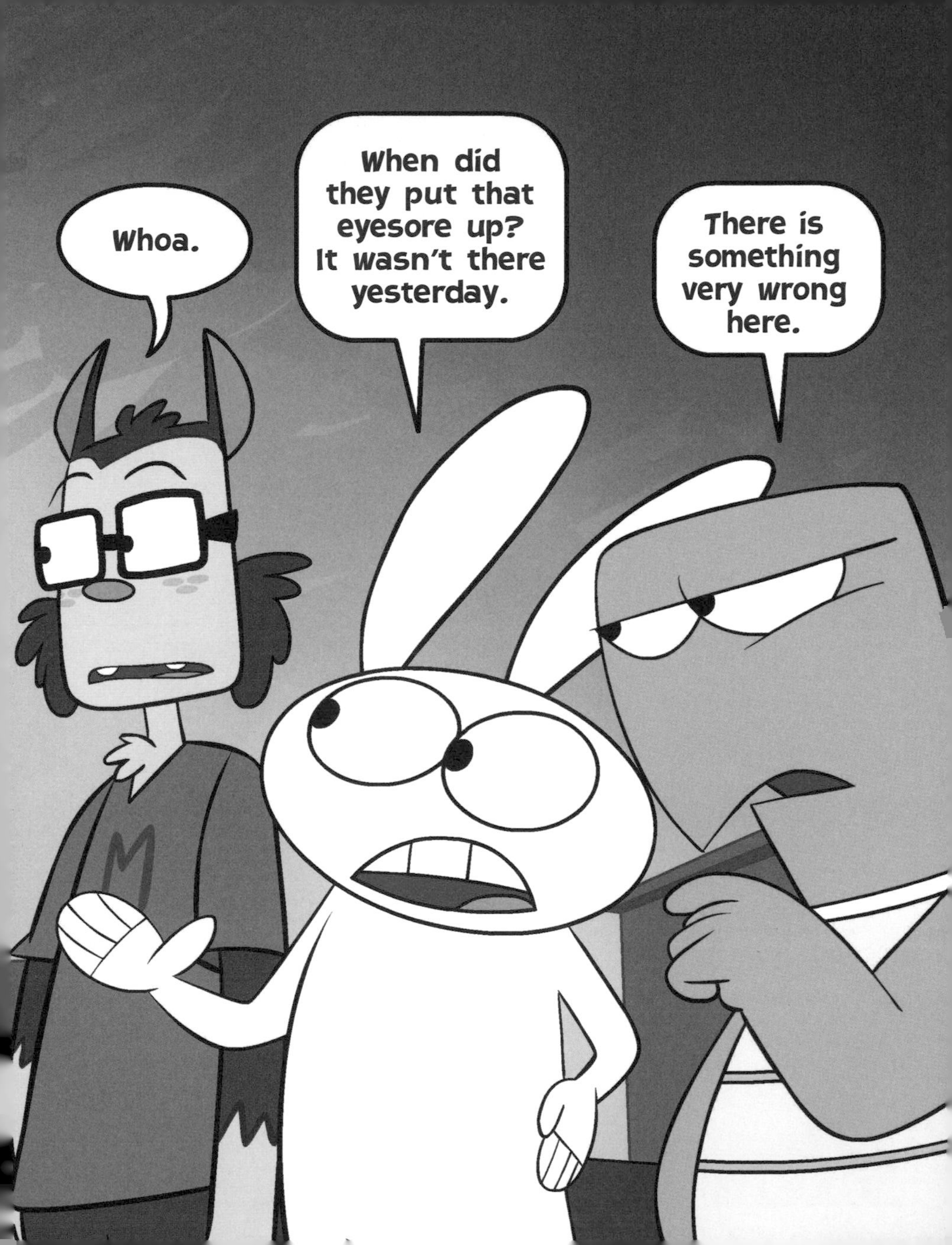
Whoa.
When did they put that eyesore up? It wasn't there yesterday.
There is something very wrong here.

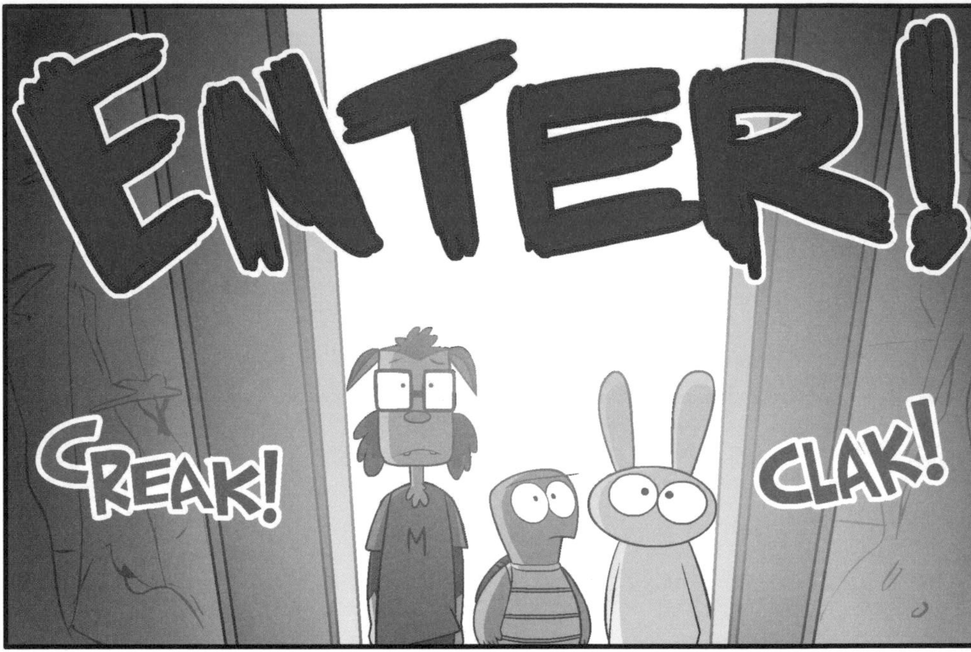
ENTER!
CREAK!
CLAK!

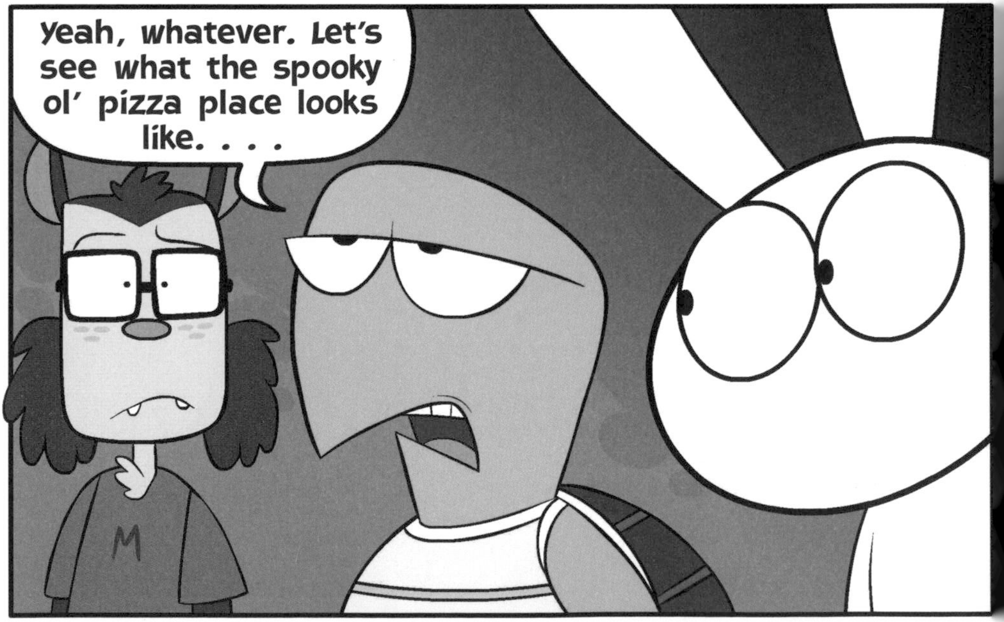
Yeah, whatever. Let's see what the spooky ol' pizza place looks like. . . .

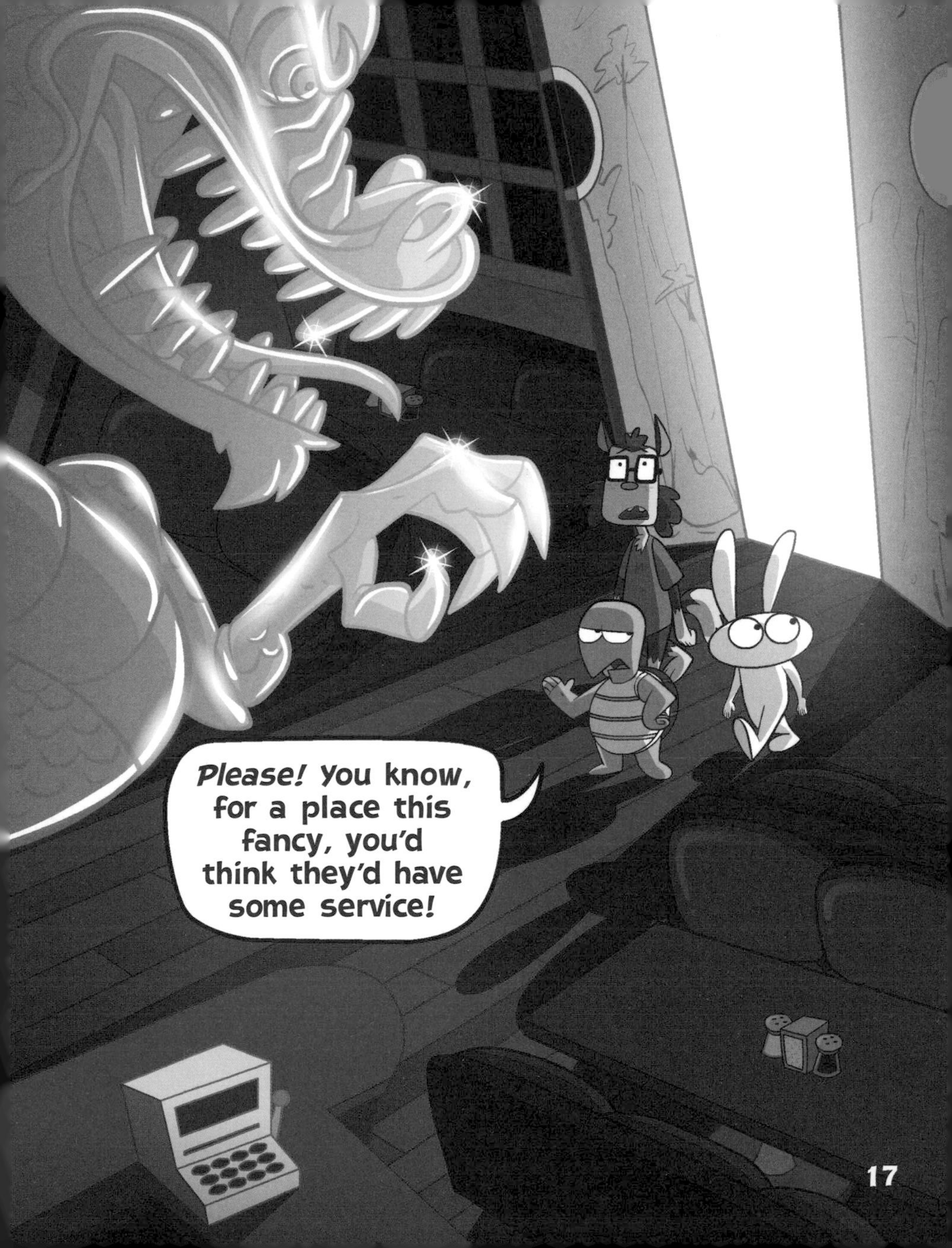
Please! You know, for a place this fancy, you'd think they'd have some service!

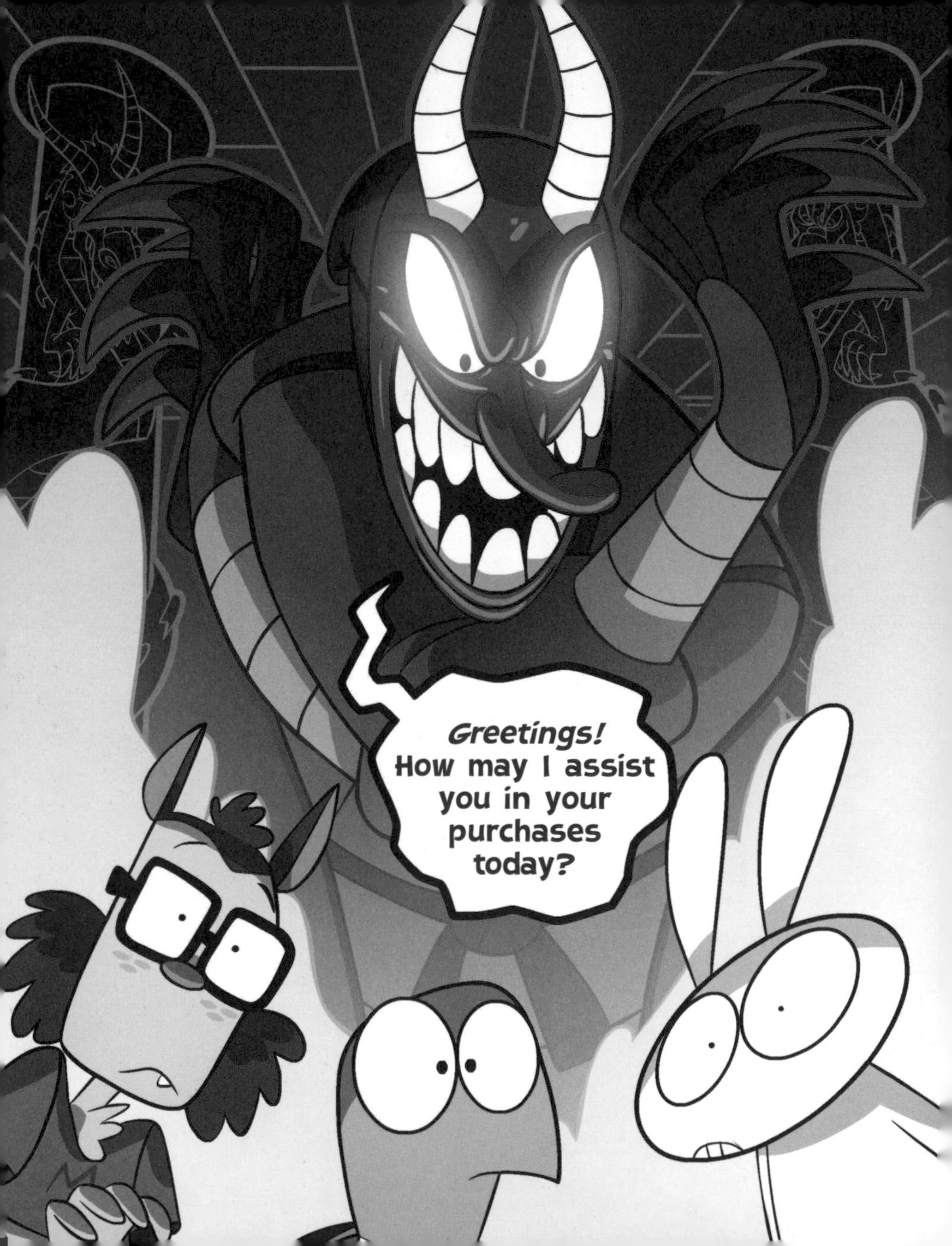
Greetings! How may I assist you in your purchases today?

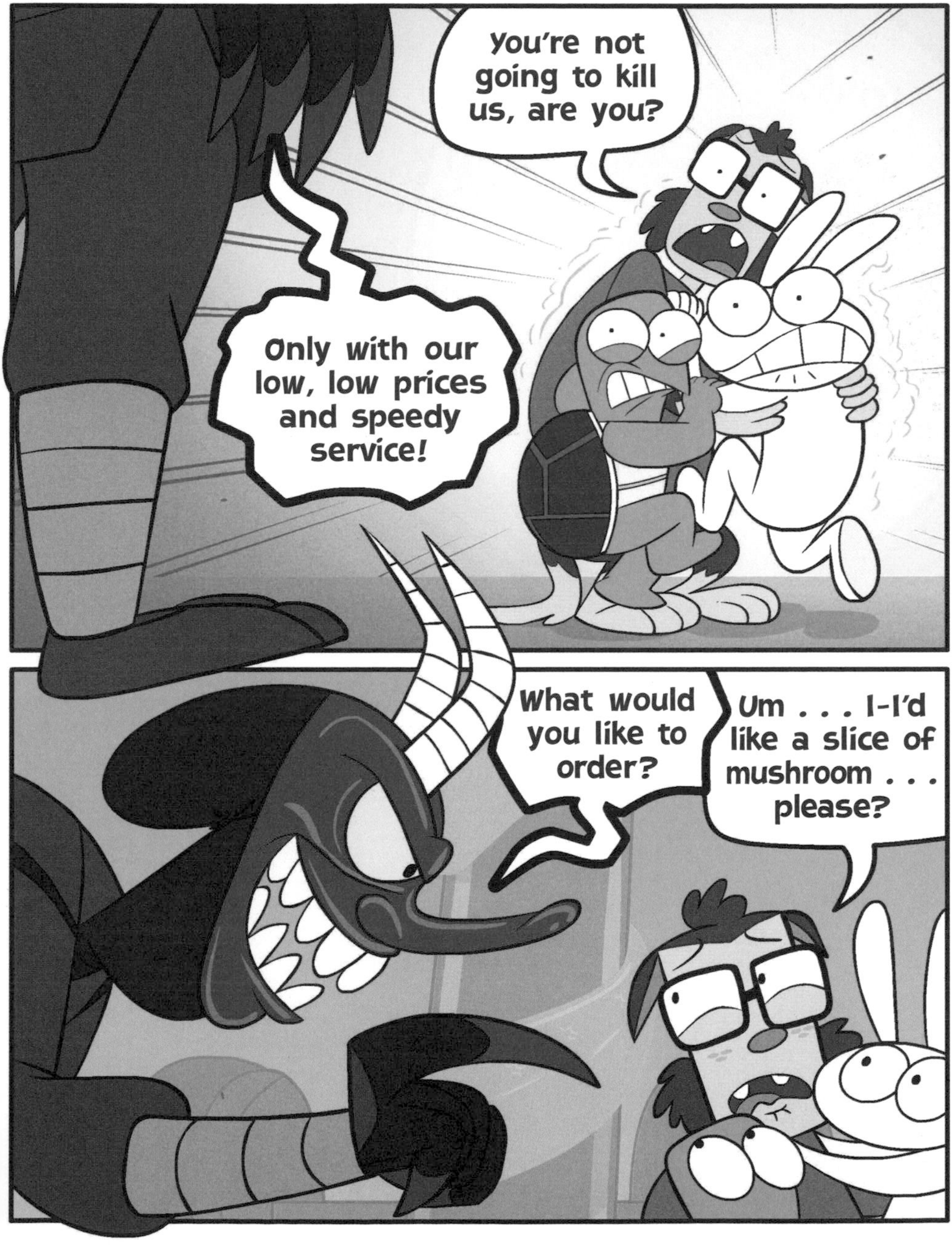
You're not going to kill us, are you?
Only with our low, low prices and speedy service!
What would you like to order?
Um . . . I-I'd like a slice of mushroom . . . please?

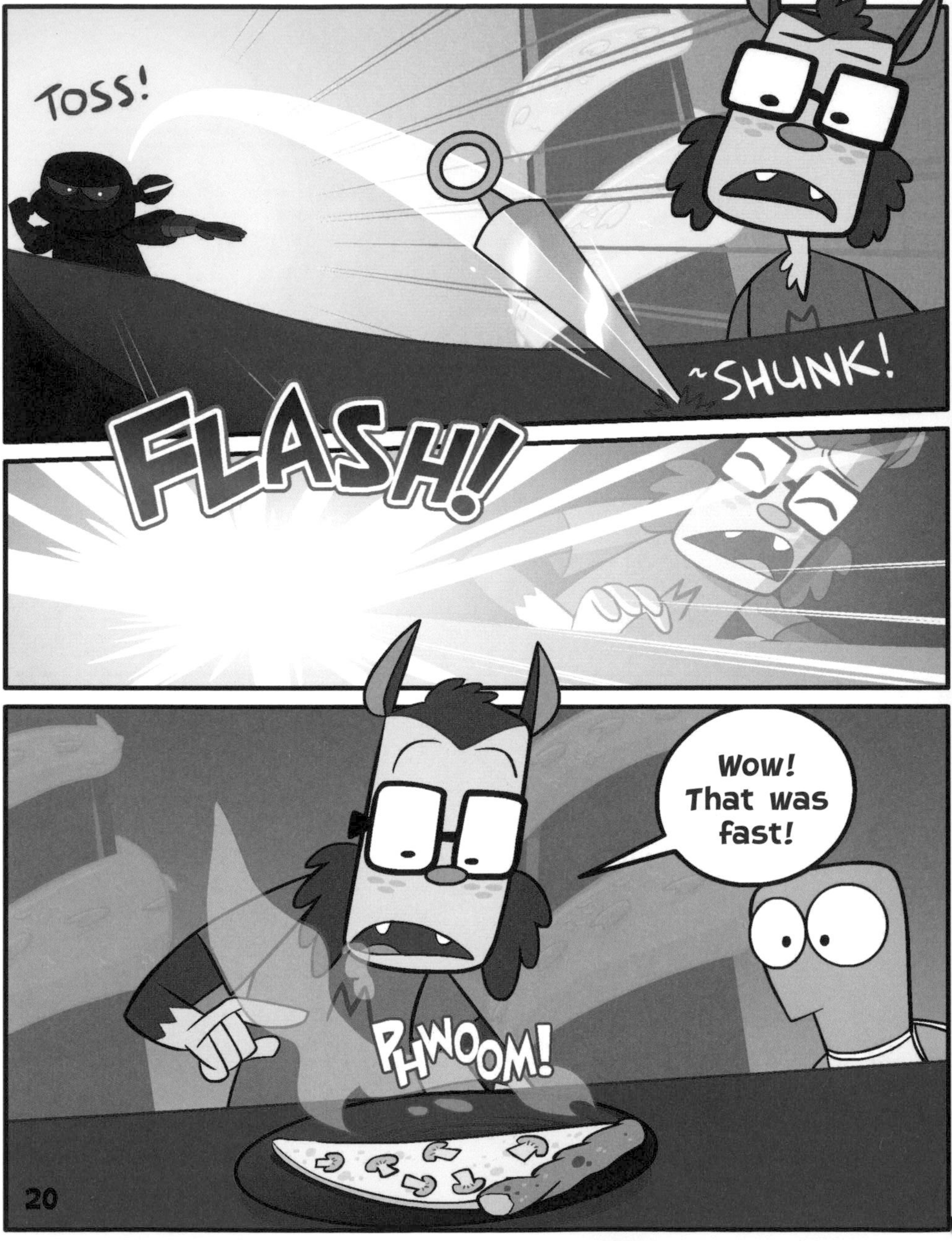
TOSS!
~SHUNK!
FLASH!
Wow! That was fast!
PHWOOM!

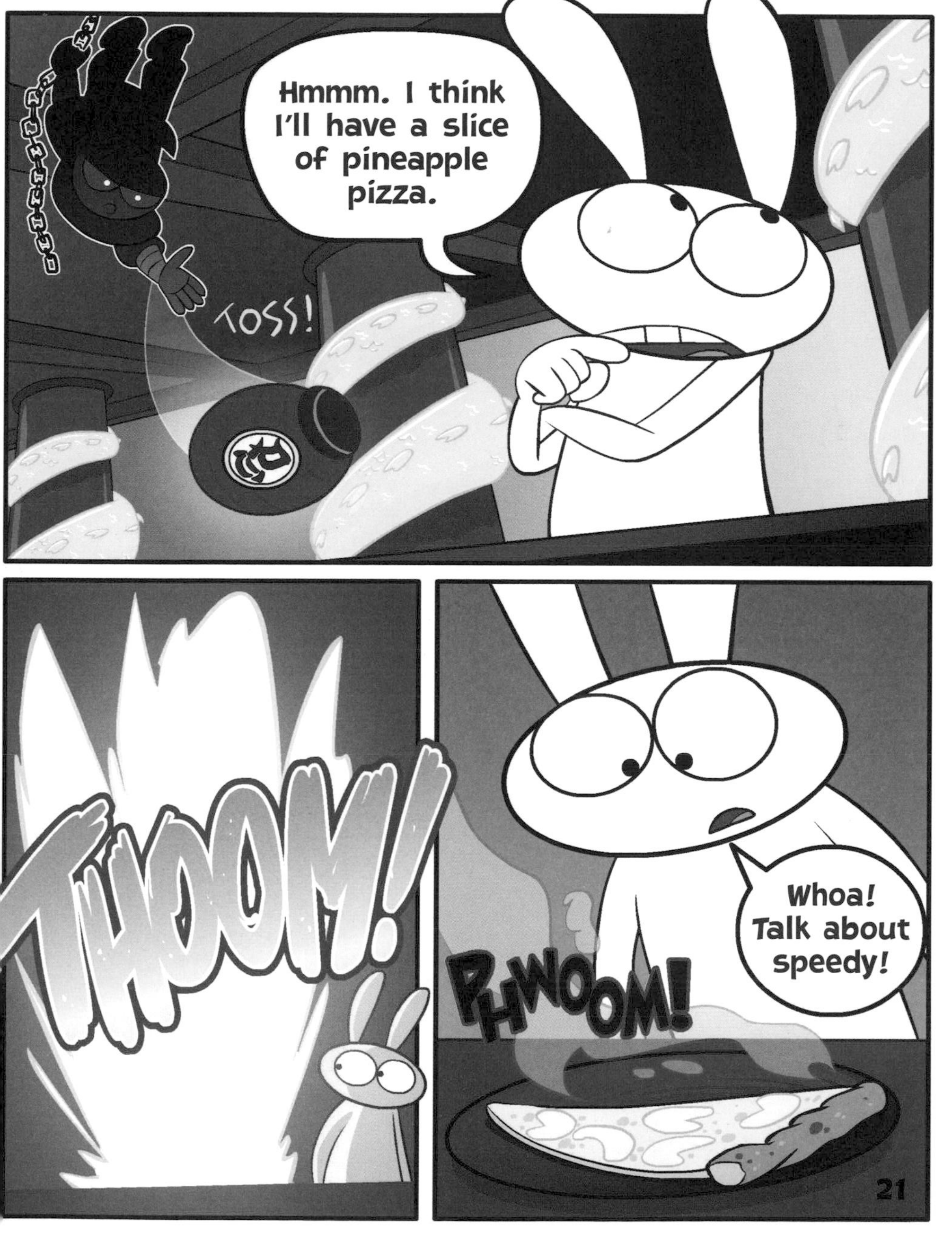
Hmmm. I think I'll have a slice of pineapple pizza.
TOSS!
THOOM!
PHWOOM!
Whoa! Talk about speedy!

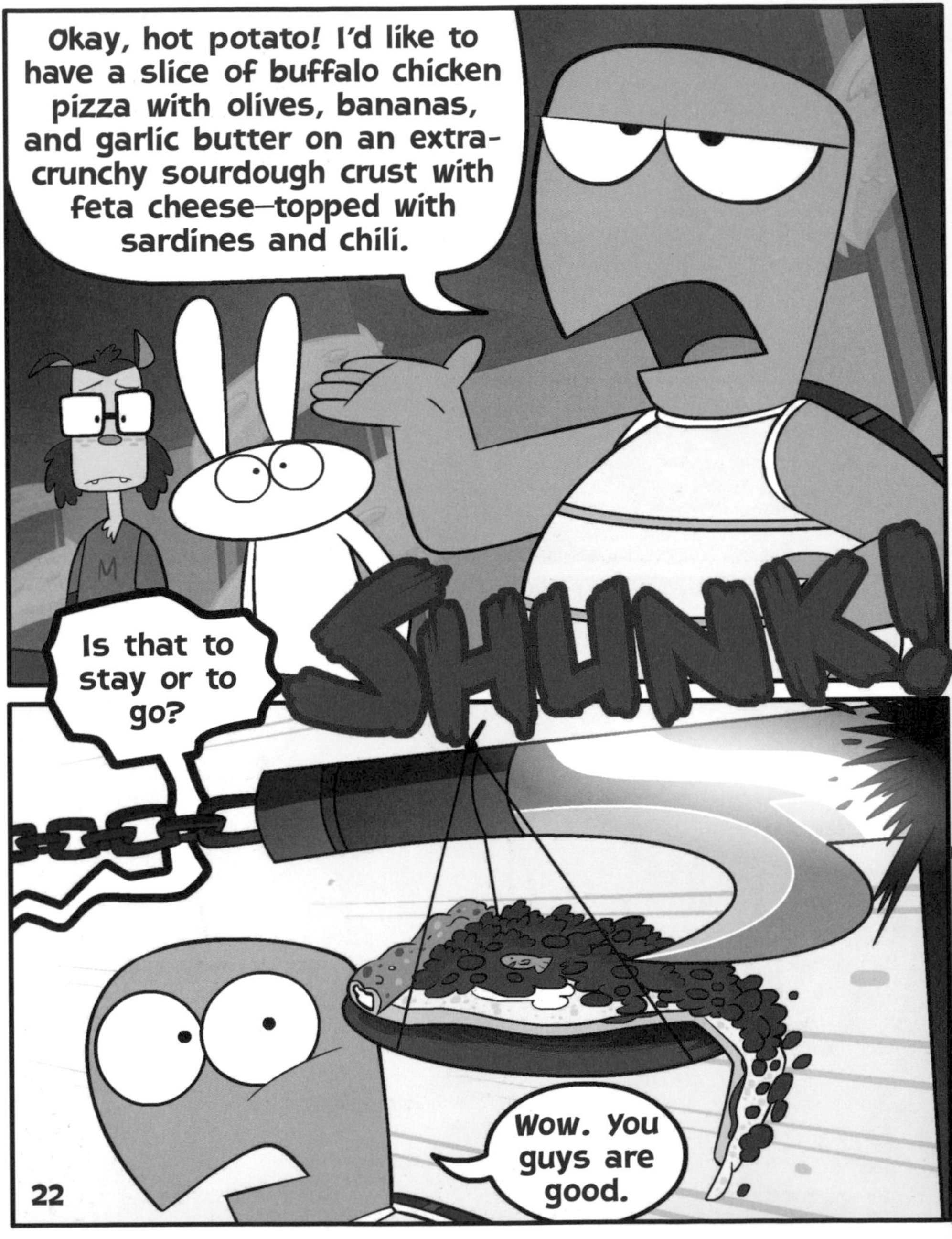
Okay, hot potato! I'd like to have a slice of buffalo chicken pizza with olives, bananas, and garlic butter on an extra-crunchy sourdough crust with feta cheese—topped with sardines and chili.
M
Is that to stay or to go?
SHUNK!
Wow. You guys are good.

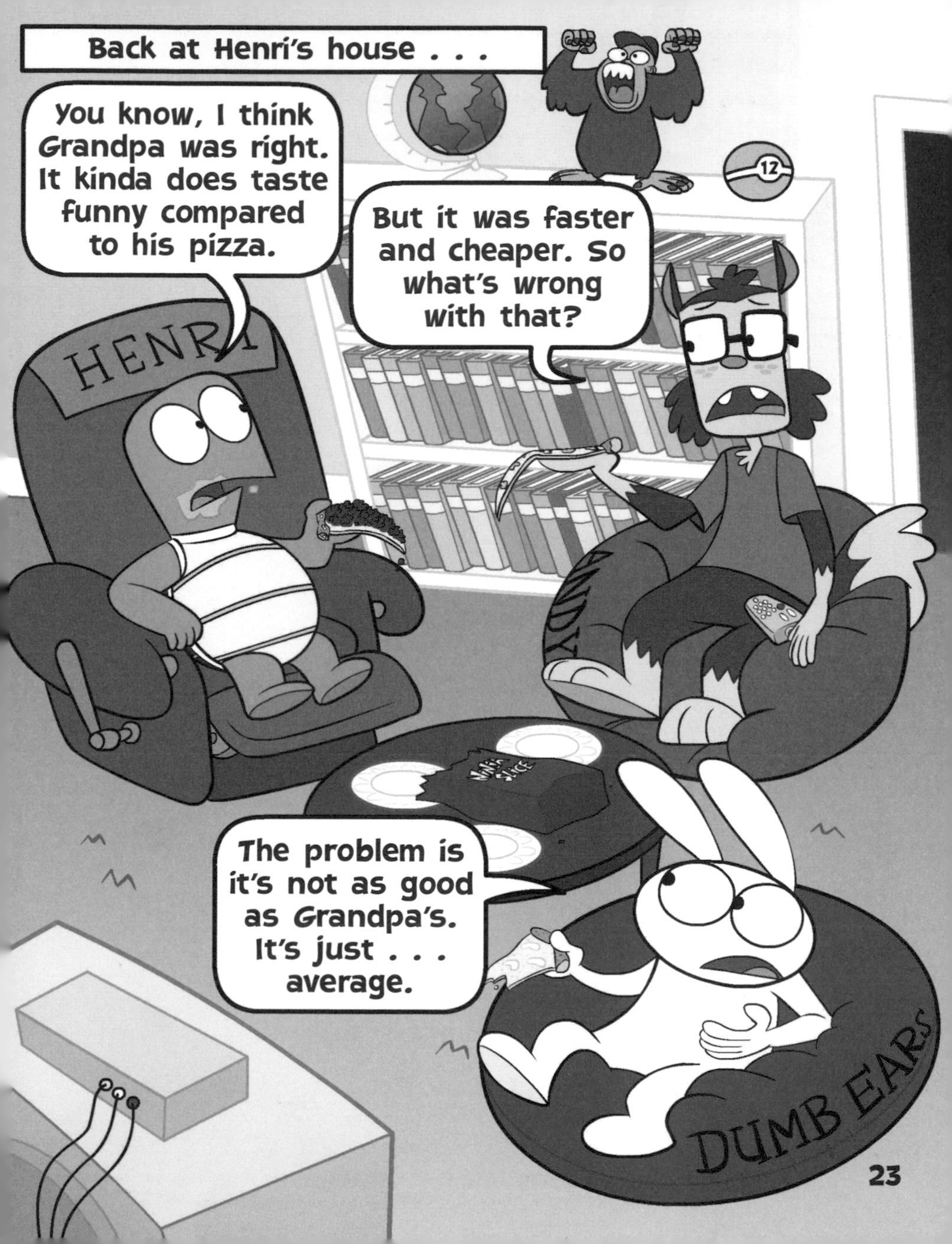
Back at Henri's house . . .
You know, I think Grandpa was right. It kinda does taste funny compared to his pizza.
But it was faster and cheaper. So what's wrong with that?
The problem is it's not as good as Grandpa's. It's just . . . average.
HENRI
ANDY
DUMB EARS

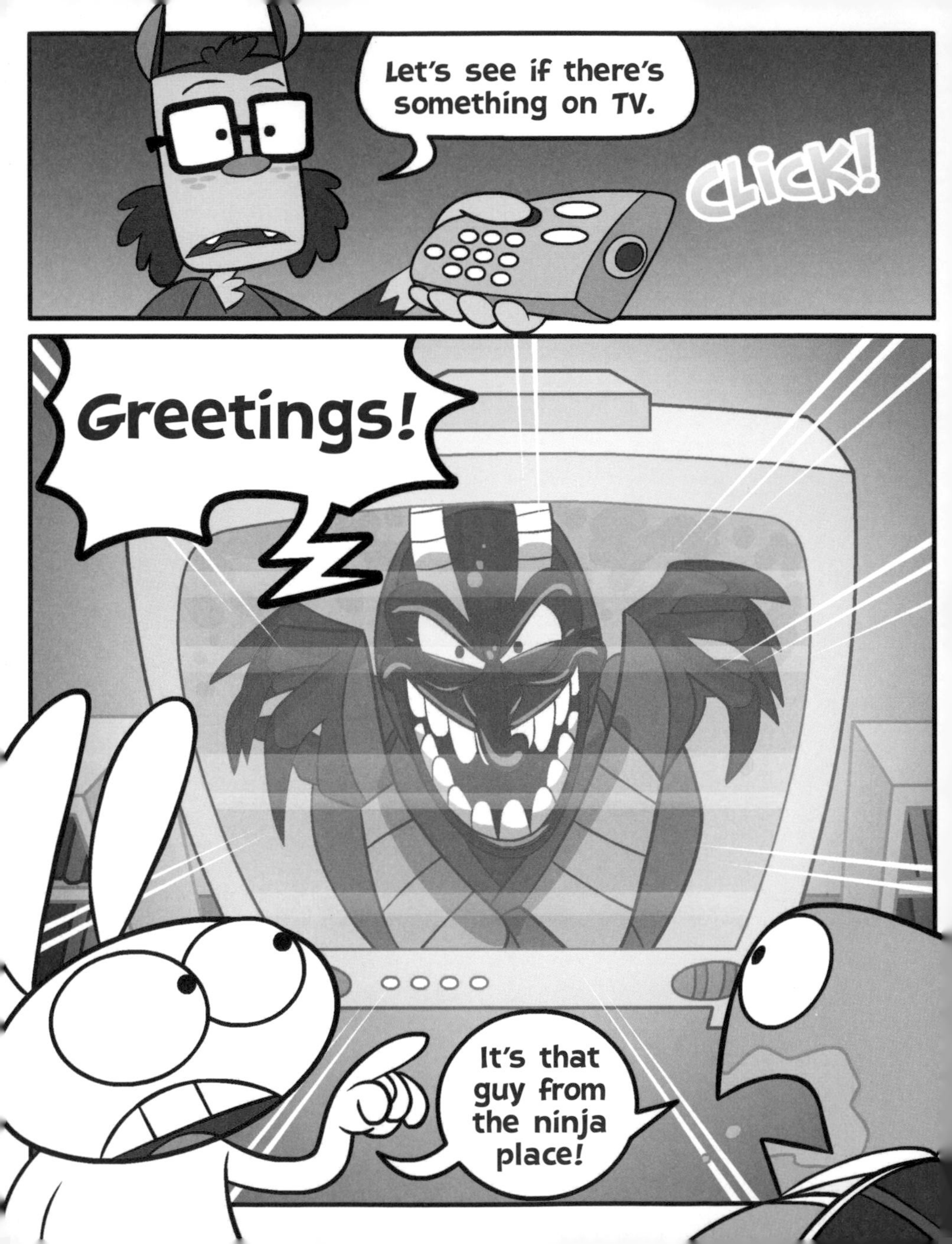
Let's see if there's something on TV.
CLICK!
Greetings!
It's that guy from the ninja place!

NINJA SLICE
Do you crave pizza? Do you yearn to slay the seven lords of hunger?
Then grab your kimonos and gallop on over to *Ninja Slice!*

Our elite shadow-warrior cooking staff are skilled in the deadly culinary arts. Over a thousand years of tradition go into each and every order.
GRAN
HOME-STY
NINJA SLICE
Pizza Dough
Pepperoni
None are faster. None are cheaper. None are . . . NINJA SLICE!
NINJA SLICE
NINJA SLICE
All major credit cards accepted!

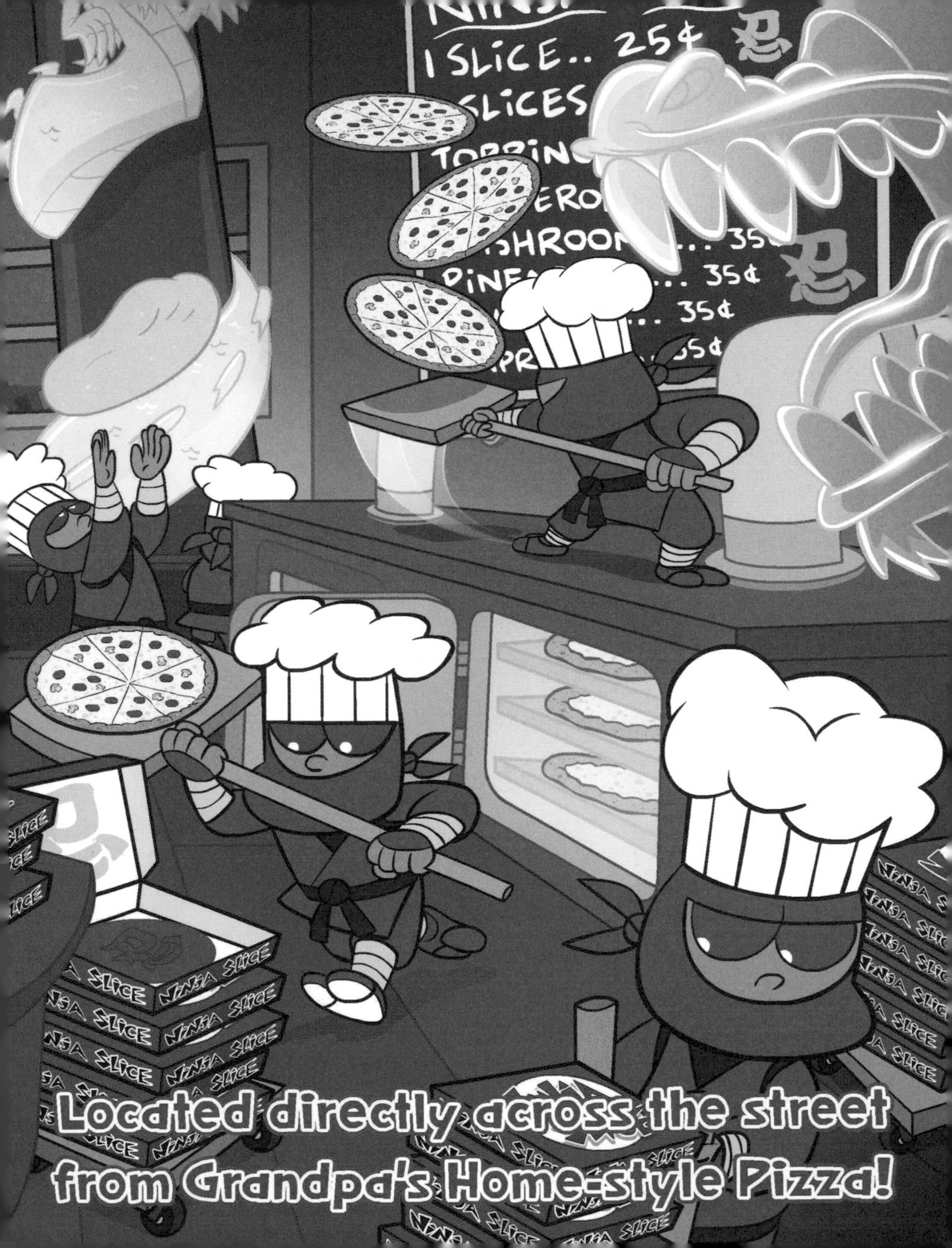

1 SLICE.. 25¢
NINJA SLICE
Located directly across the street from Grandpa's Home-style Pizza!

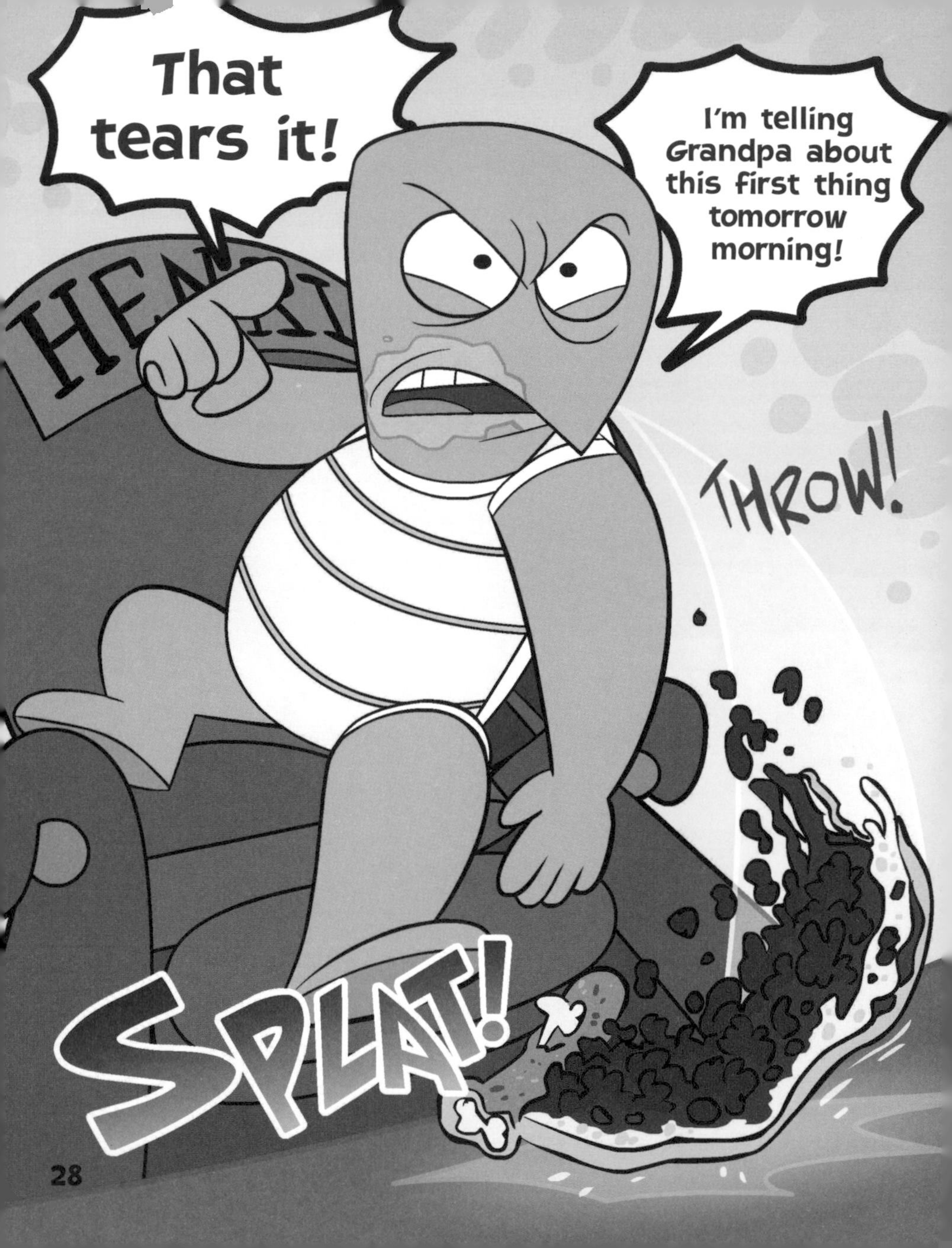
That tears it!
I'm telling Grandpa about this first thing tomorrow morning!
THROW!
SPLAT!

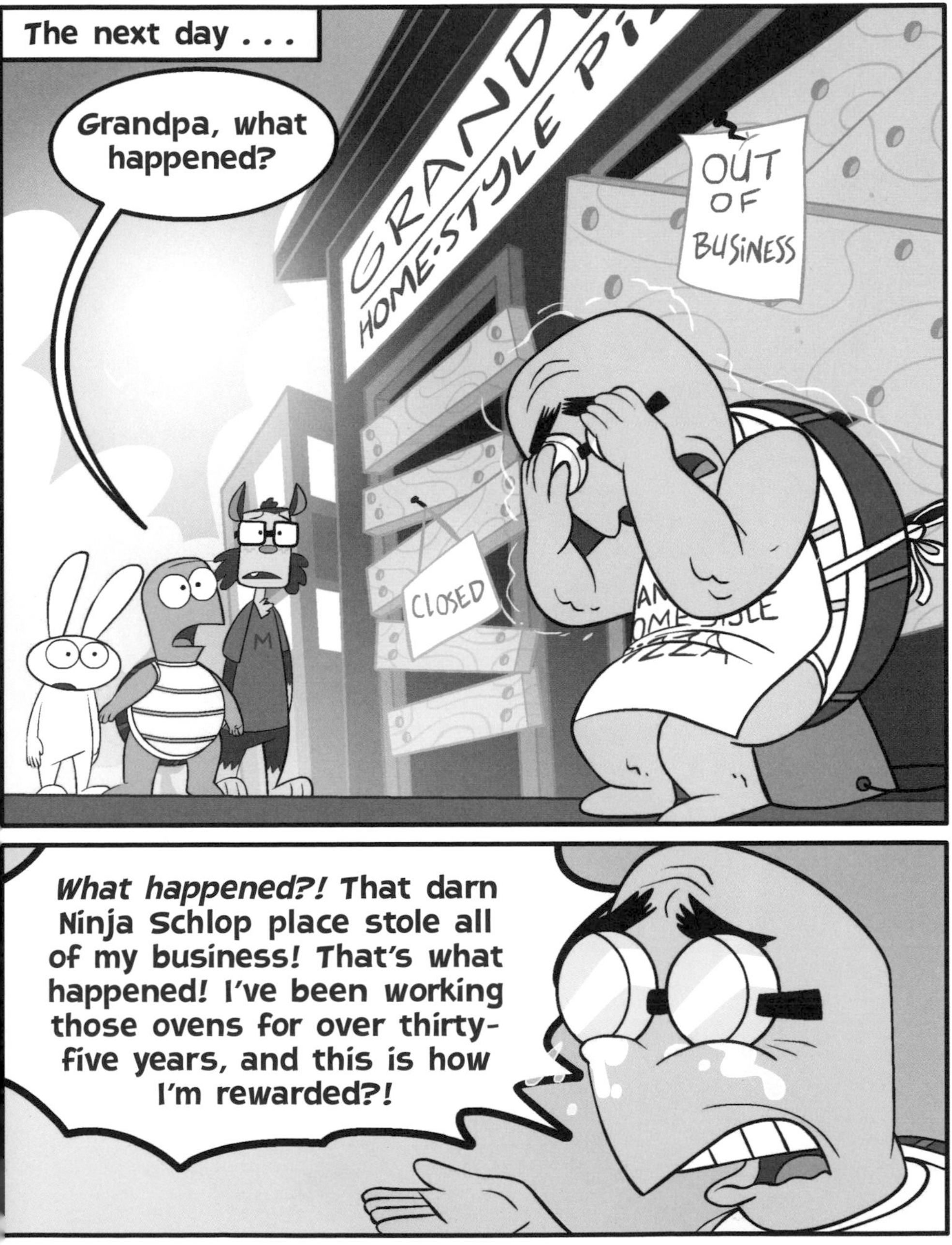
The next day . . .
Grandpa, what happened?
OUT OF BUSINESS
CLOSED
What happened?! That darn Ninja Schlop place stole all of my business! That's what happened! I've been working those ovens for over thirty-five years, and this is how I'm rewarded?!

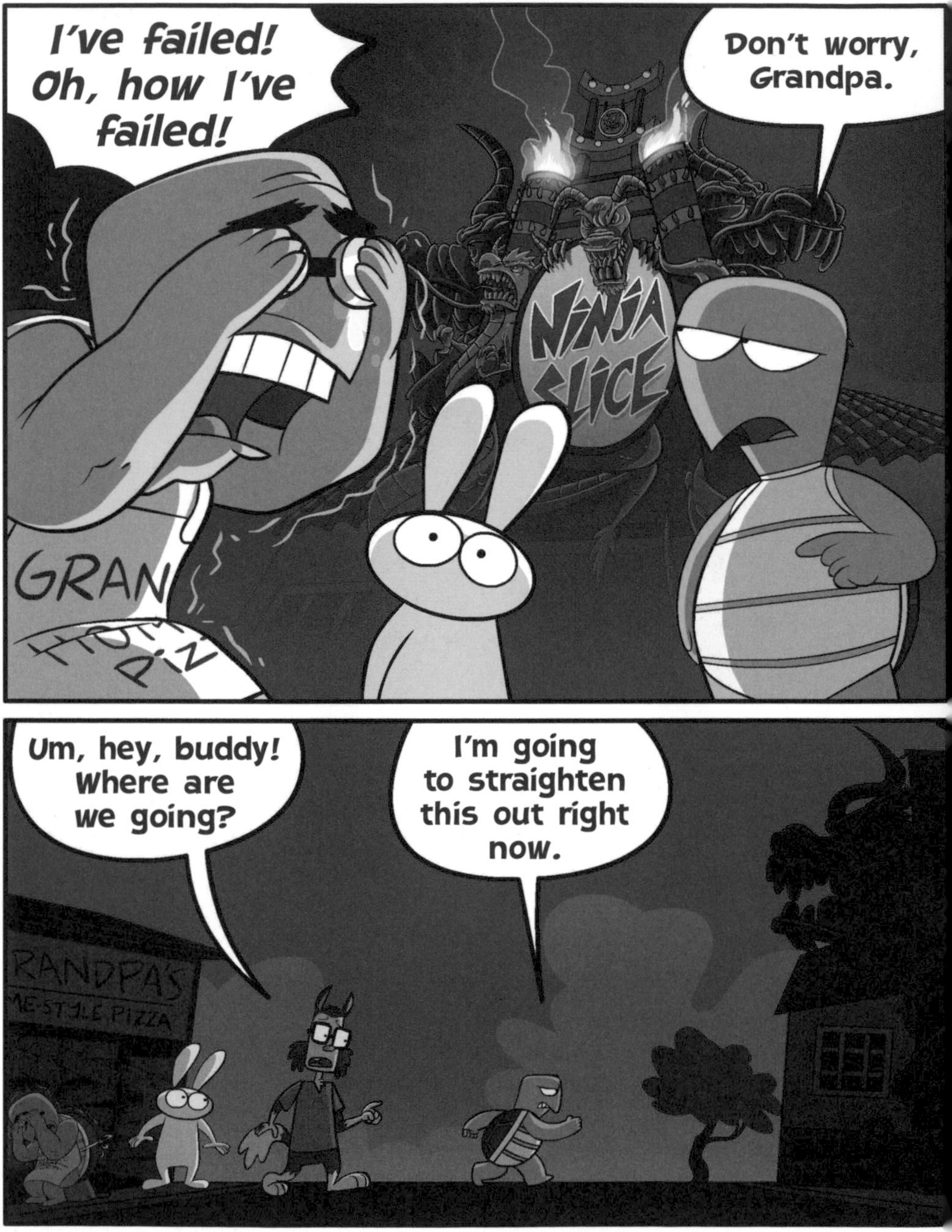
I've failed! Oh, how I've failed!
Don't worry, Grandpa.
NINJA SLICE
GRAN
Um, hey, buddy! Where are we going?
I'm going to straighten this out right now.
RANDPA'S
ME-STYLE PIZZA

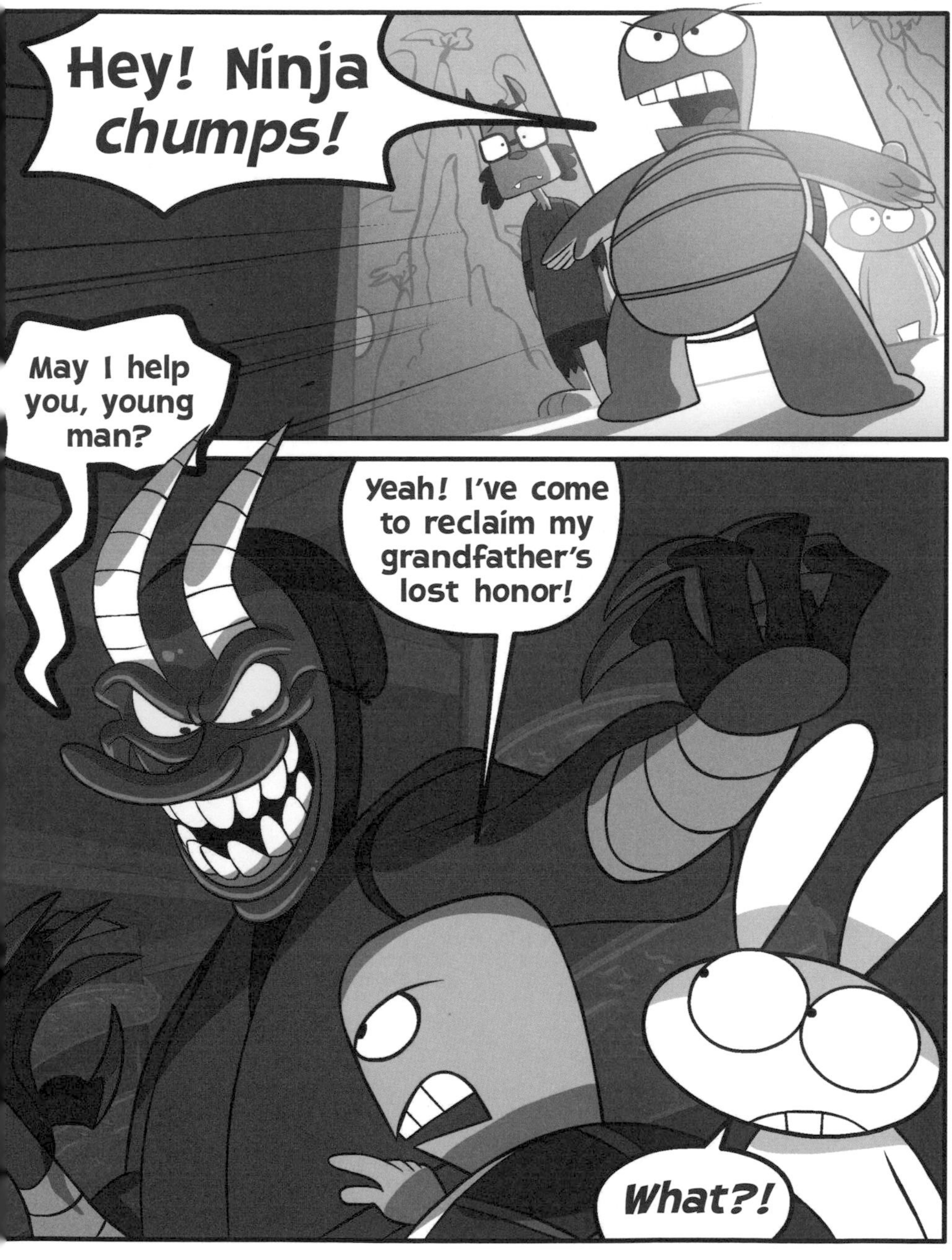
Hey! Ninja chumps!
May I help you, young man?
Yeah! I've come to reclaim my grandfather's lost honor!
What?!

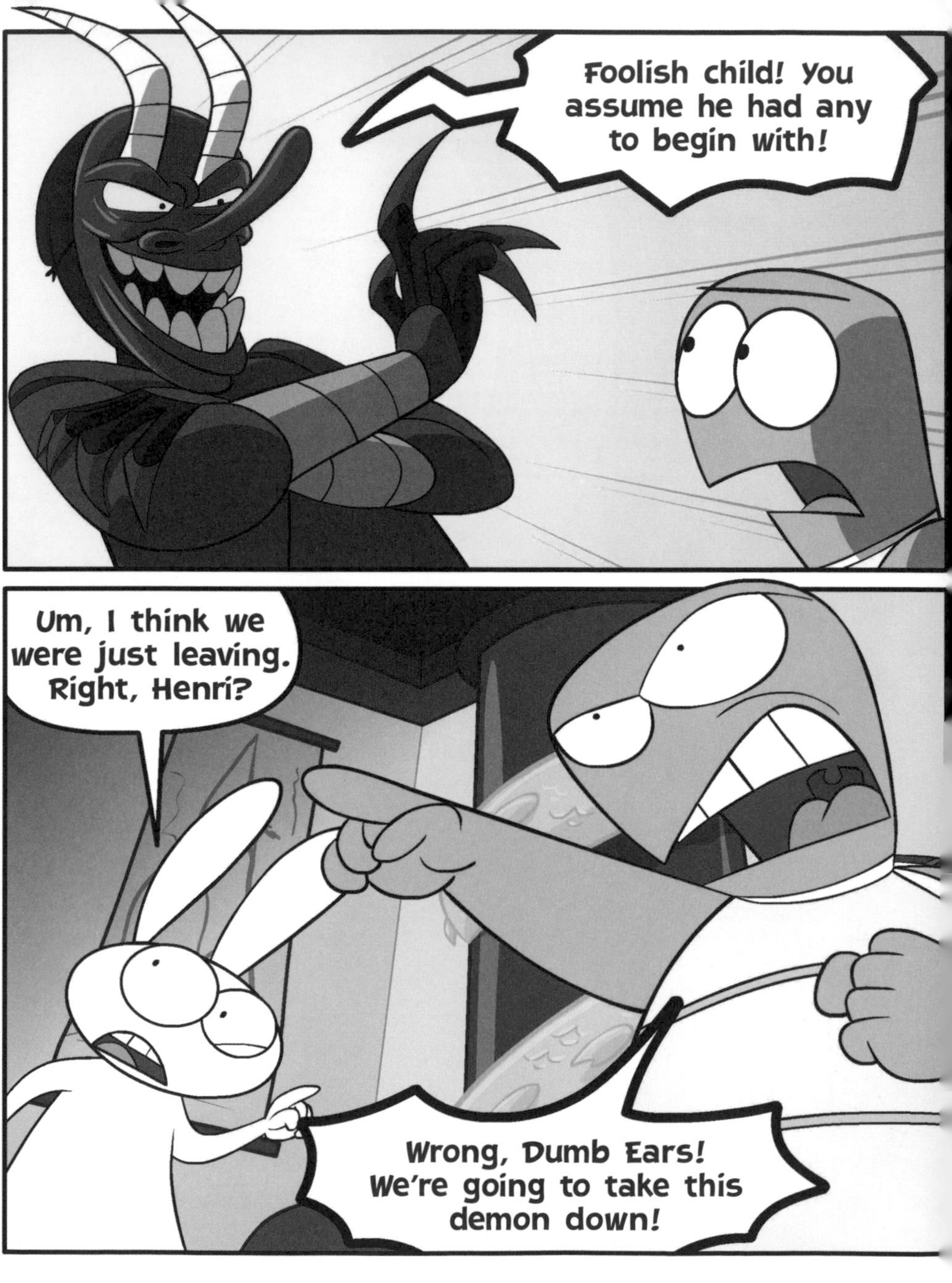
Foolish child! You assume he had any to begin with!
Um, I think we were just leaving. Right, Henri?
Wrong, Dumb Ears! We're going to take this demon down!

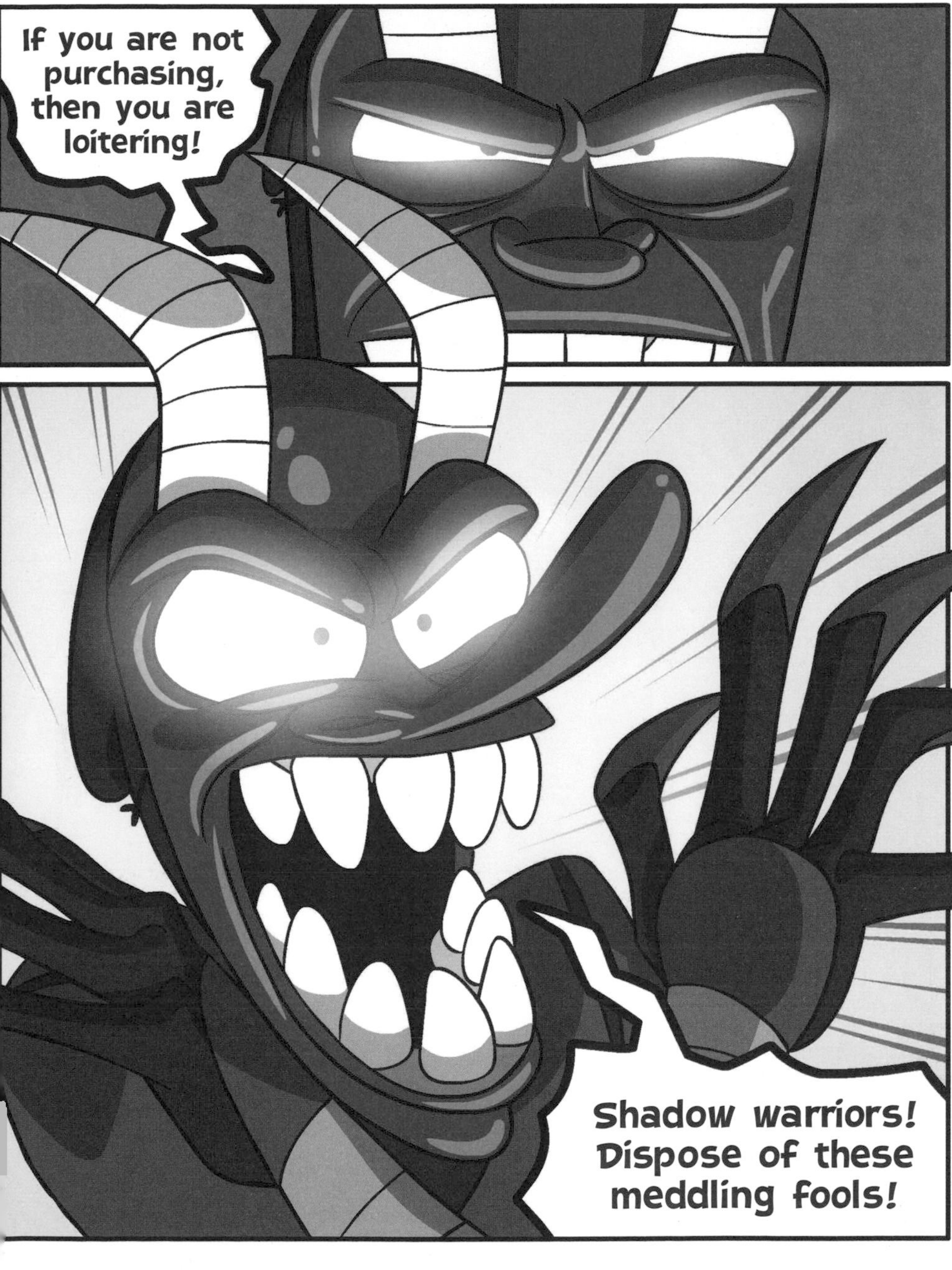
If you are not purchasing, then you are loitering!
Shadow warriors! Dispose of these meddling fools!

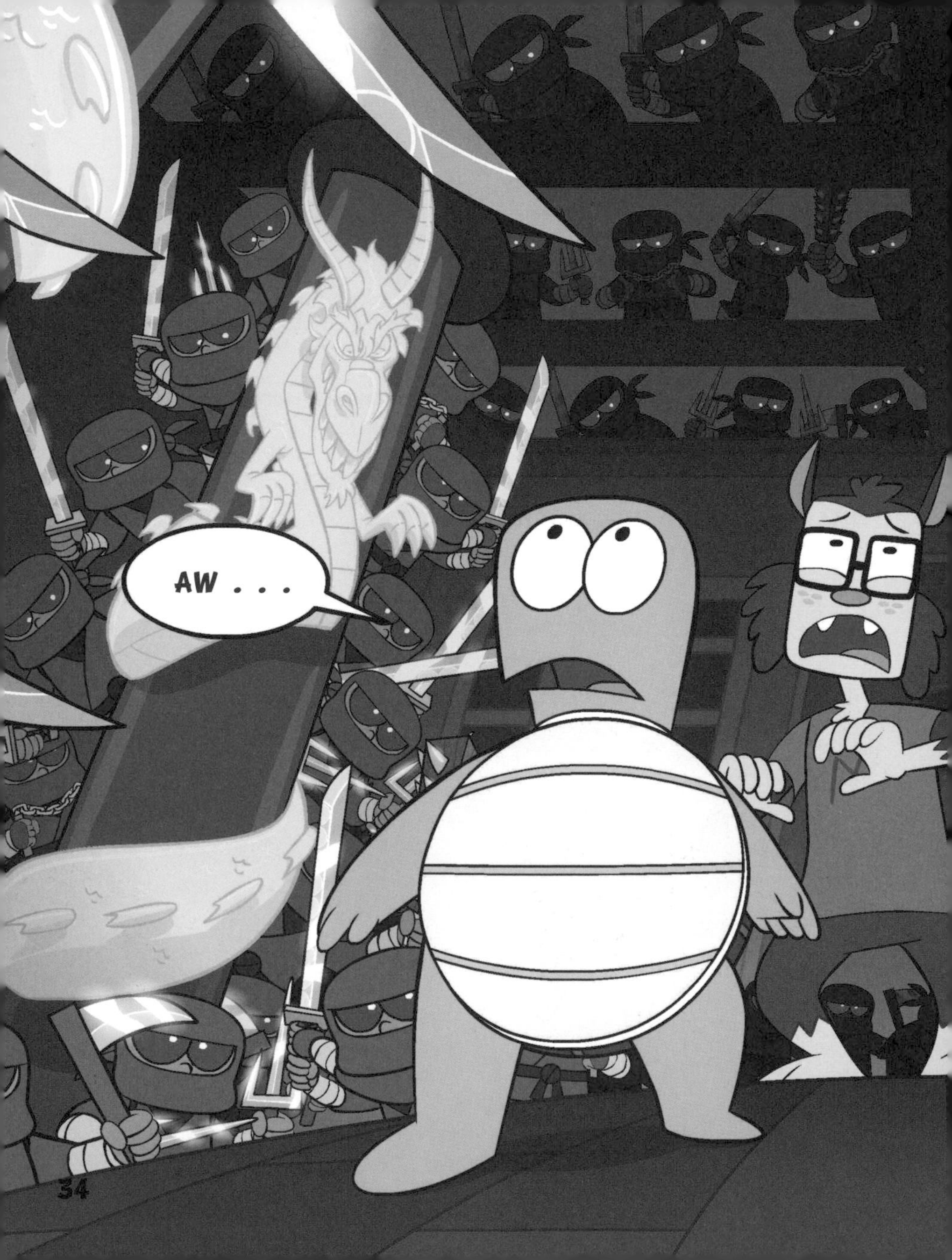
AW . . .

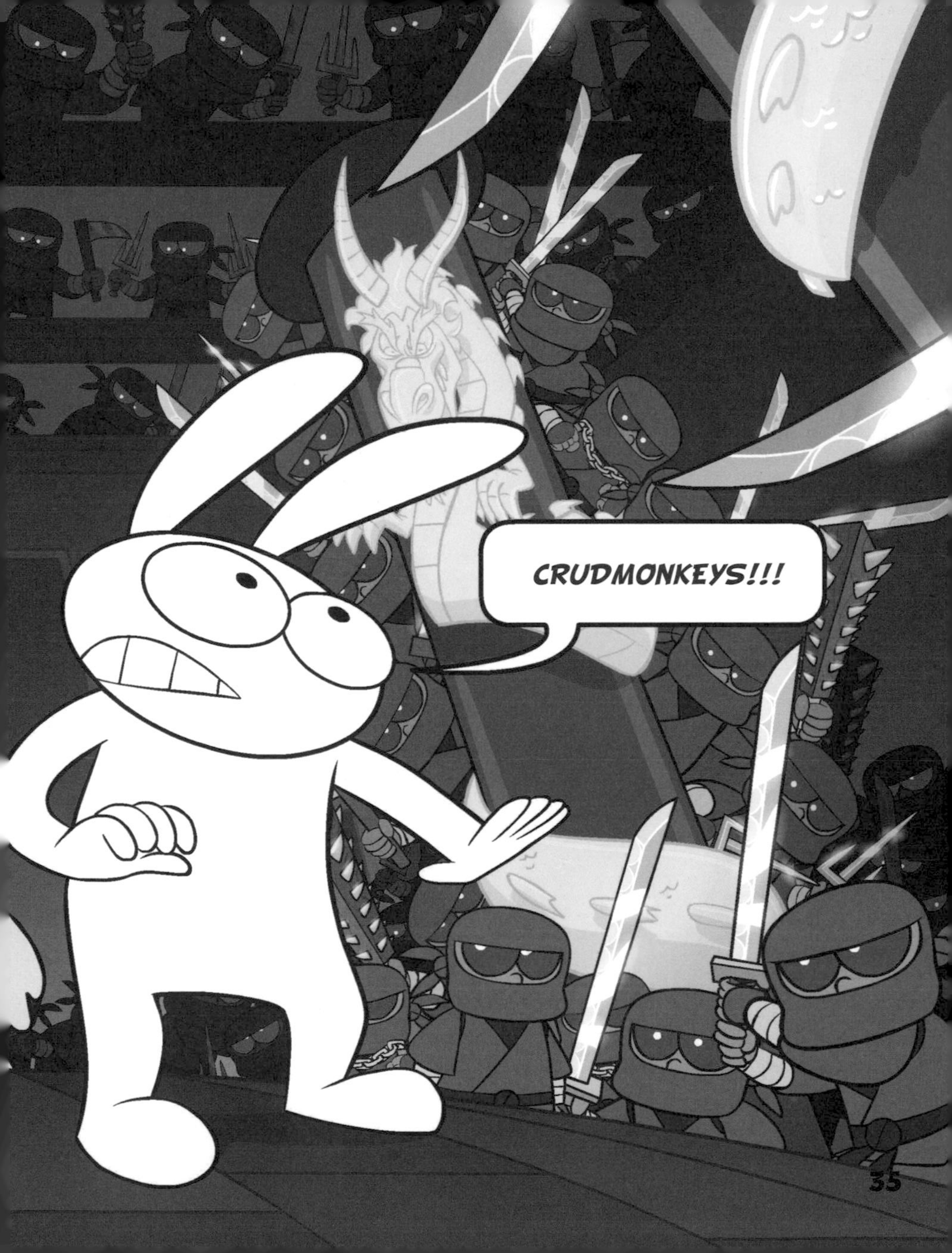
CRUDMONKEYS!!!

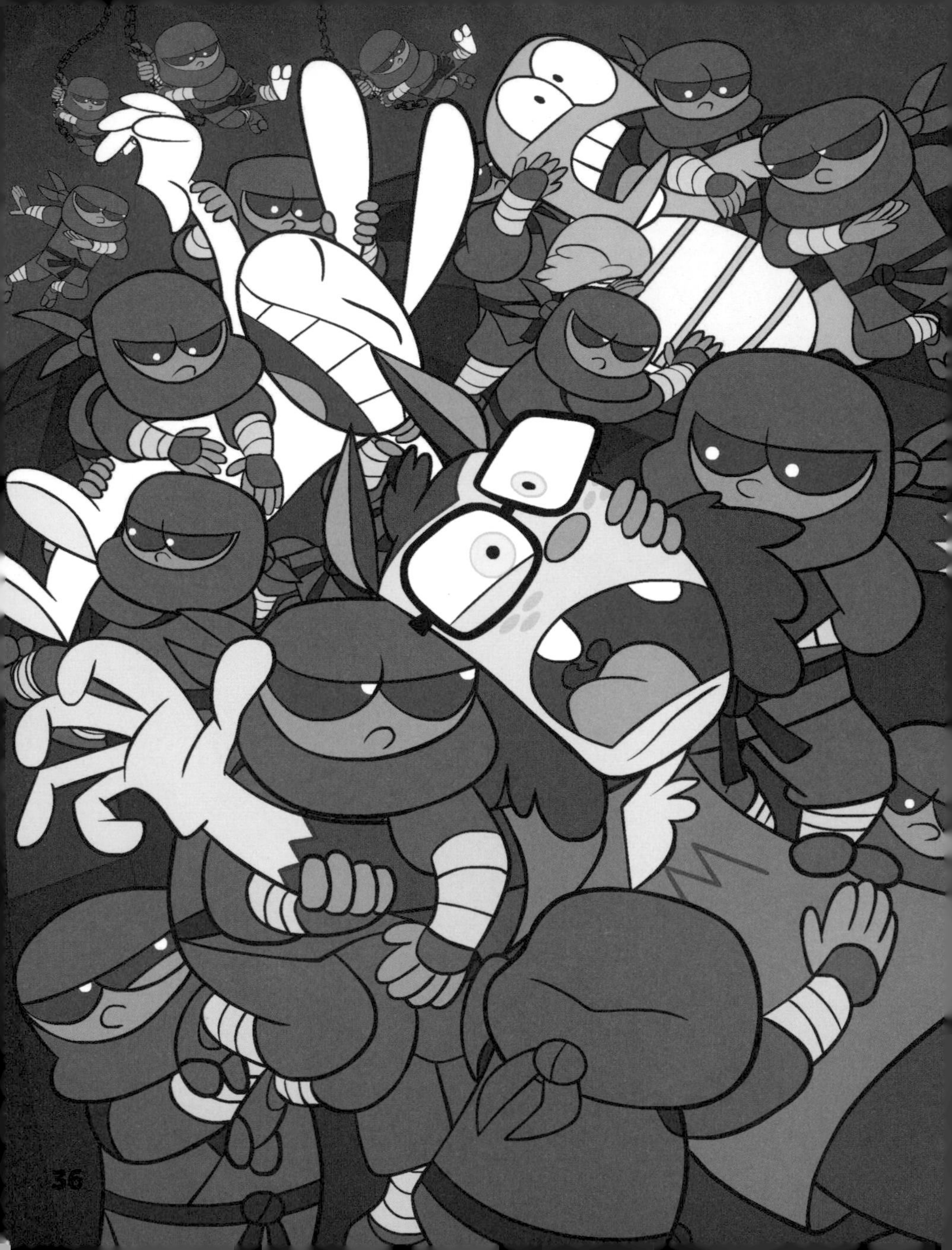

Ugh . . . hey, guys? I had the craziest dream . . .
. . . that there was this crazy ninja place . . .
. . . and it was filled with ninjas, and we got our butts kicked pretty hard. . . .

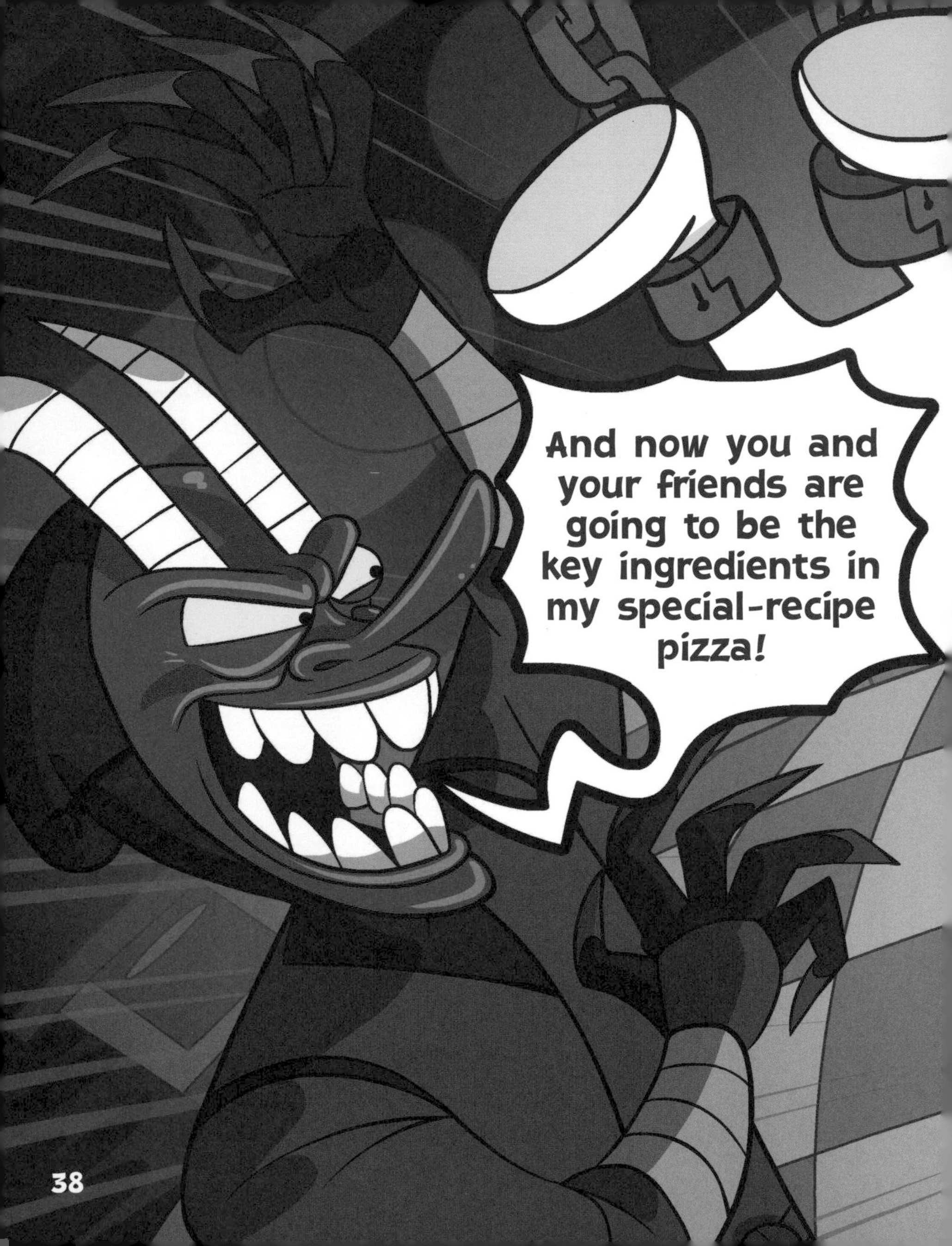
And now you and your friends are going to be the key ingredients in my special-recipe pizza!

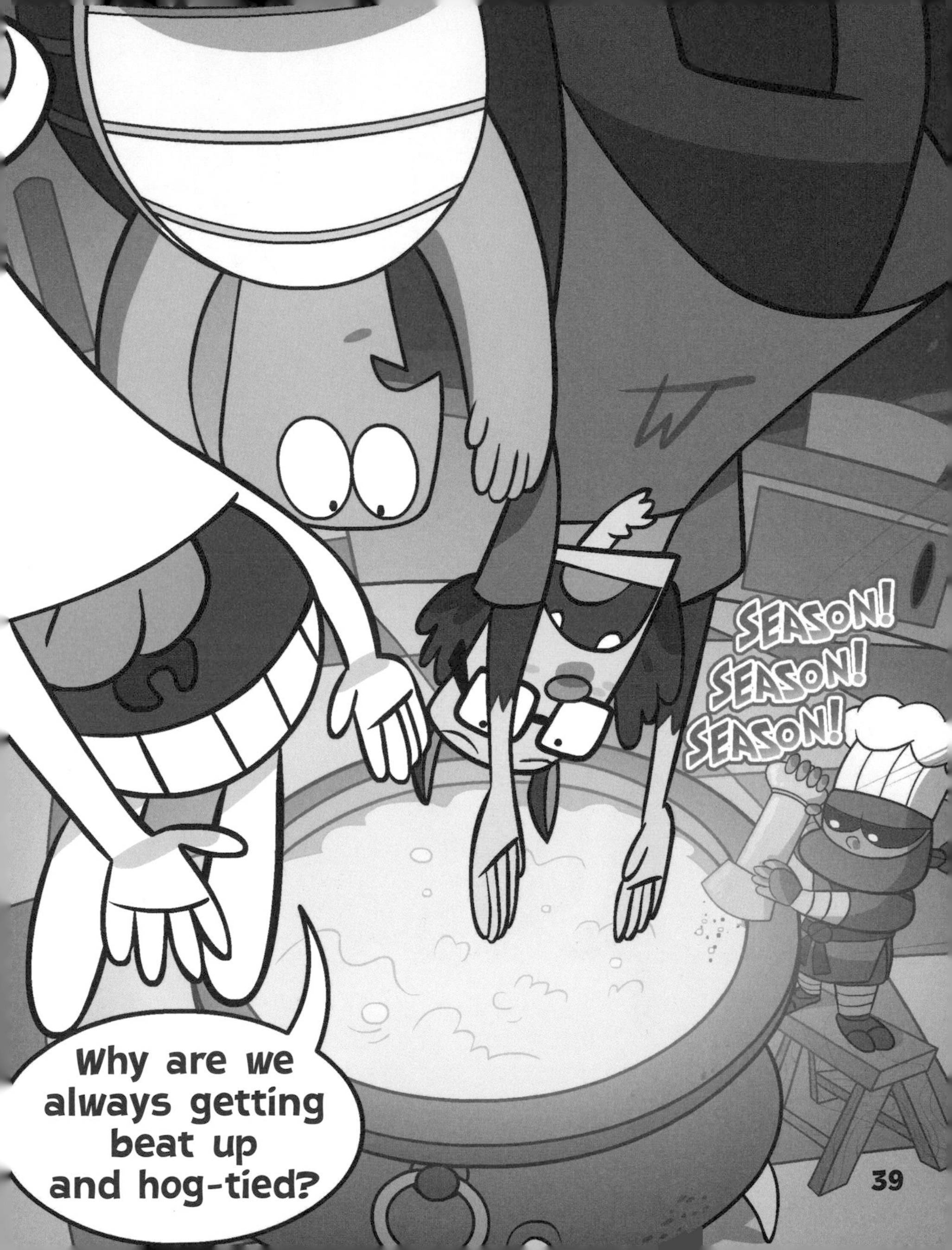
SEASON! SEASON! SEASON!
Why are we always getting beat up and hog-tied?

Because you're worthless and weak!
And technically speaking, you're *chained*—not tied like so many hogs!
How can things possibly get any *worse*?!

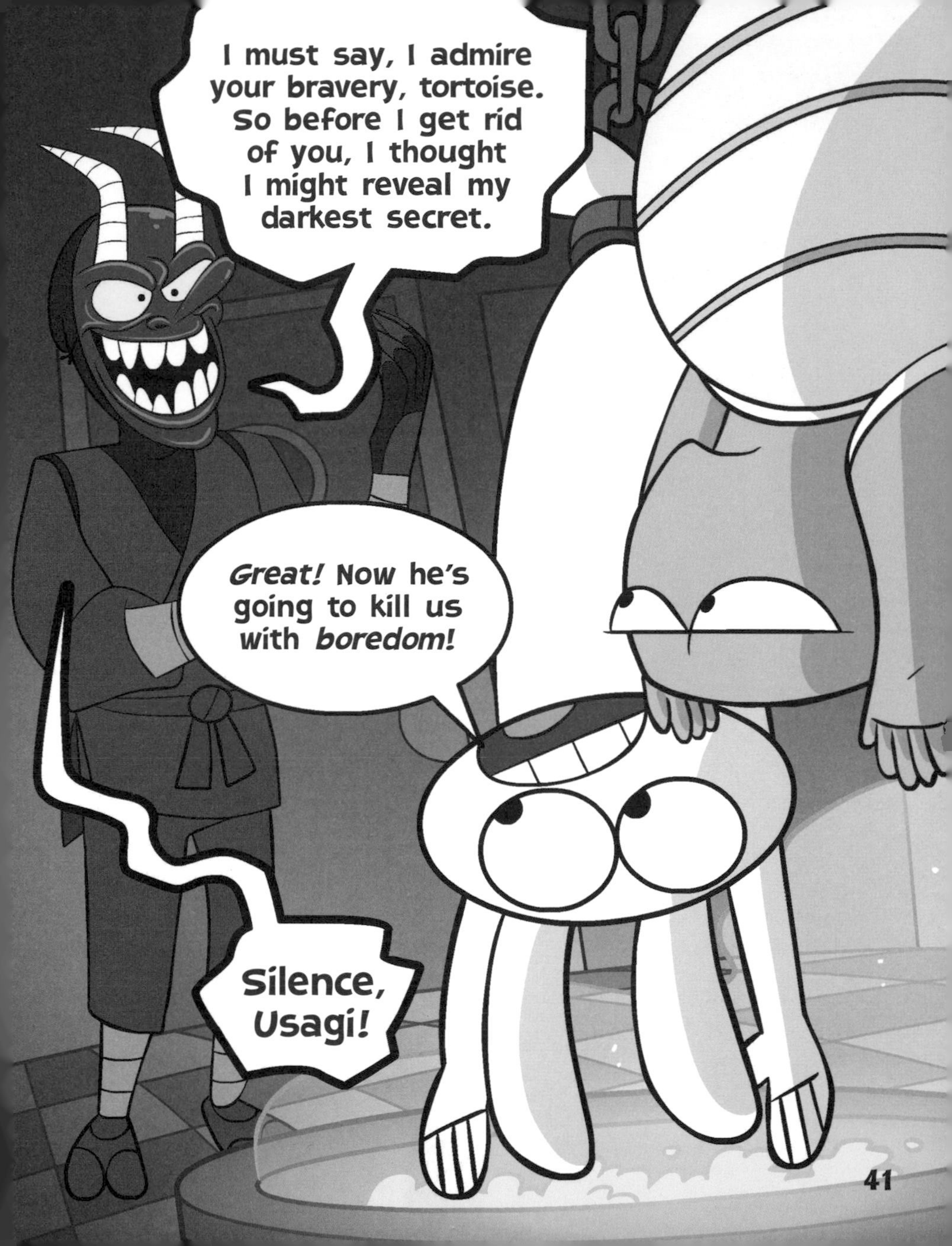
I must say, I admire your bravery, tortoise. So before I get rid of you, I thought I might reveal my darkest secret.
Great! Now he's going to kill us with *boredom!*
Silence, Usagi!

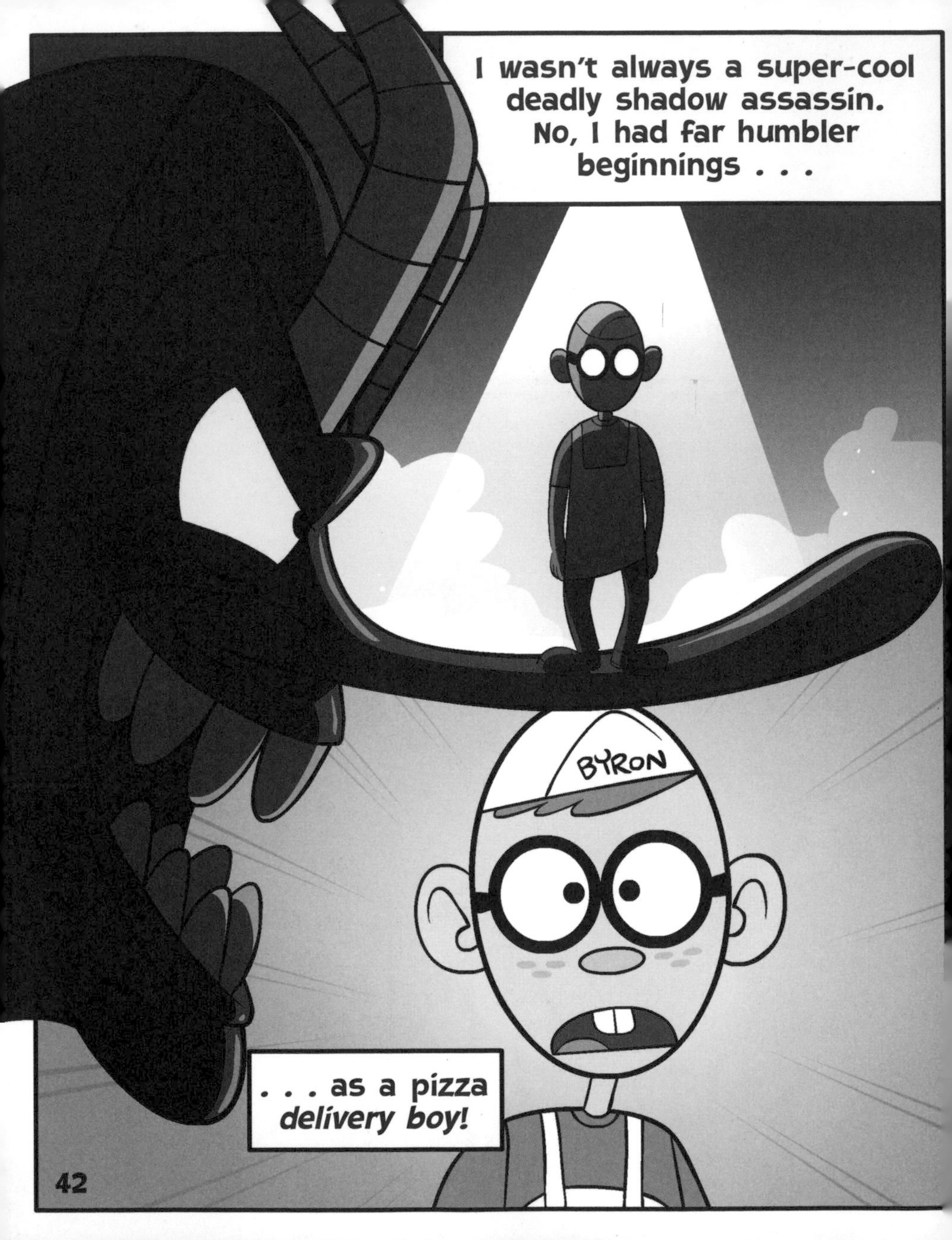
I wasn't always a super-cool deadly shadow assassin. No, I had far humbler beginnings . . .
BYRON
. . . as a pizza *delivery boy!*

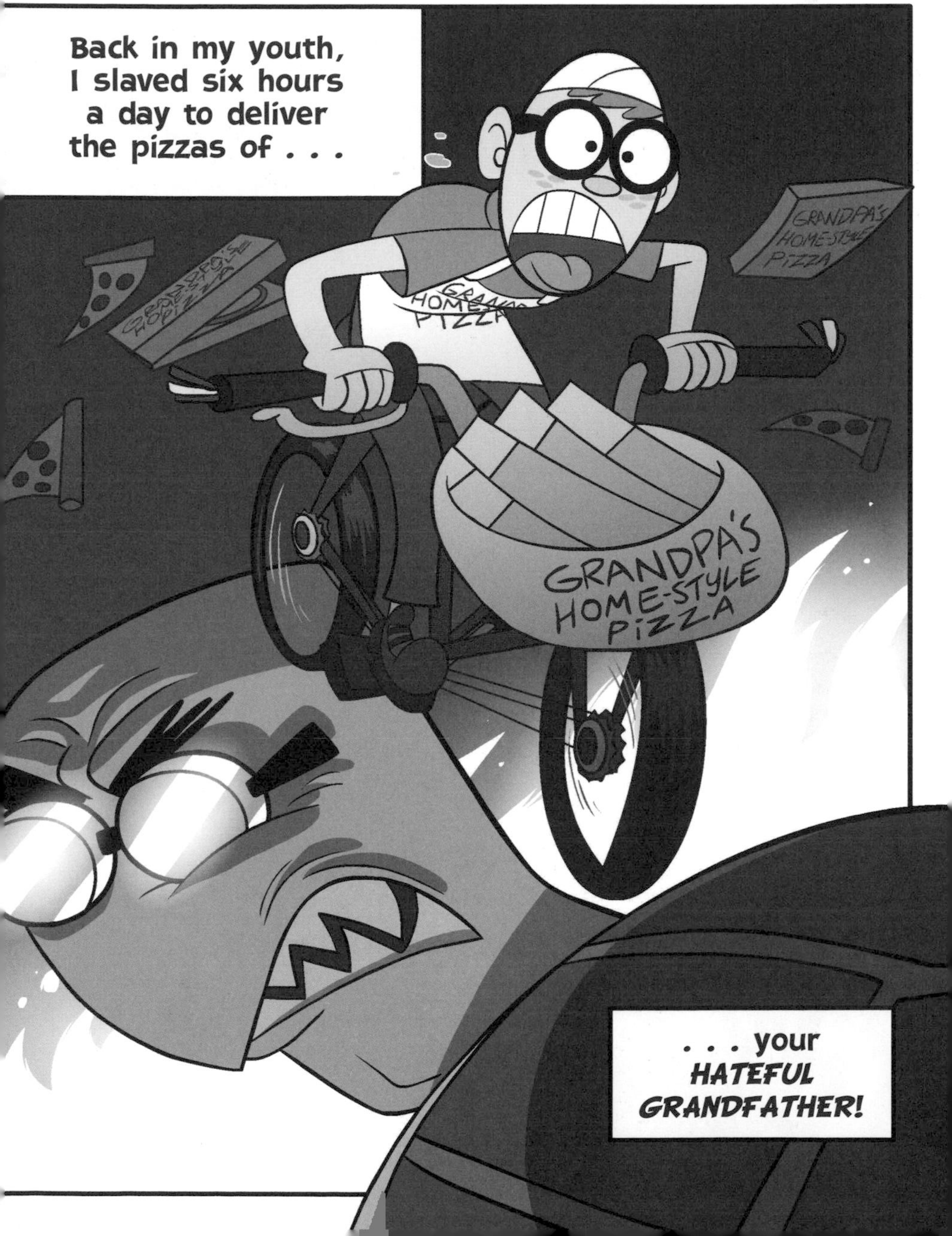
Back in my youth, I slaved six hours a day to deliver the pizzas of . . .
GRANDPA'S HOME-STYLE PIZZA
GRANDPA'S HOME-STYLE PIZZA
. . . your *HATEFUL* *GRANDFATHER!*

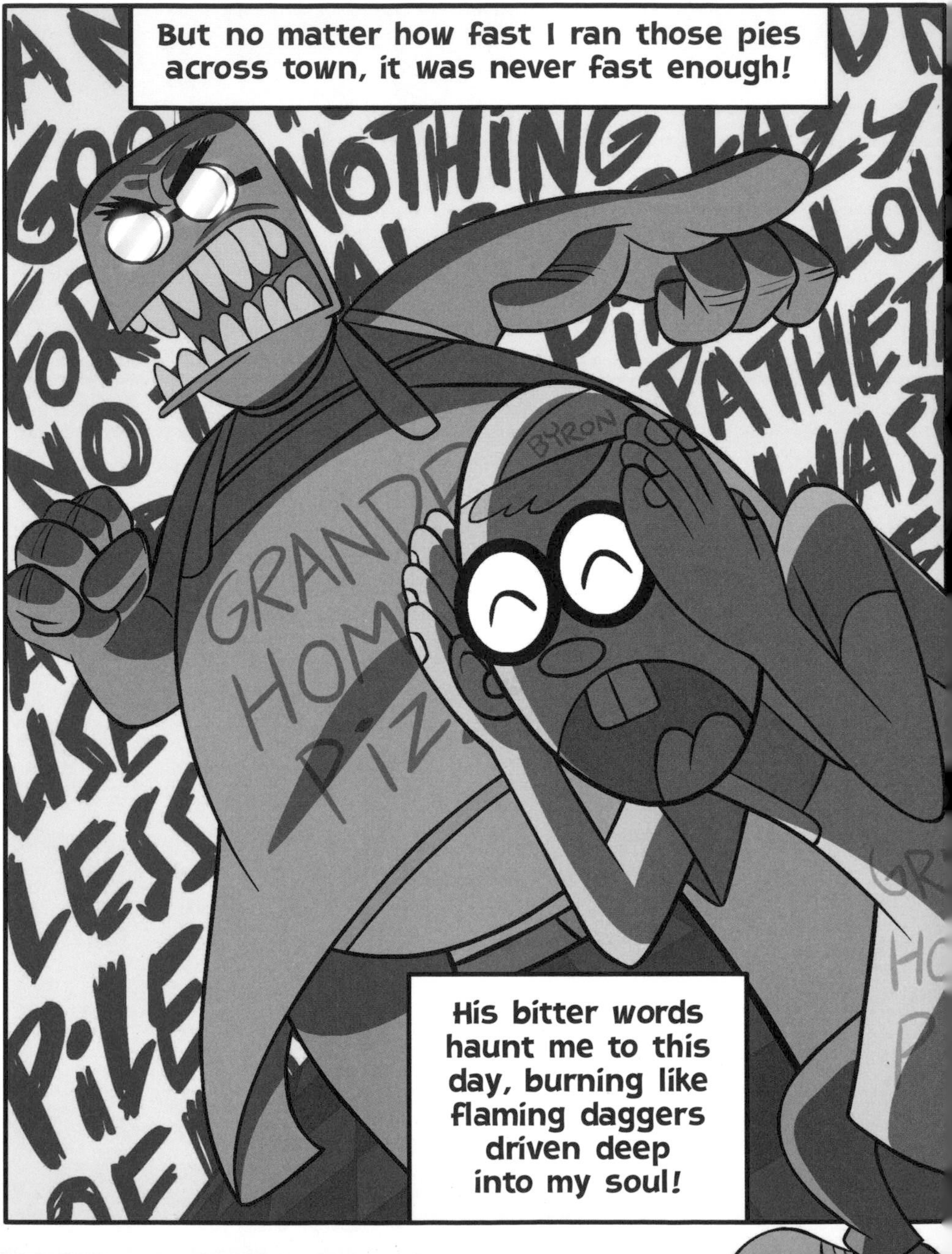
But no matter how fast I ran those pies across town, it was never fast enough!
NOTHING
BYRON
His bitter words haunt me to this day, burning like flaming daggers driven deep into my soul!

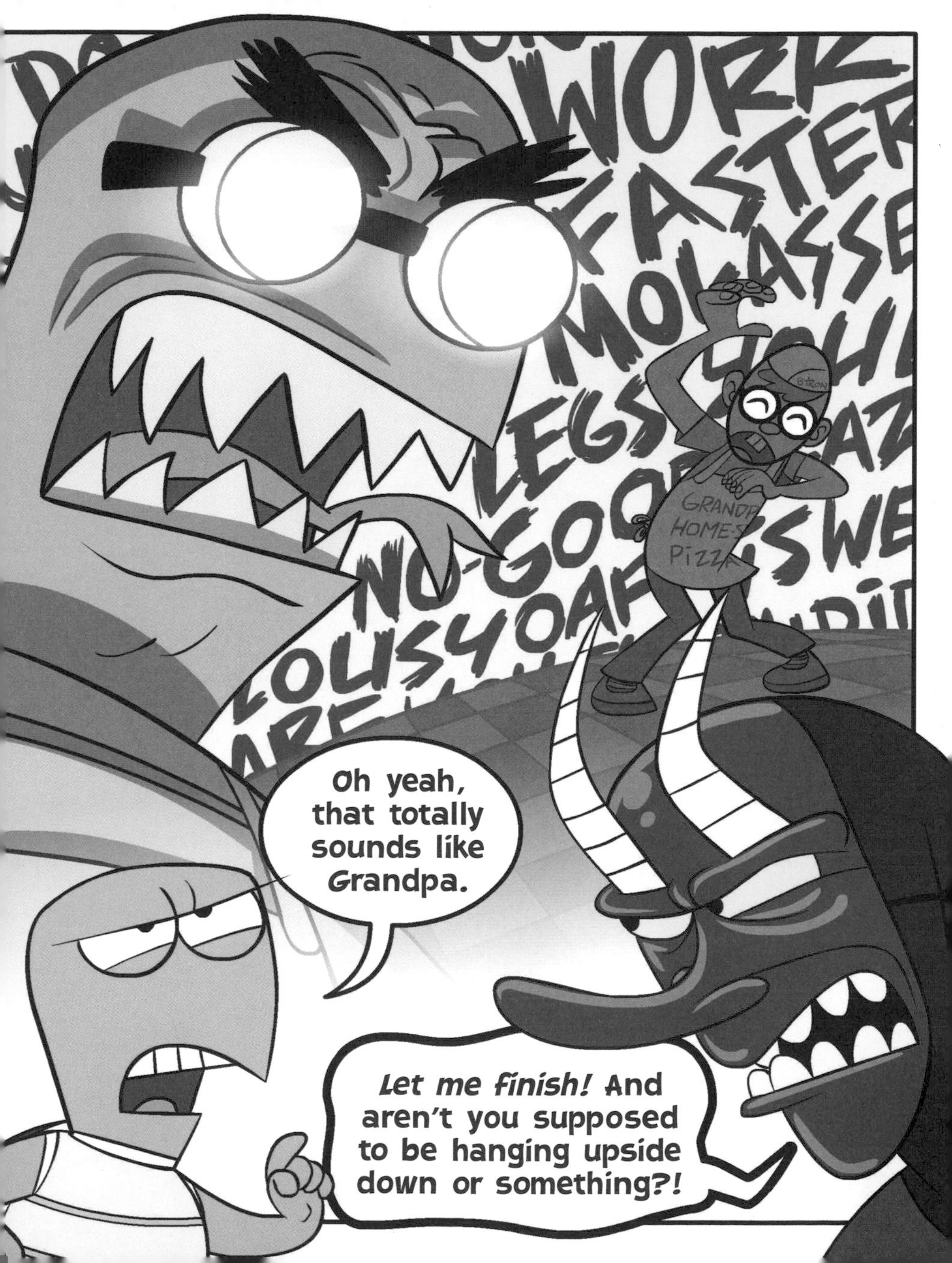
WORK
FASTER
Oh yeah, that totally sounds like Grandpa.
Let me finish! And aren't you supposed to be hanging upside down or something?!

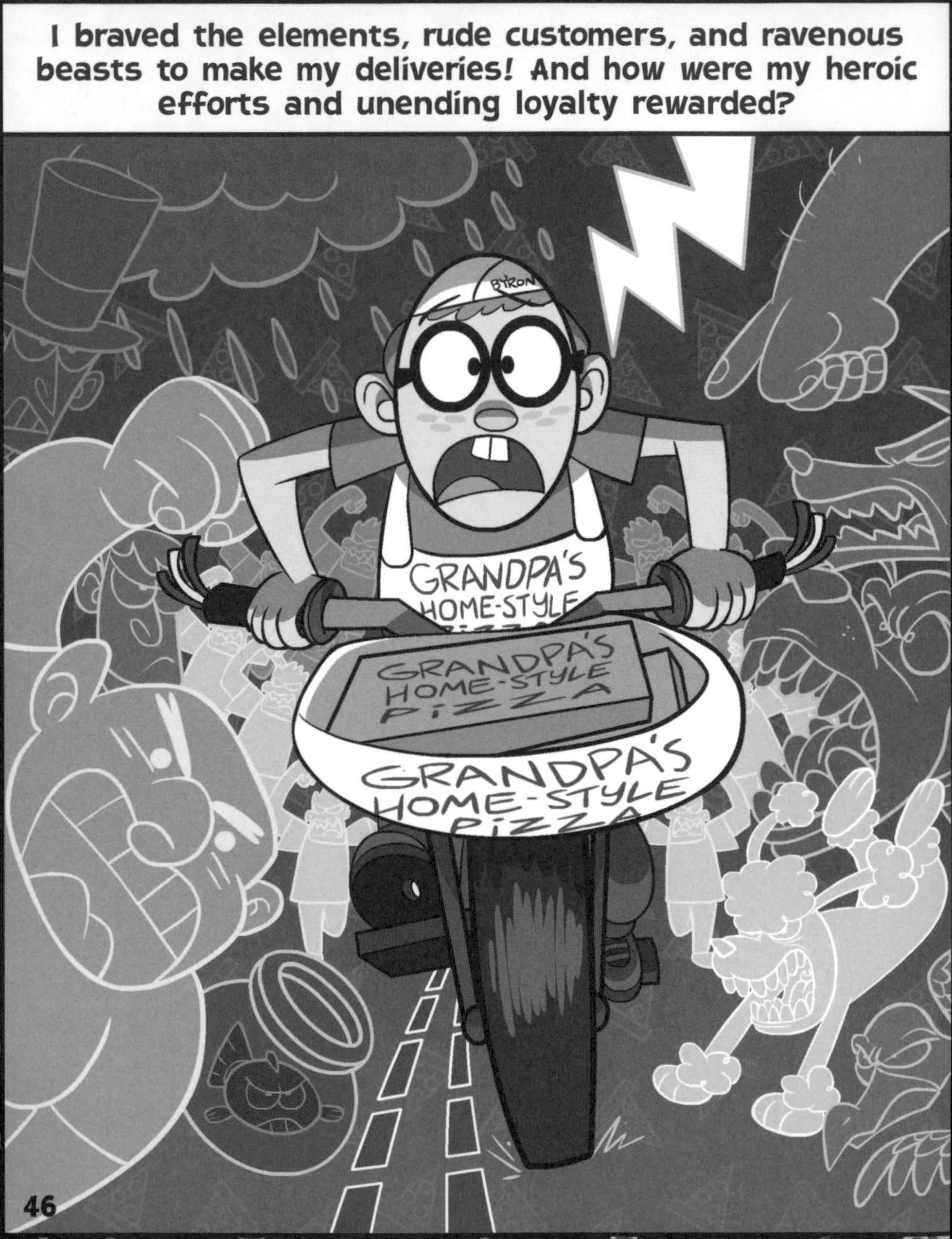
I braved the elements, rude customers, and ravenous beasts to make my deliveries! And how were my heroic efforts and unending loyalty rewarded?
BYRON
GRANDPA'S
HOME-STYLE
GRANDPA'S
HOME-STYLE
PIZZA
GRANDPA'S
HOME-STYLE

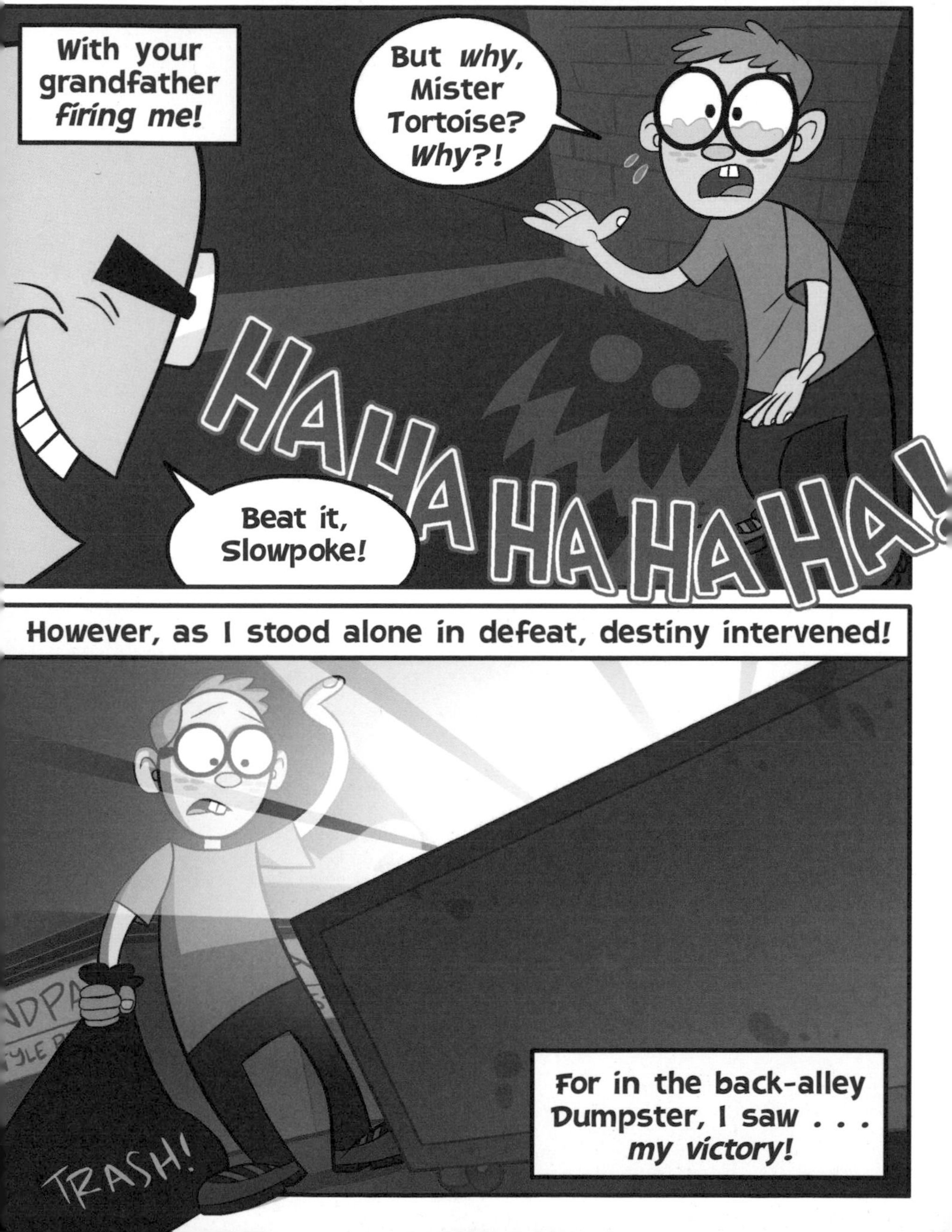
With your grandfather firing me!
But *why*, Mister Tortoise? *Why?!*
HAHAHAHAHAHAHA!
Beat it, Slowpoke!
However, as I stood alone in defeat, destiny intervened!
TRASH!
For in the back-alley Dumpster, I saw . . . *my victory!*

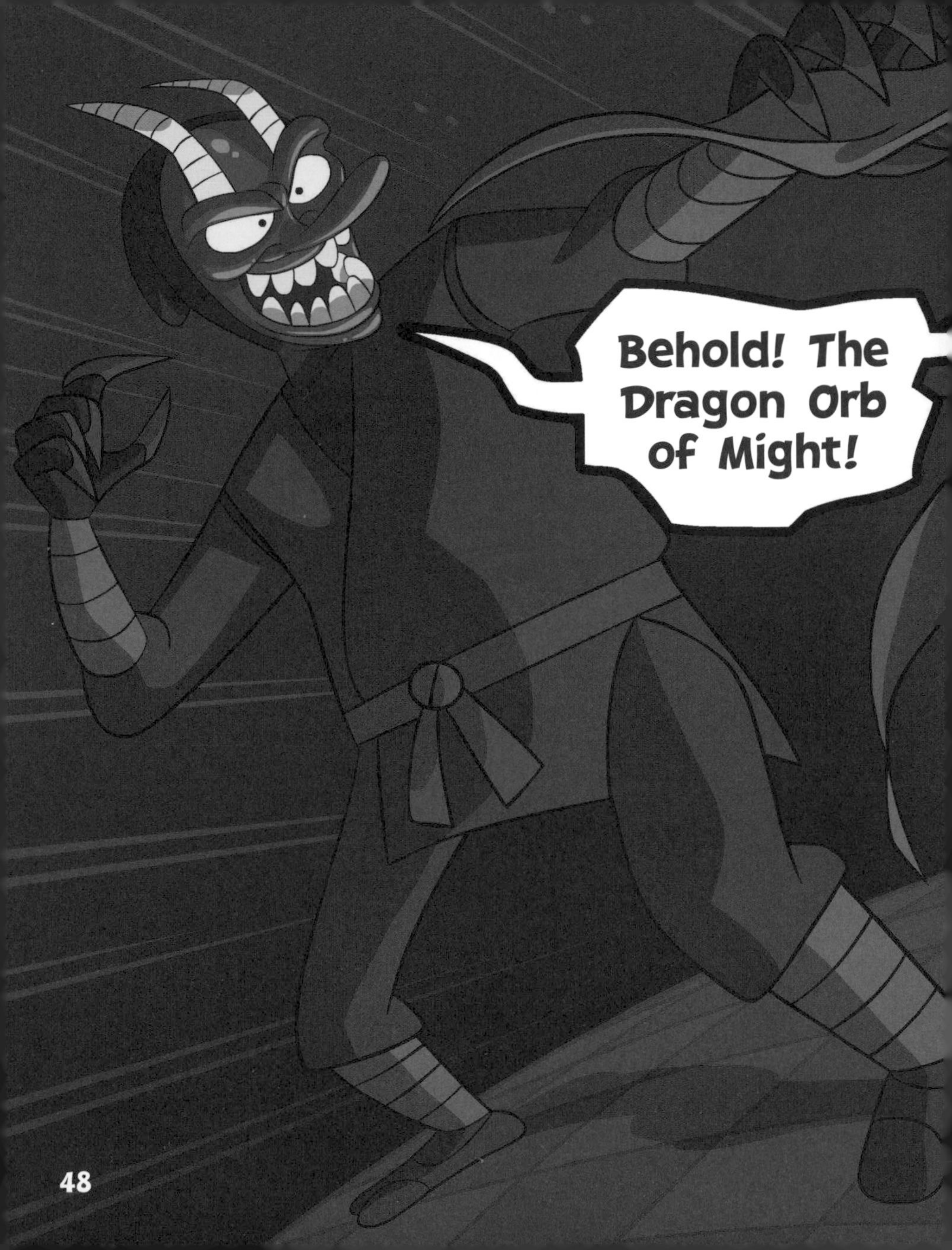
Behold! The Dragon Orb of Might!

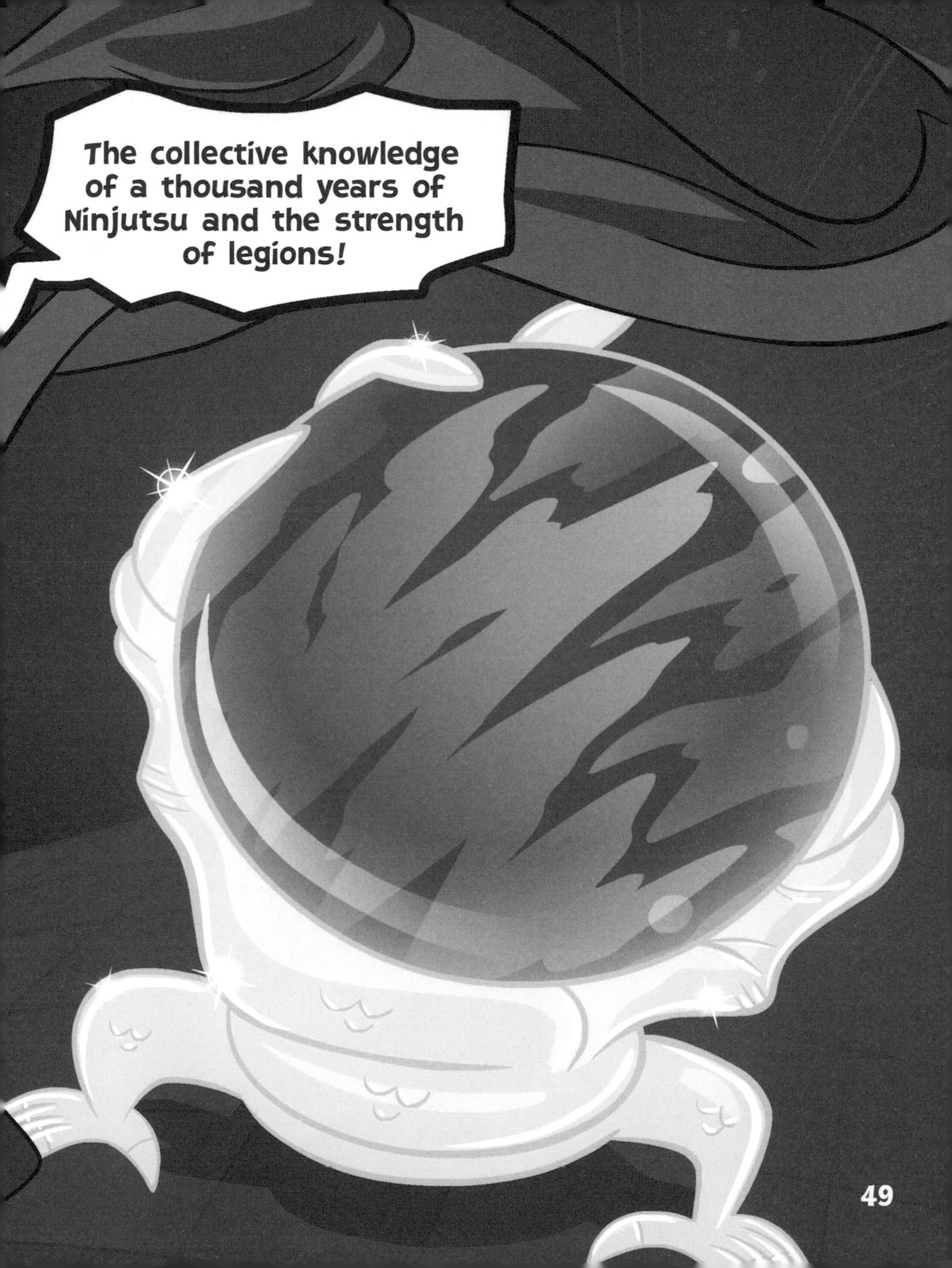
The collective knowledge of a thousand years of Ninjutsu and the strength of legions!

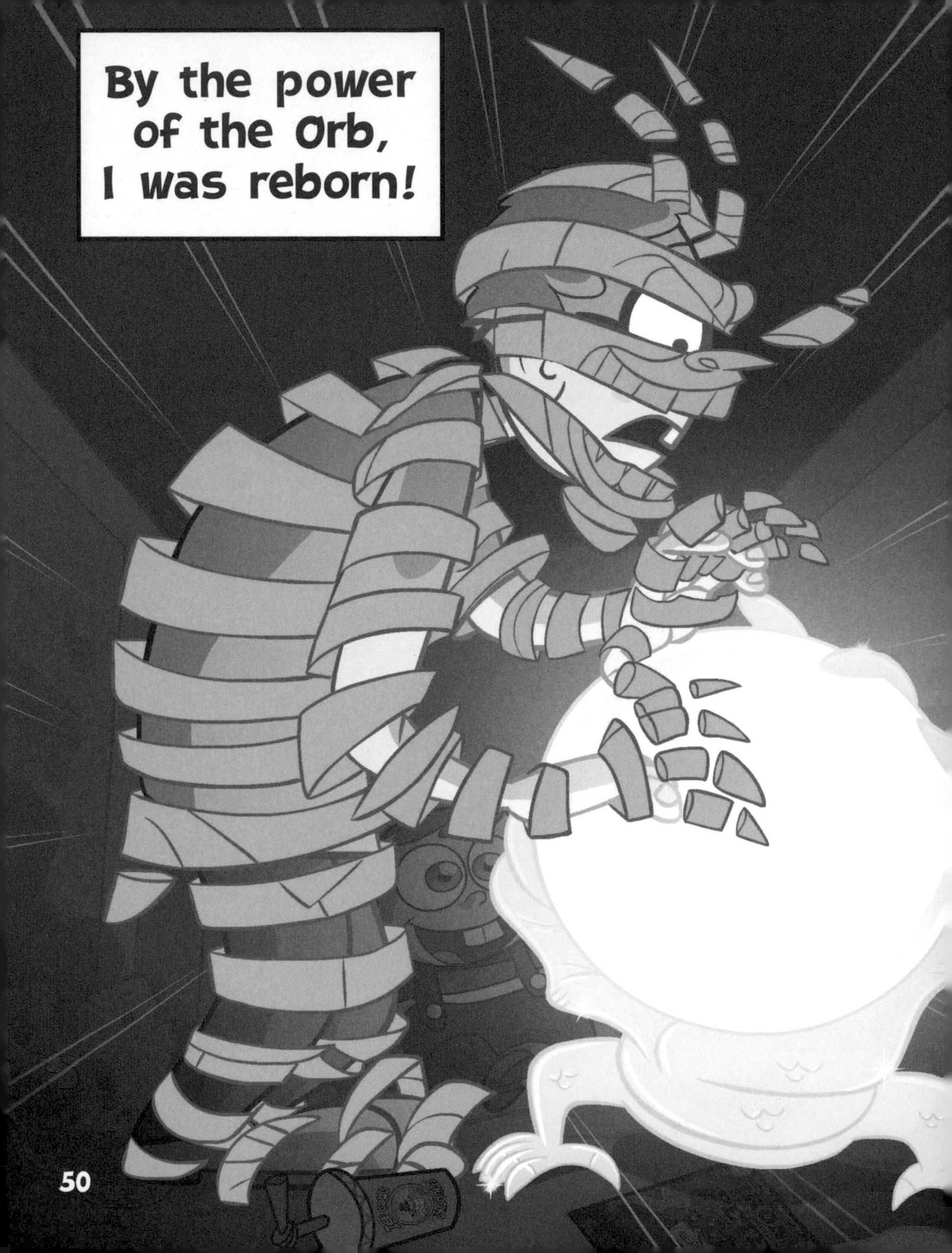
By the power of the Orb, I was reborn!

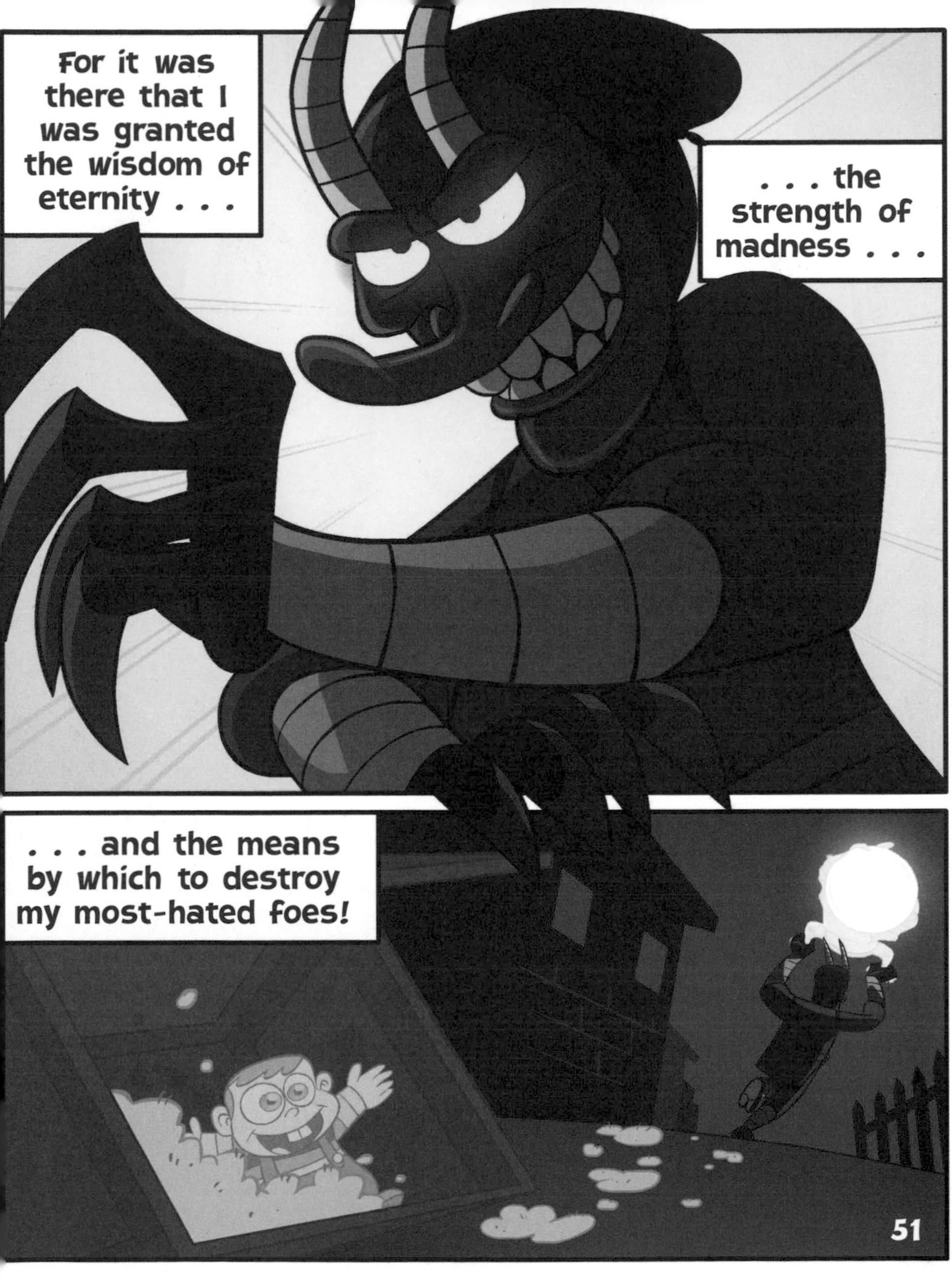
For it was there that I was granted the wisdom of eternity . . .
. . . the strength of madness . . .
. . . and the means by which to destroy my most-hated foes!

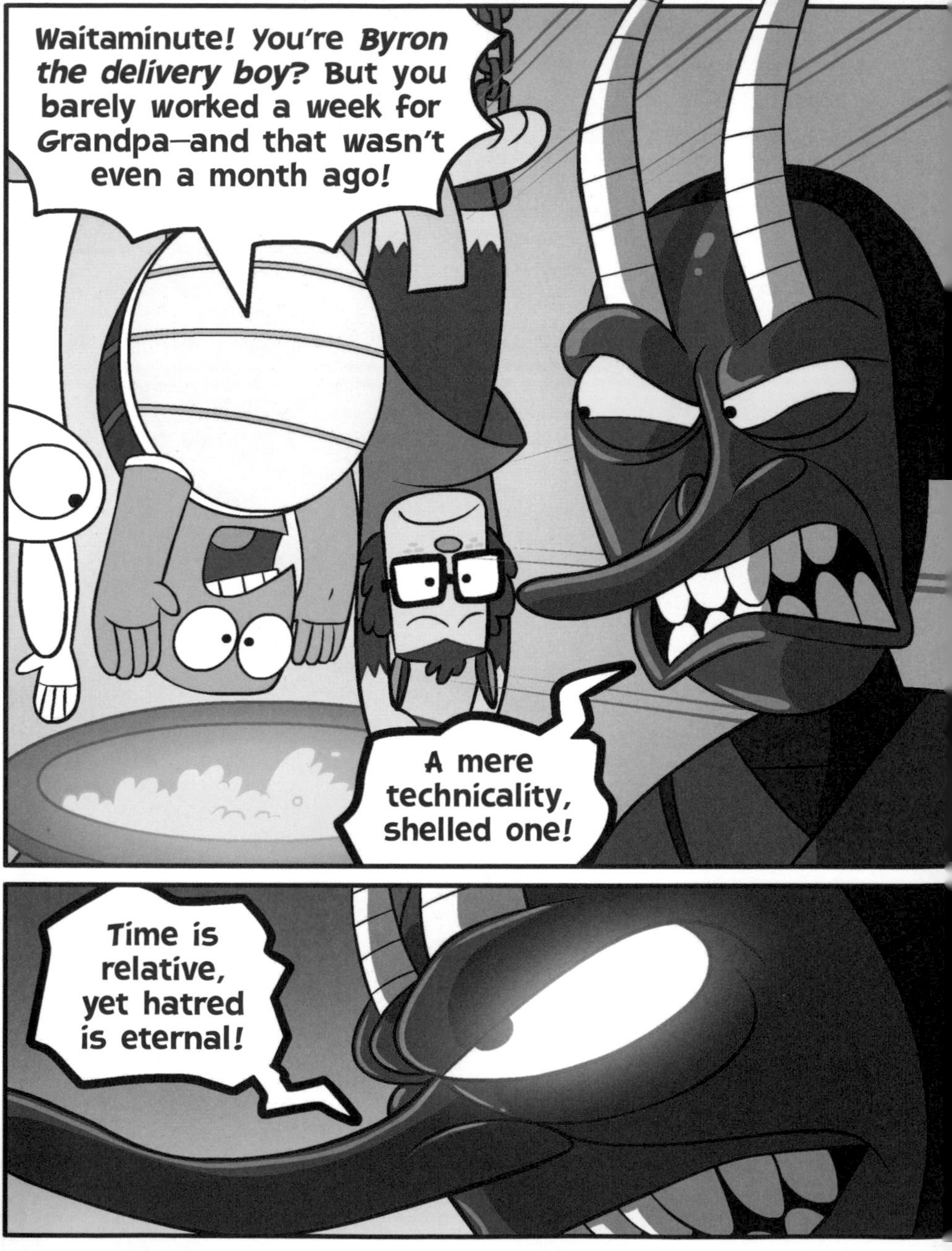
Waitaminute! *You're* ***Byron the delivery boy?*** But you barely worked a week for Grandpa—and that wasn't even a month ago!
A mere technicality, shelled one!
Time is relative, yet hatred is eternal!

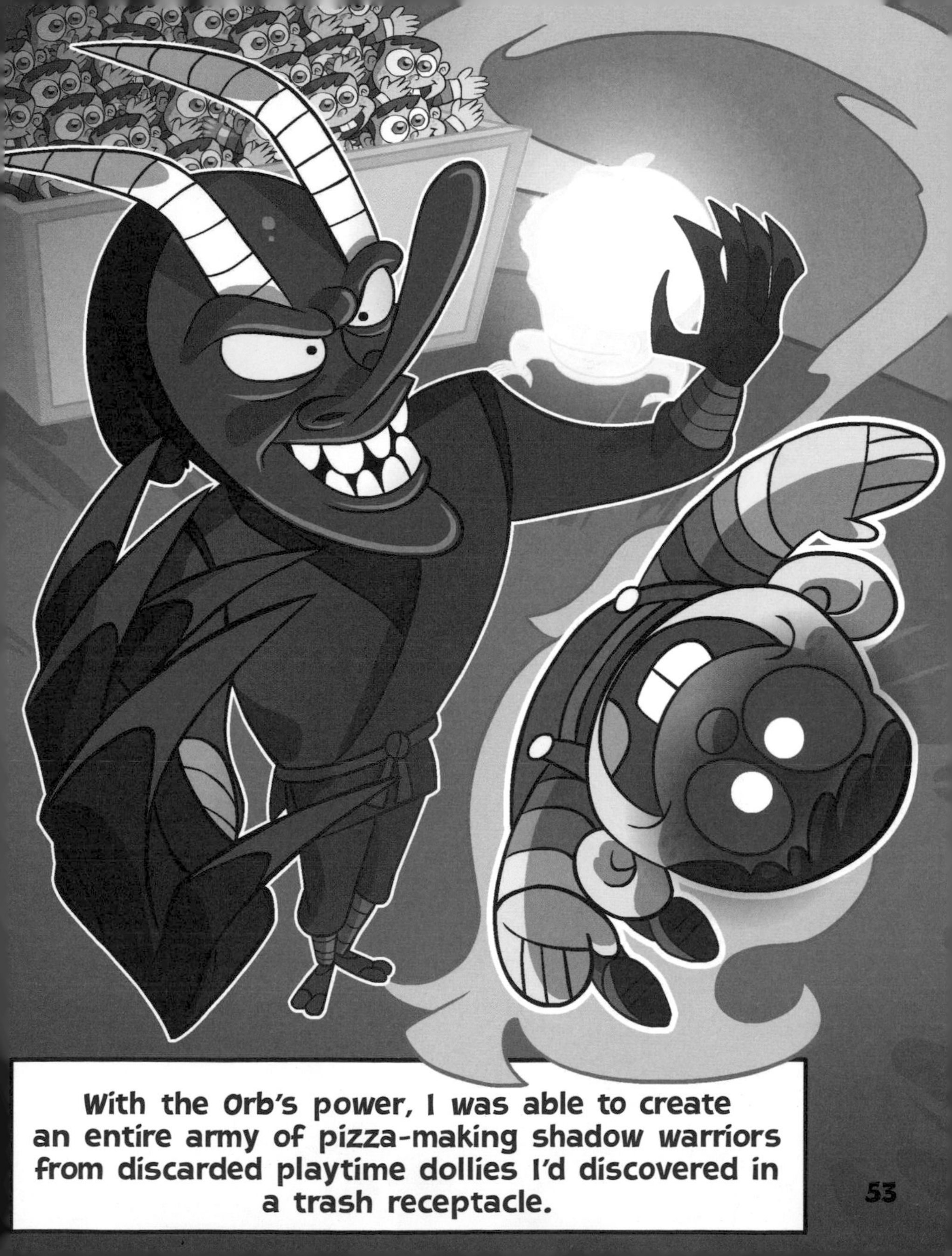

With the Orb's power, I was able to create an entire army of pizza-making shadow warriors from discarded playtime dollies I'd discovered in a trash receptacle.

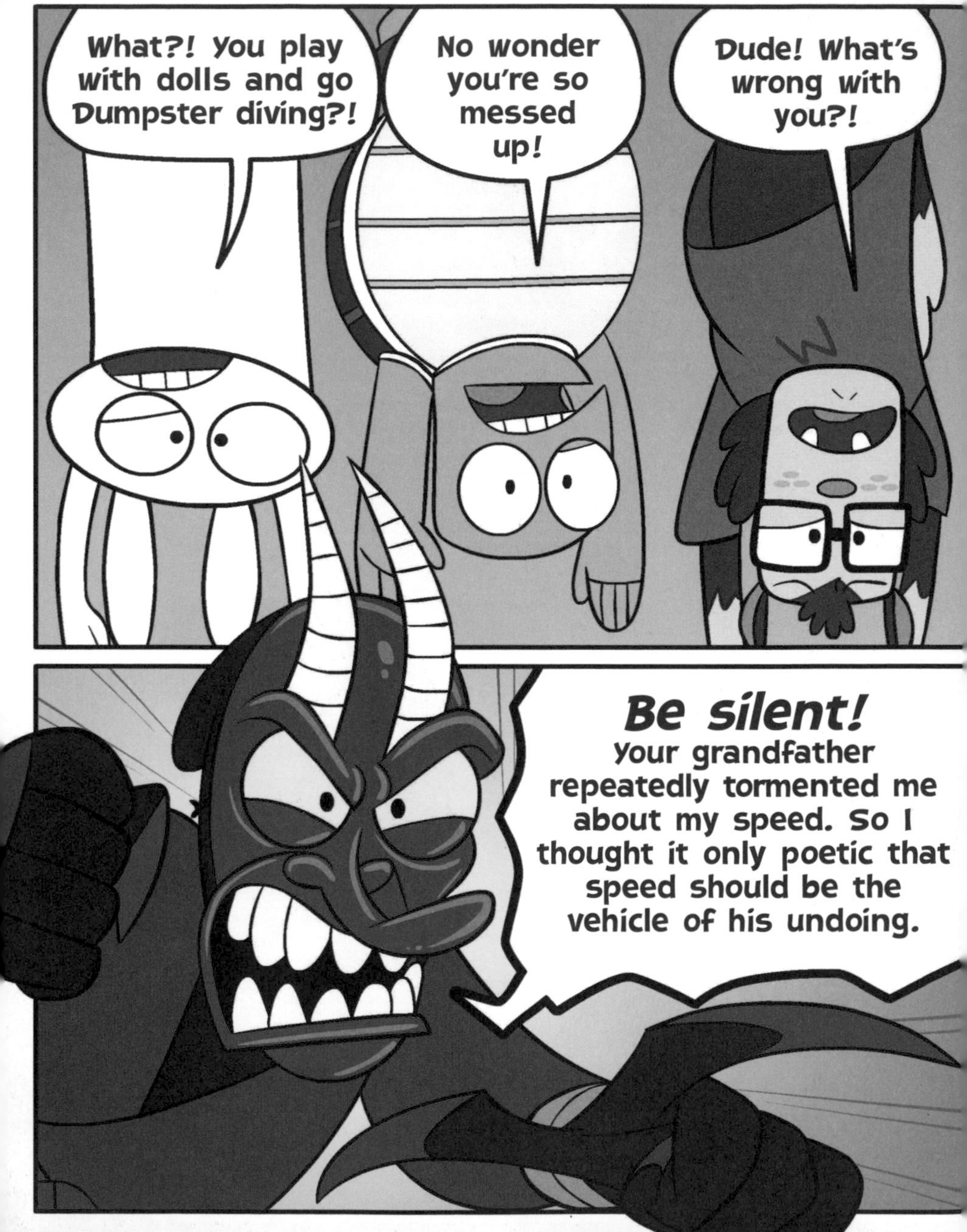
What?! You play with dolls and go Dumpster diving?!
No wonder you're so messed up!
Dude! What's wrong with you?!
Be silent! Your grandfather repeatedly tormented me about my speed. So I thought it only poetic that speed should be the vehicle of his undoing.

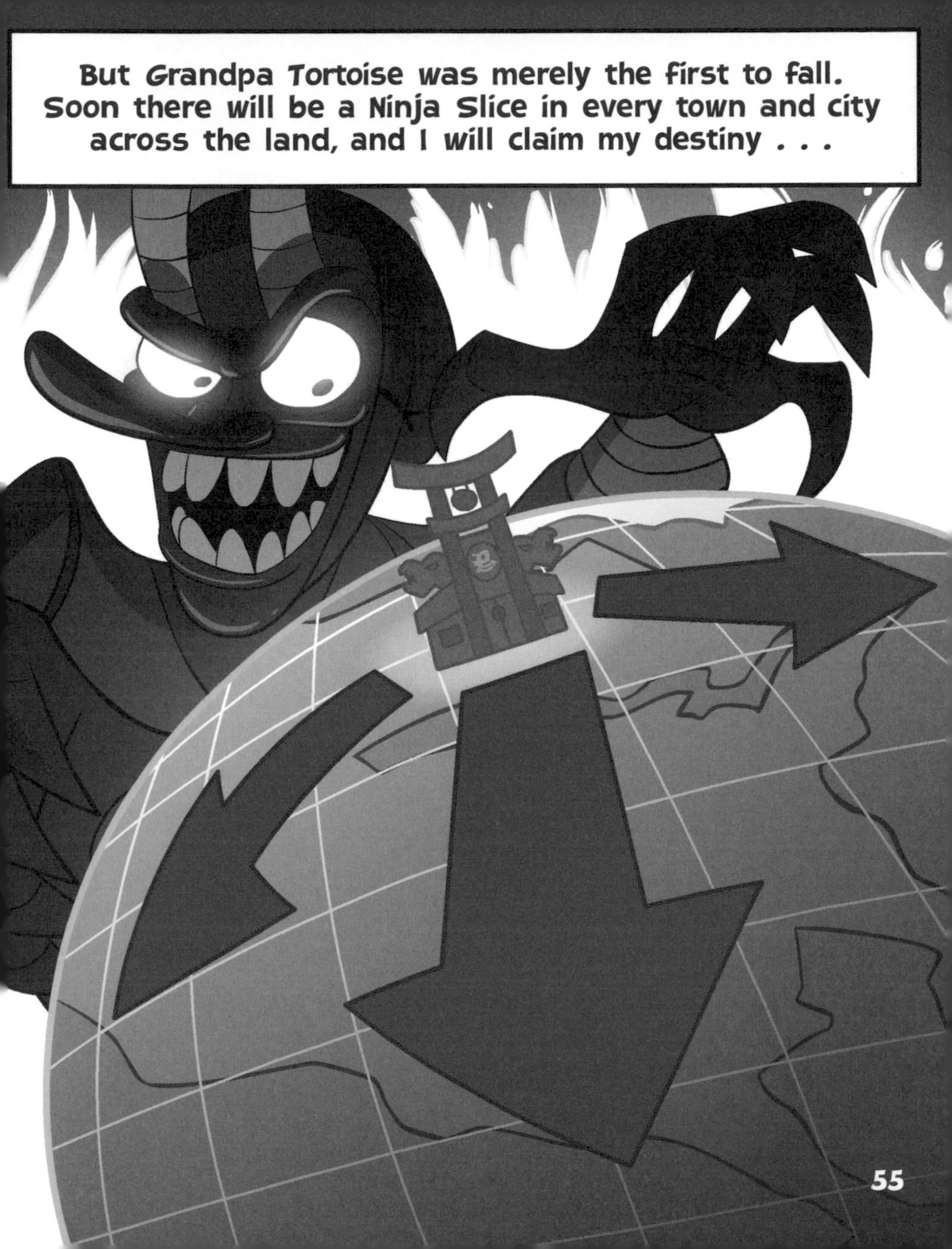
But Grandpa Tortoise was merely the first to fall. Soon there will be a Ninja Slice in every town and city across the land, and I will claim my destiny . . .

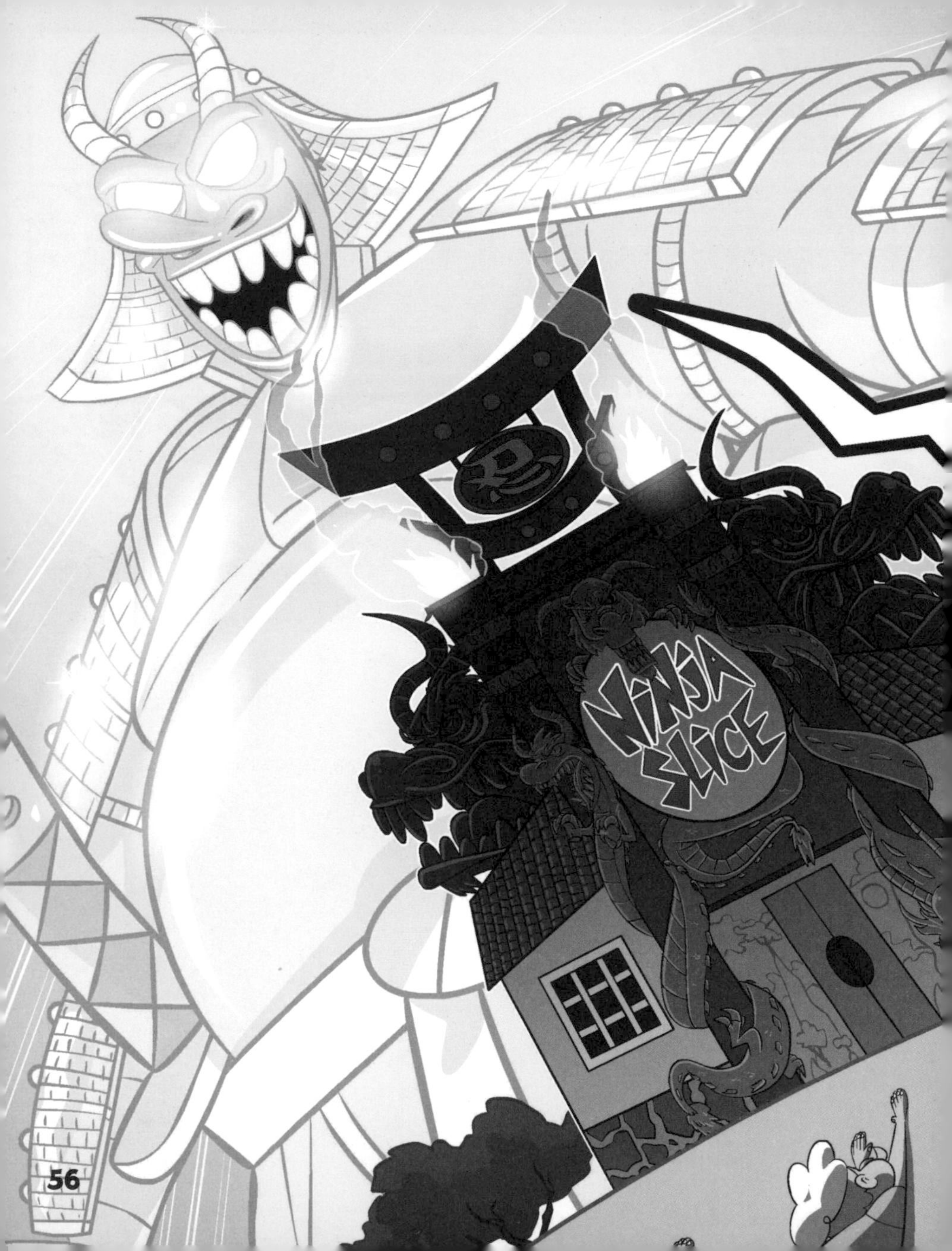
NINJA SLICE

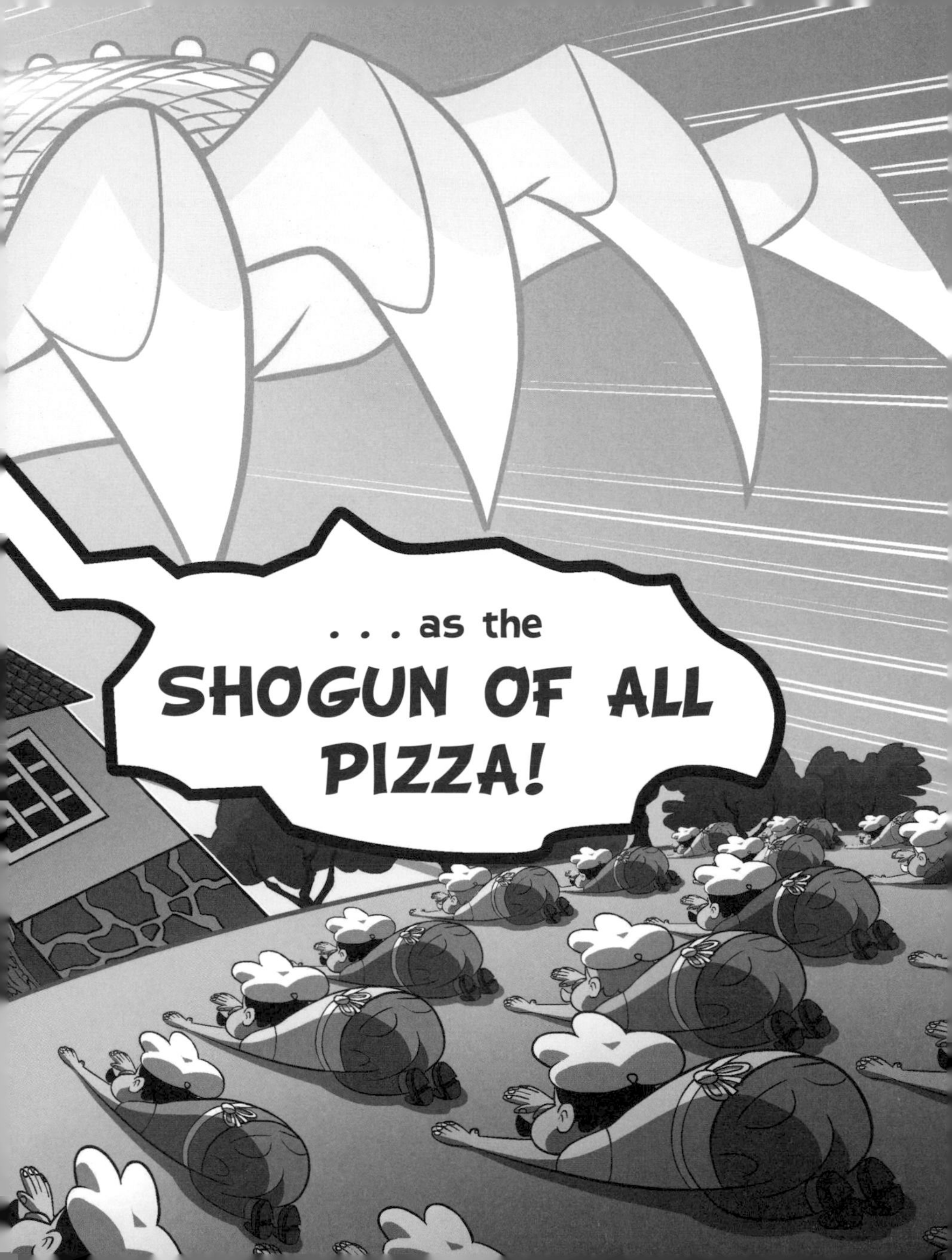
. . . as the SHOGUN OF ALL PIZZA!

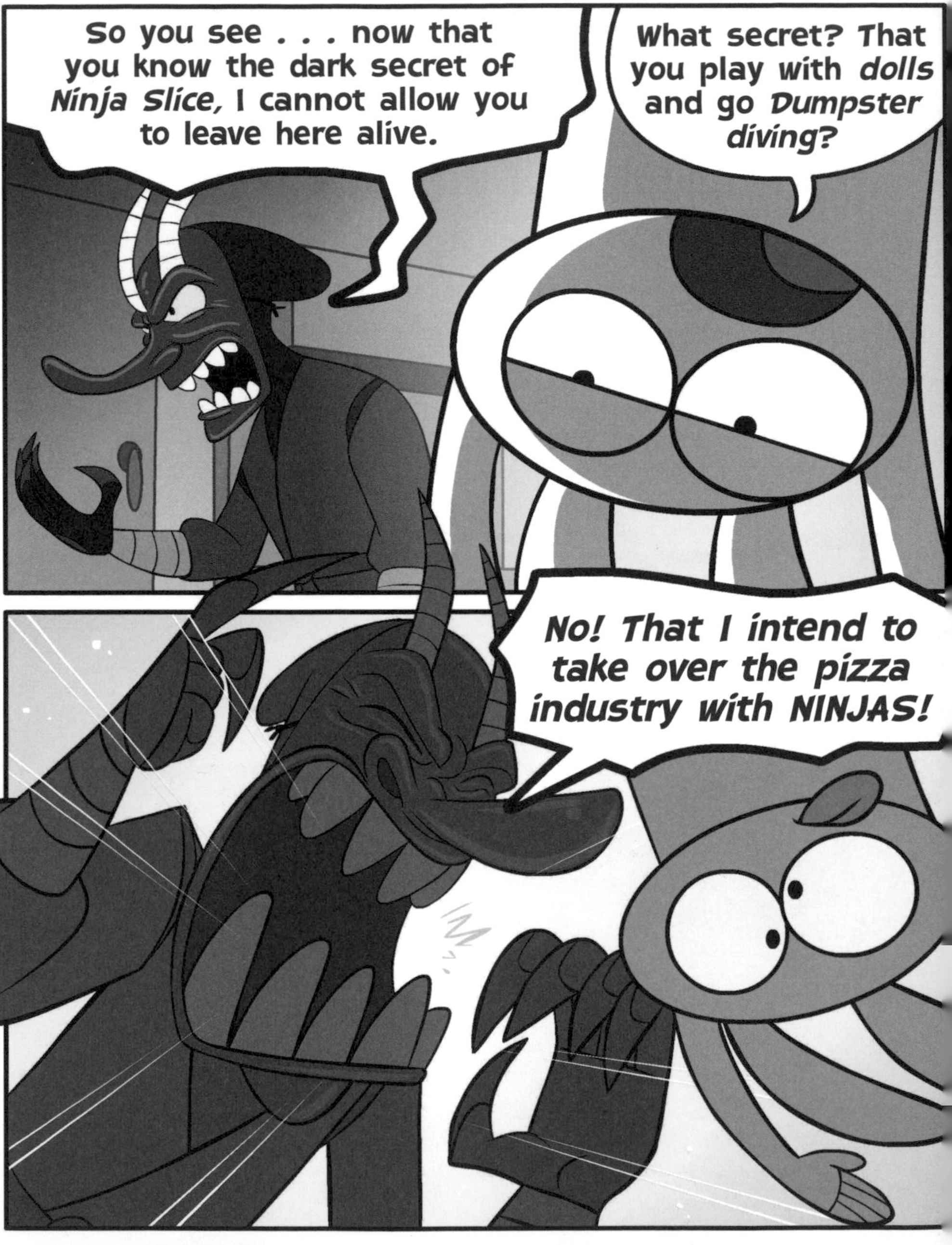
So you see . . . now that you know the dark secret of *Ninja Slice,* I cannot allow you to leave here alive.
What secret? That you play with *dolls* and go *Dumpster diving?*
No! That I intend to take over the pizza industry with NINJAS!

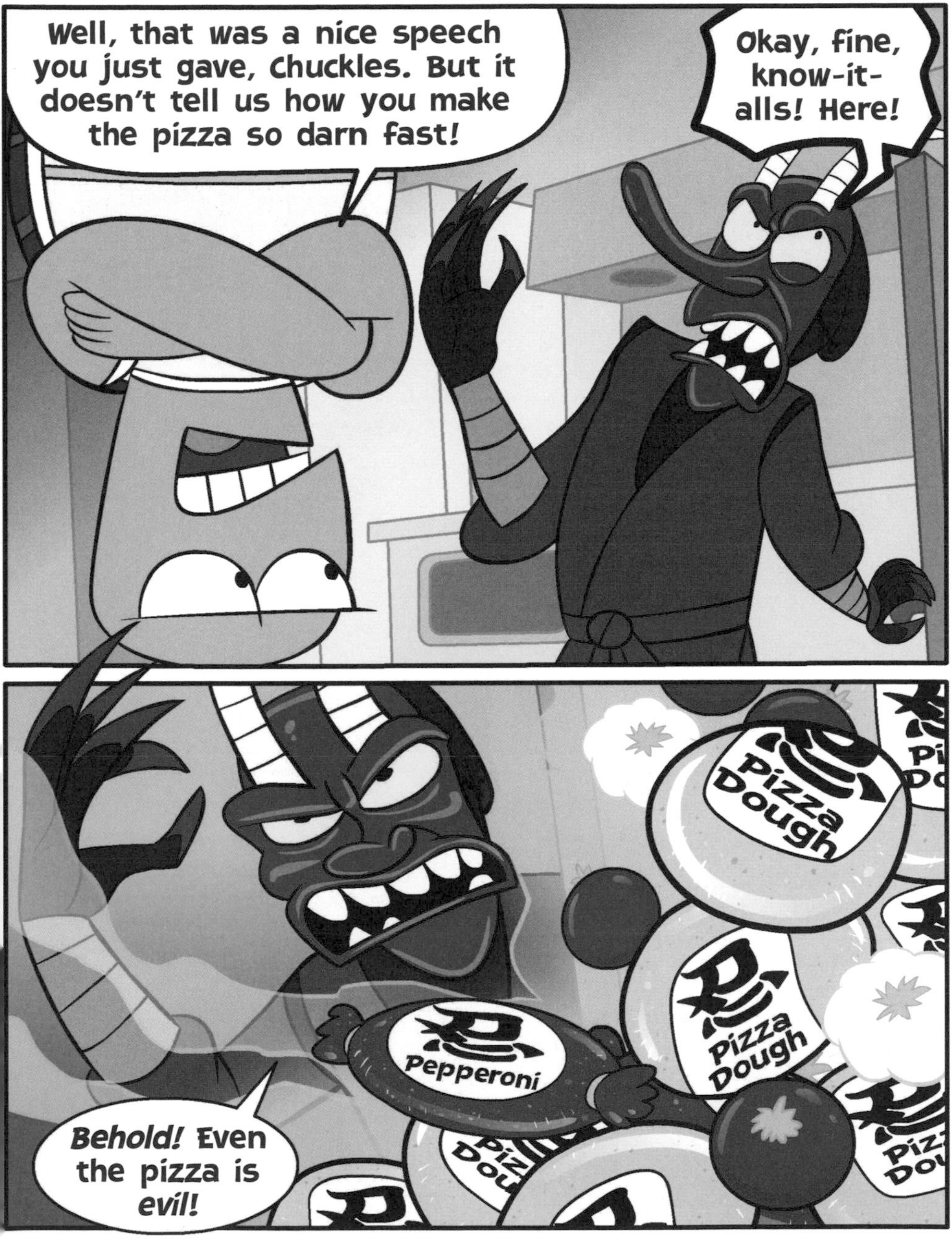
Well, that was a nice speech you just gave, Chuckles. But it doesn't tell us how you make the pizza so darn fast!
Okay, fine, know-it-alls! Here!
Pizza Dough
Pepperoni
Pizza Dough
Behold! Even the pizza is *evil!*

By combining the dark magic of the Orb with the latest in dehydrated cooking products, I can now cook pizza in an instant with a mere drop of water! All that my minions do afterward is add toppings and serve.

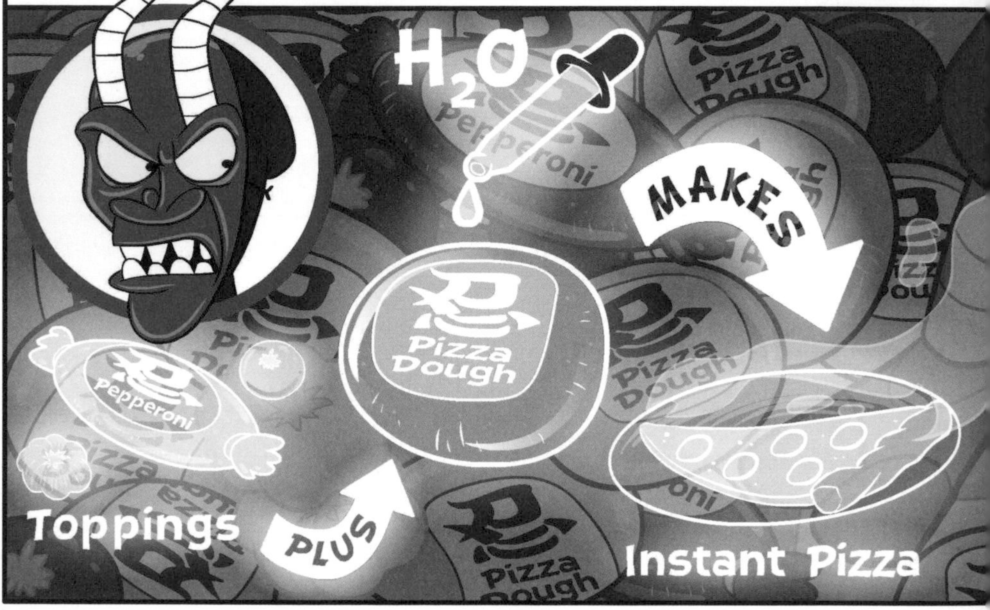
H_2O
MAKES
Pizza Dough
Pepperoni
Toppings
PLUS
Instant Pizza

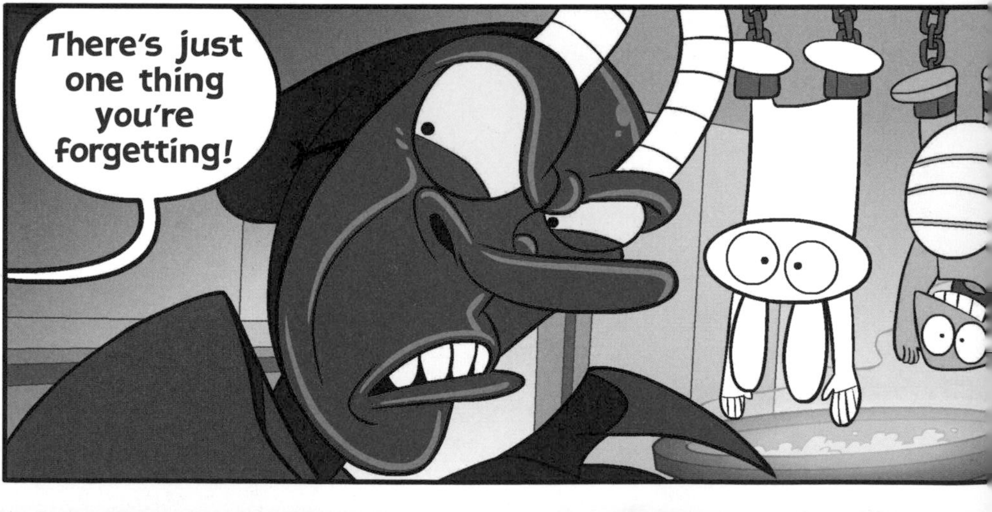
There's just one thing you're forgetting!

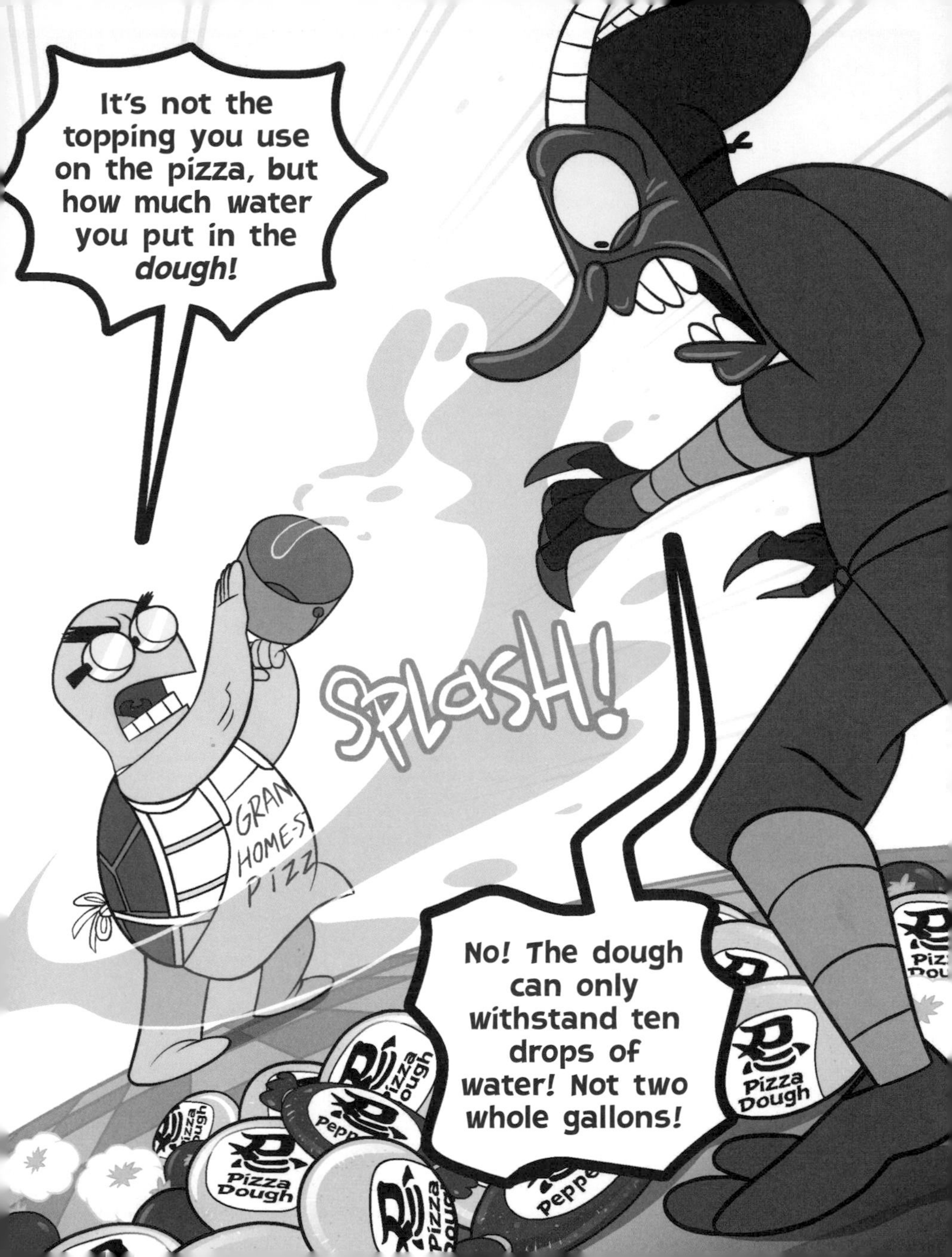
It's not the topping you use on the pizza, but how much water you put in the *dough!*
SPLASH!
GRAN HOME-ST PIZZ
No! The dough can only withstand ten drops of water! Not two whole gallons!
Pizza Dough
Pizza Dough
Pizza Dough
Pizza Dough
Pizza Dough
Pizza Dough

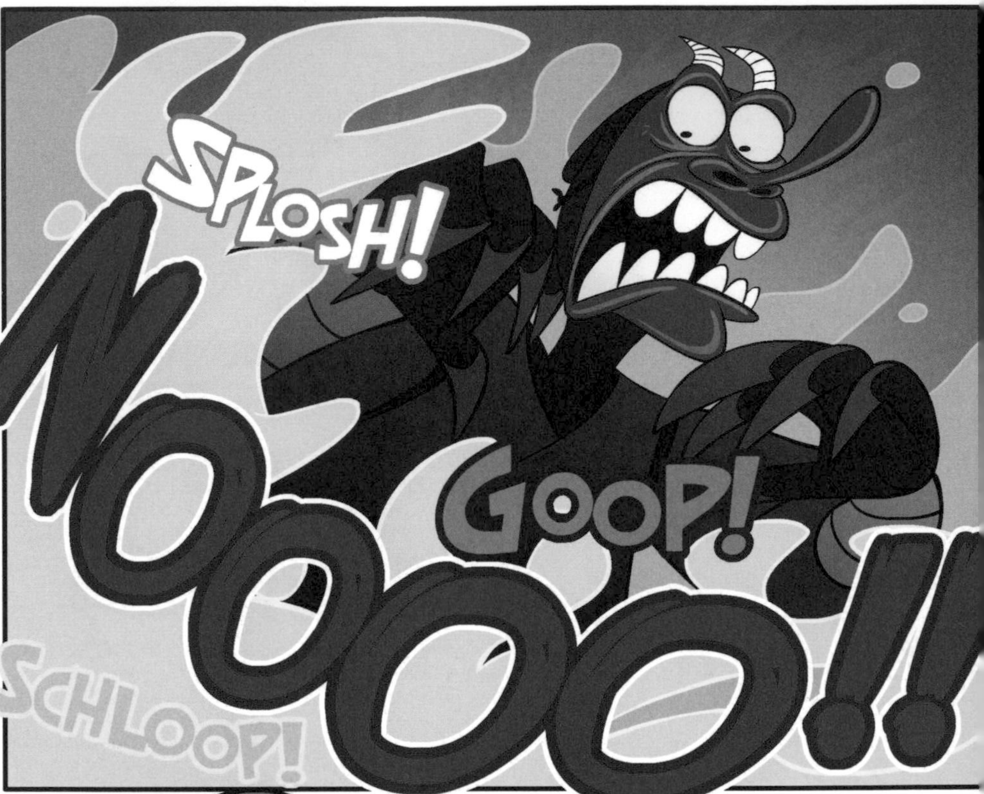
SPLOSH!
NOOOOO!!
GOOP!
SCHLOOP!

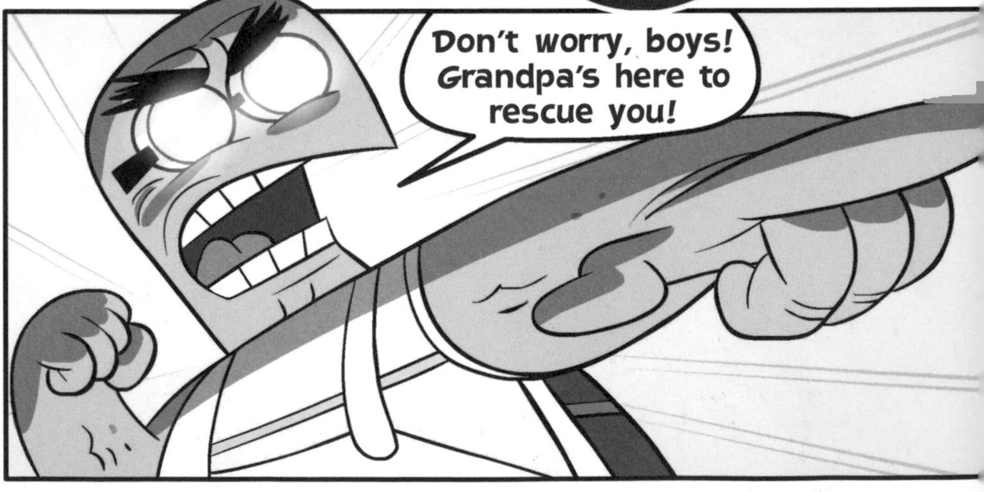
Don't worry, boys! Grandpa's here to rescue you!

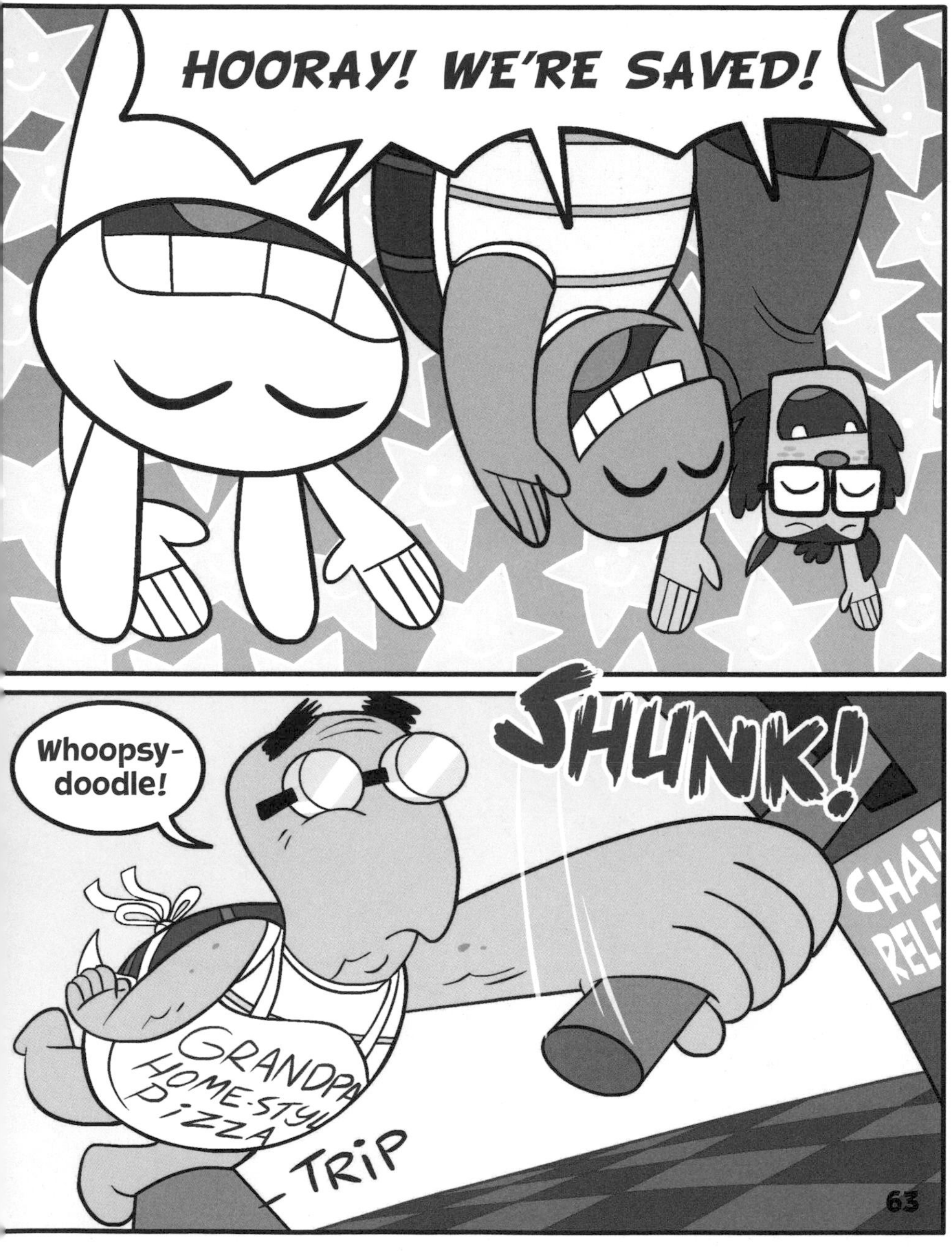
HOORAY! WE'RE SAVED!
Whoopsy-doodle!
SHUNK!
CHAI
RELE
GRANDPA HOME-STYL PIZZA
TRIP

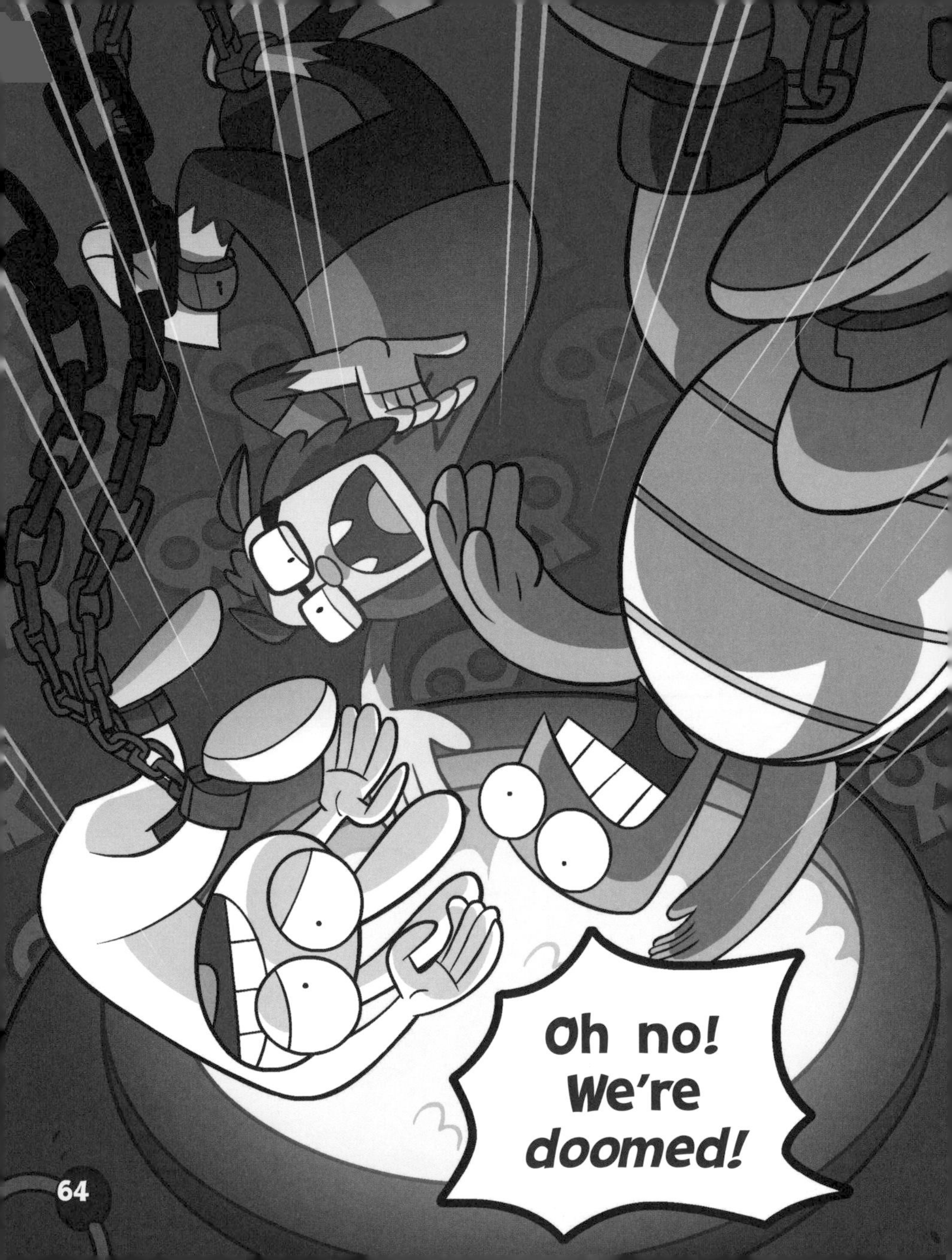
Oh no! We're doomed!

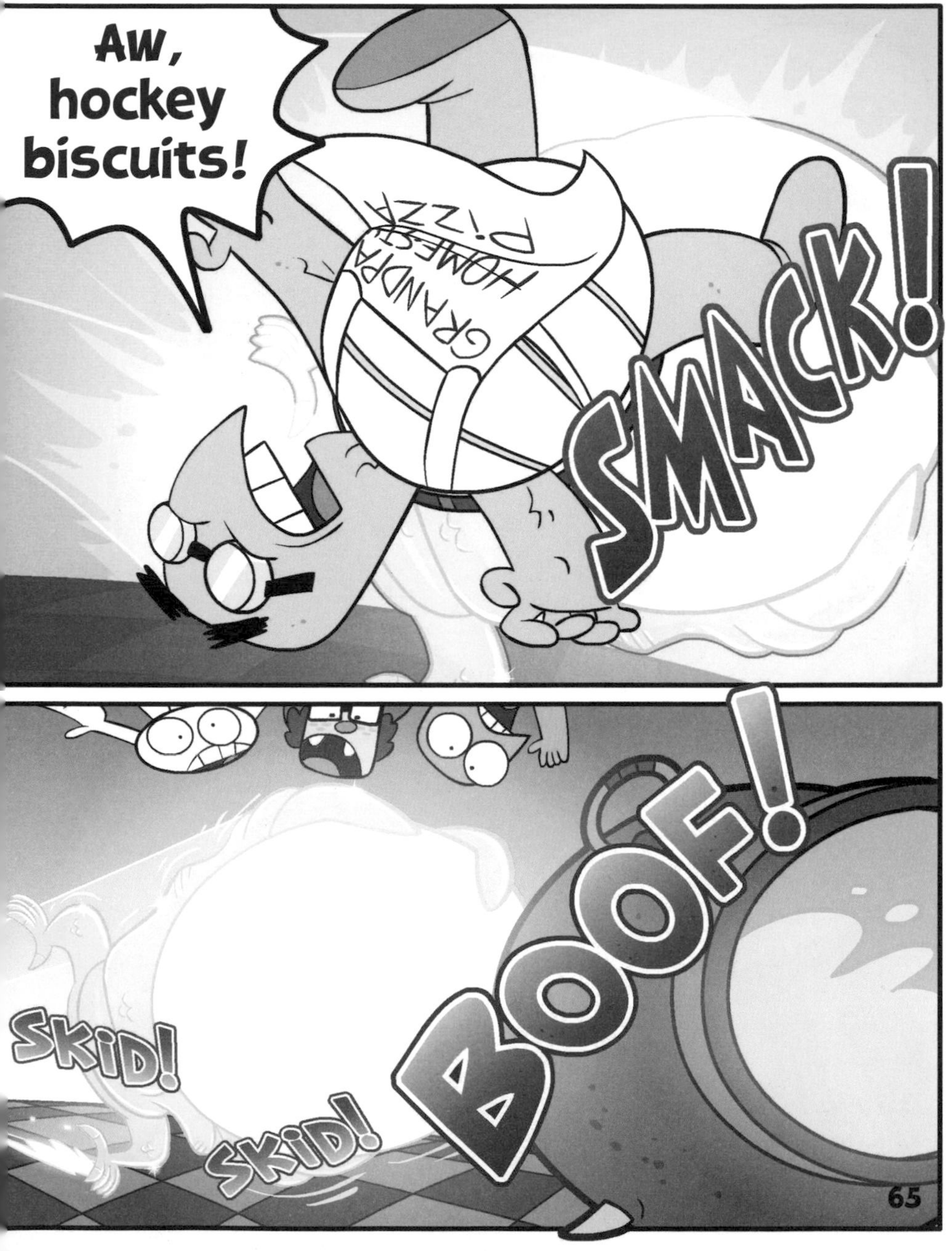

Aw, hockey biscuits!
SMACK!
SKID!
SKID!
BOOF!

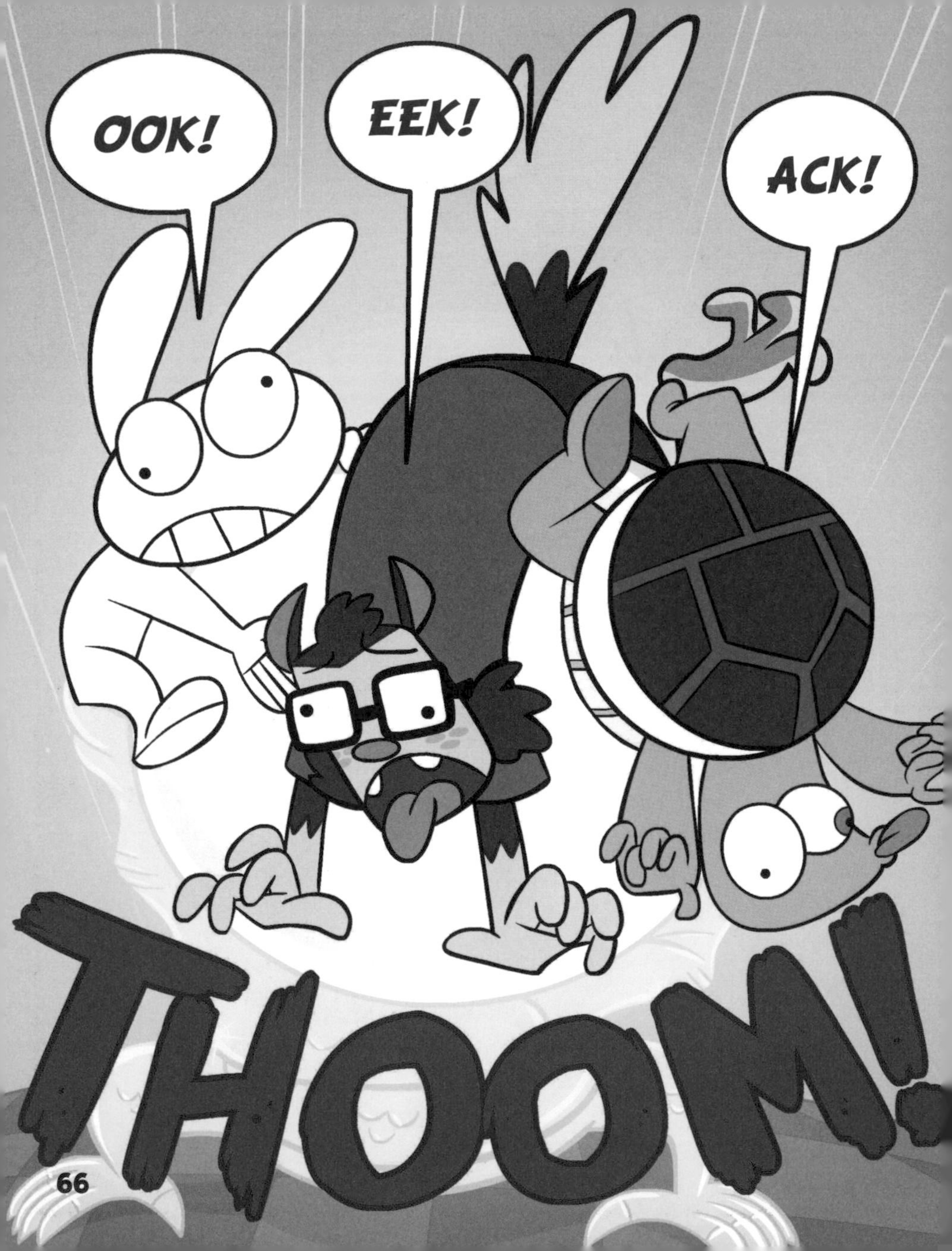
OOK!
EEK!
ACK!
THOOM!

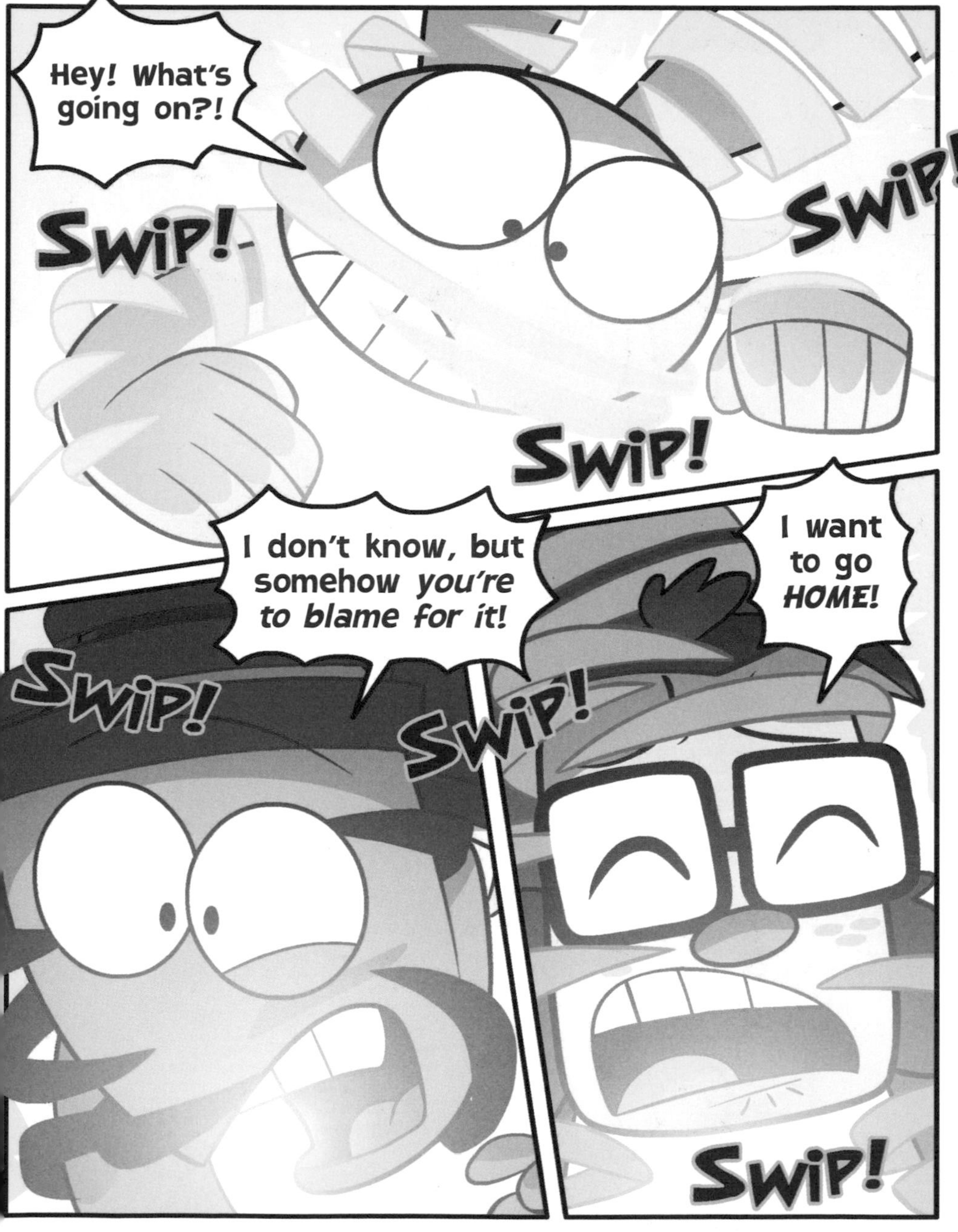
Hey! What's going on?!
SWIP!
SWIP!
SWIP!
I don't know, but somehow *you're to blame for it!*
I want to go *HOME!*
SWIP!
SWIP!
SWIP!

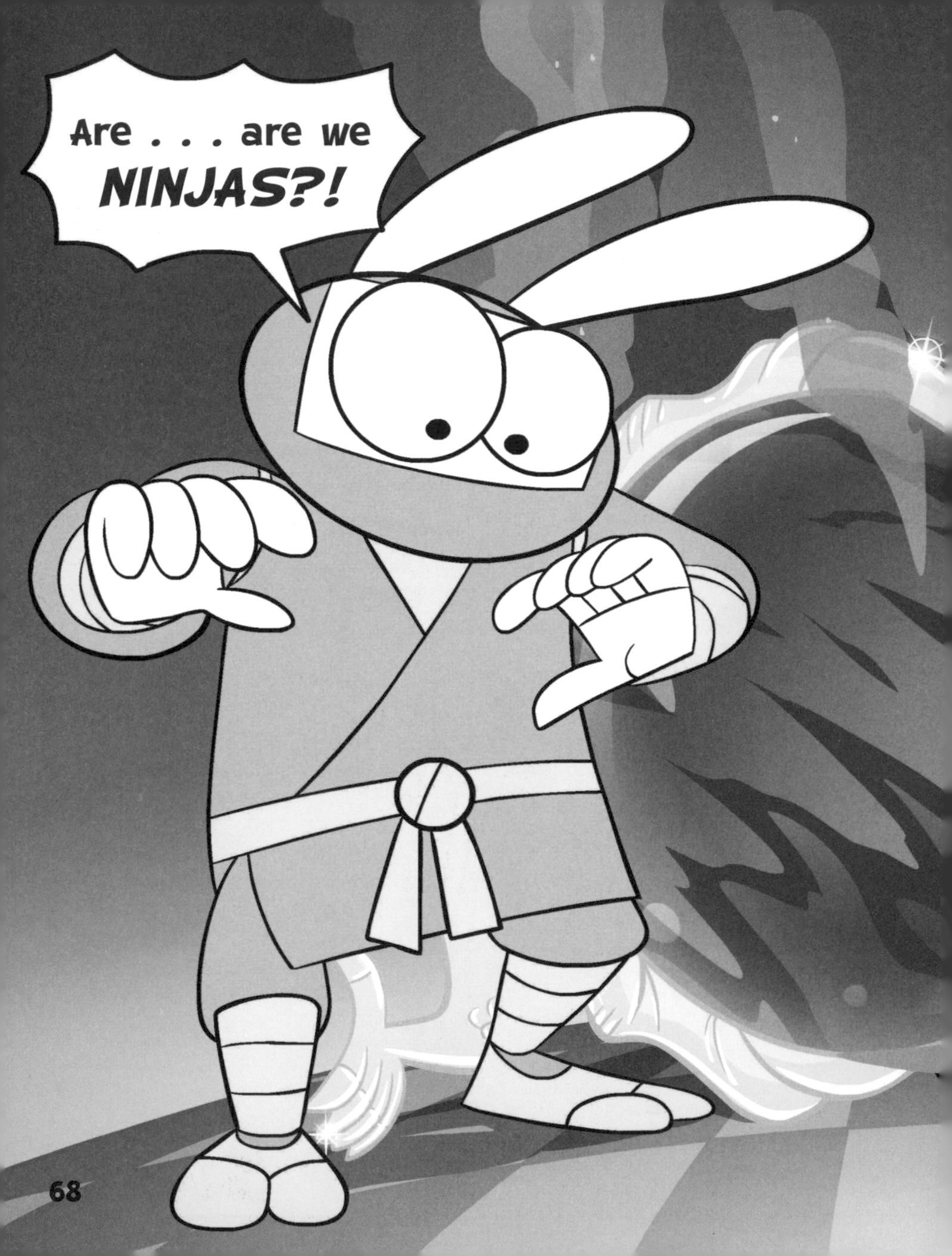
Are . . . are we NINJAS?!

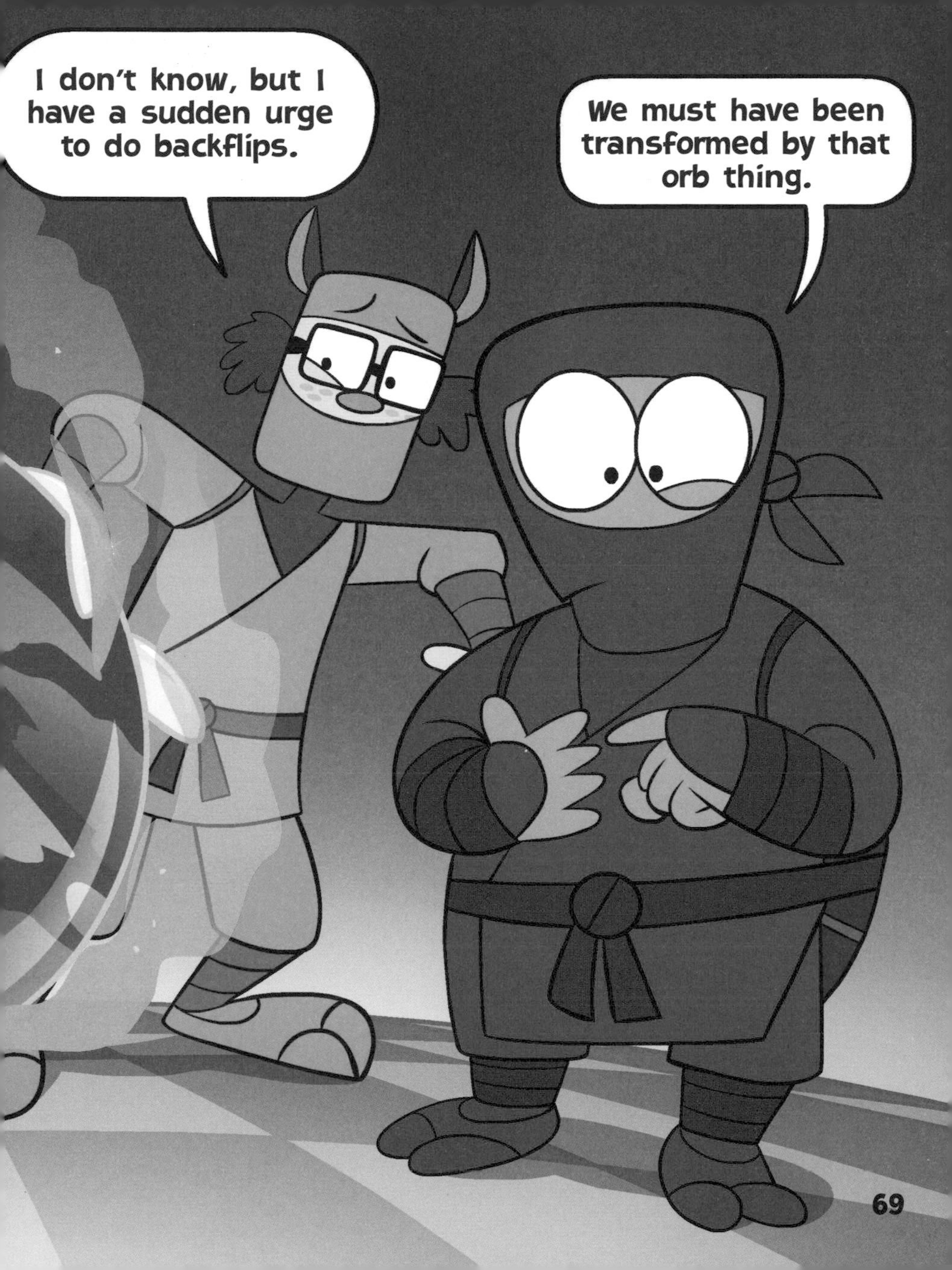
I don't know, but I have a sudden urge to do backflips.
We must have been transformed by that orb thing.

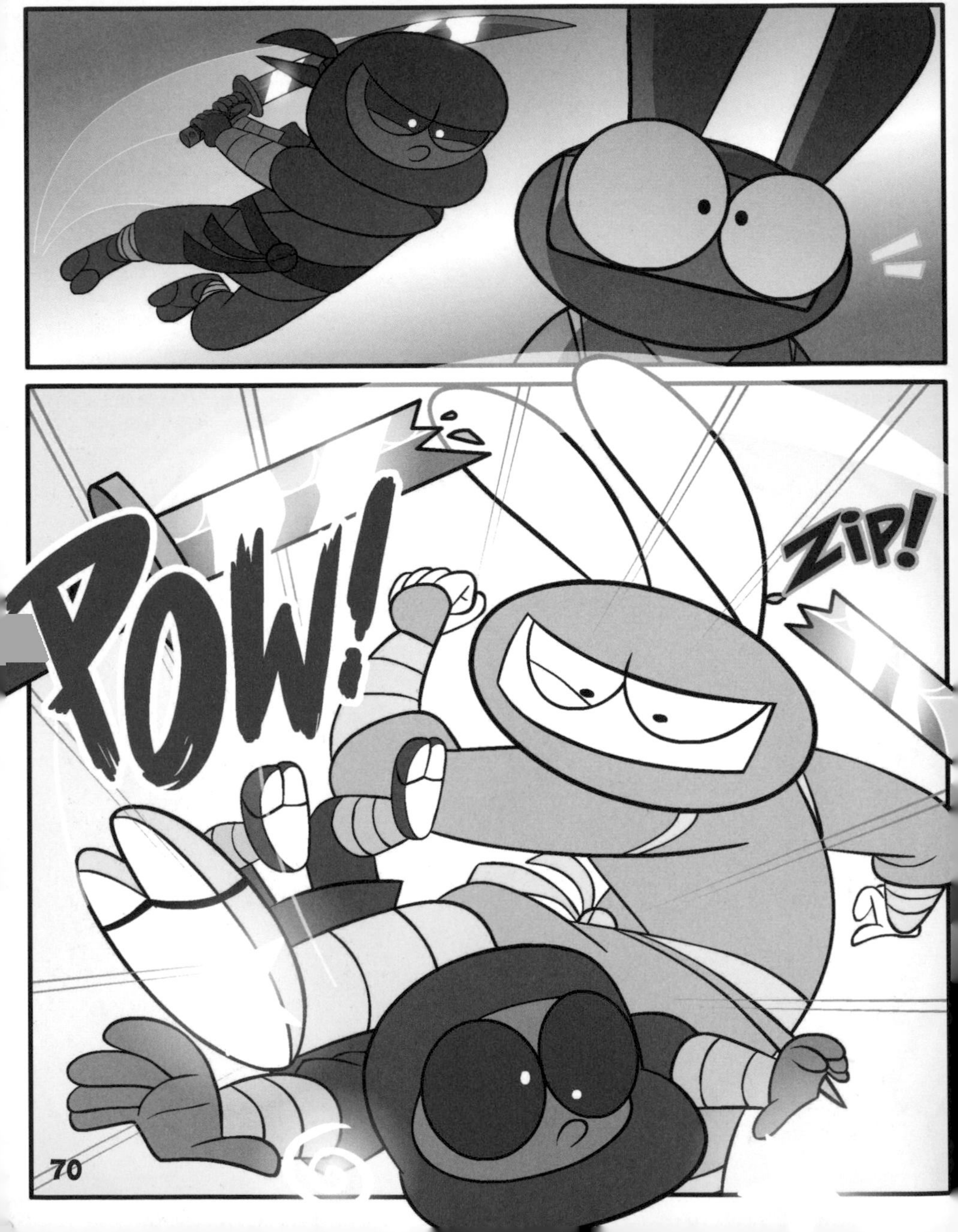
POW!
ZIP!

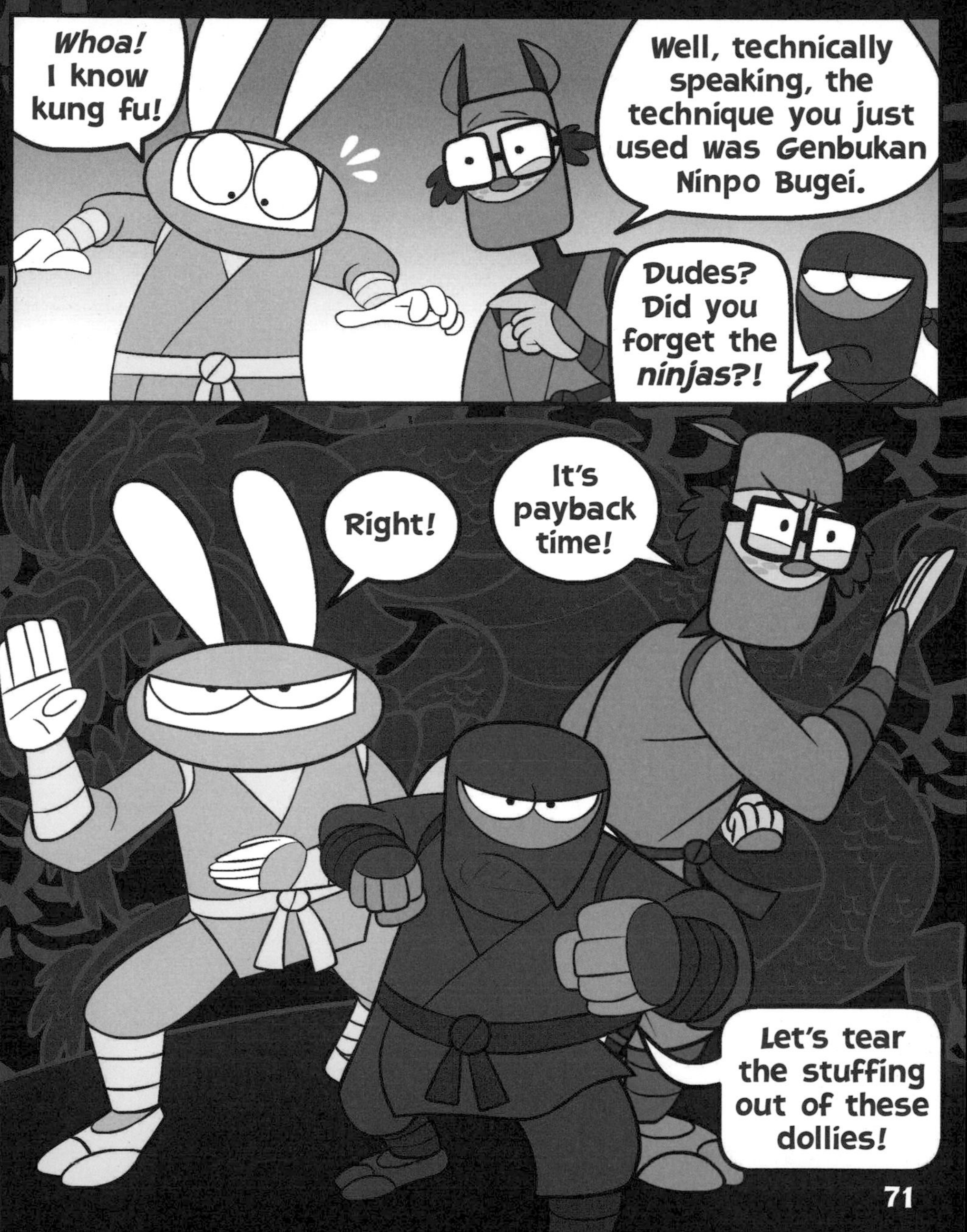
Whoa! I know kung fu!
Well, technically speaking, the technique you just used was Genbukan Ninpo Bugei.
Dudes? Did you forget the *ninjas?!*
Right!
It's payback time!
Let's tear the stuffing out of these dollies!

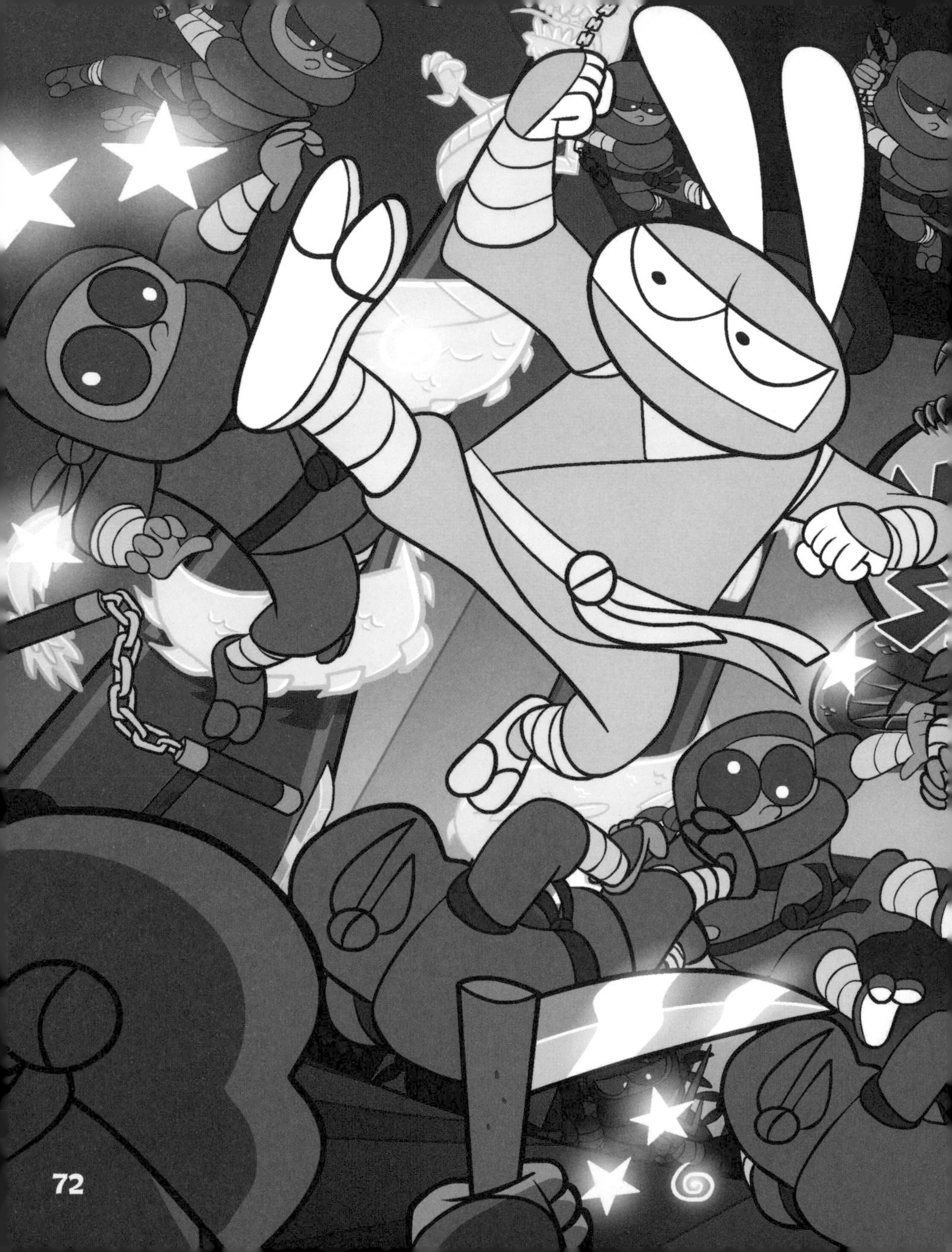

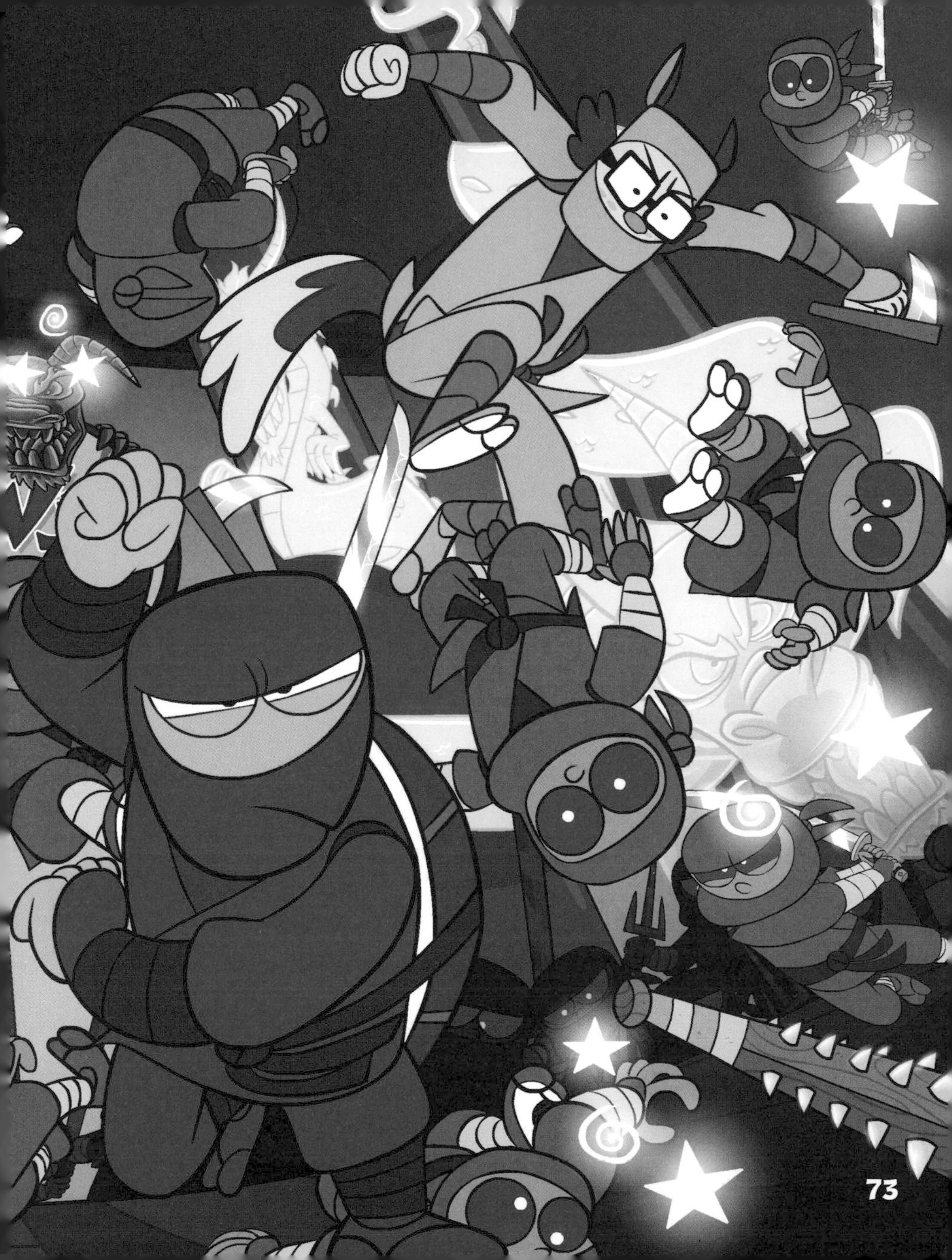

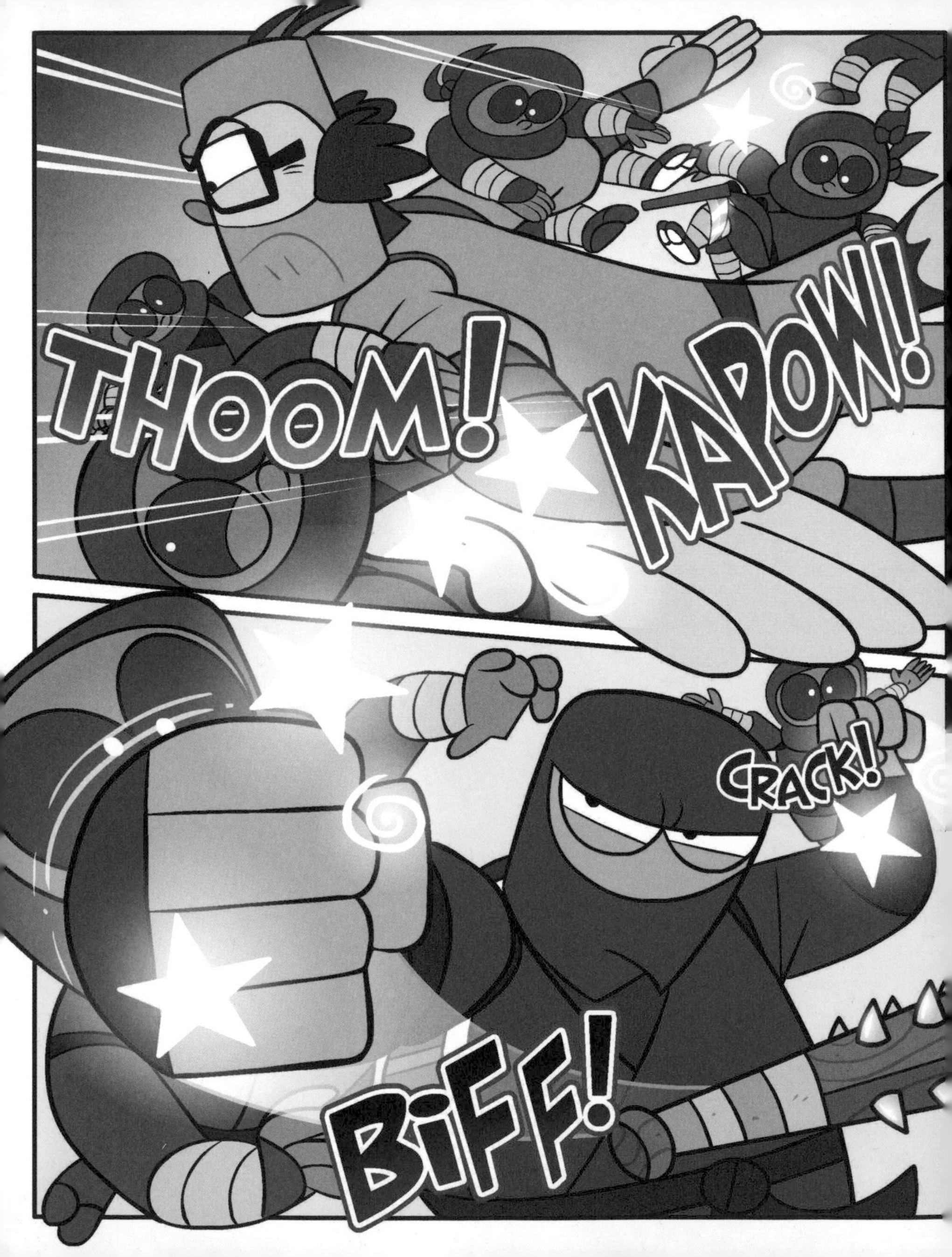
THOOM!
KAPOW!
CRACK!
BIFF!

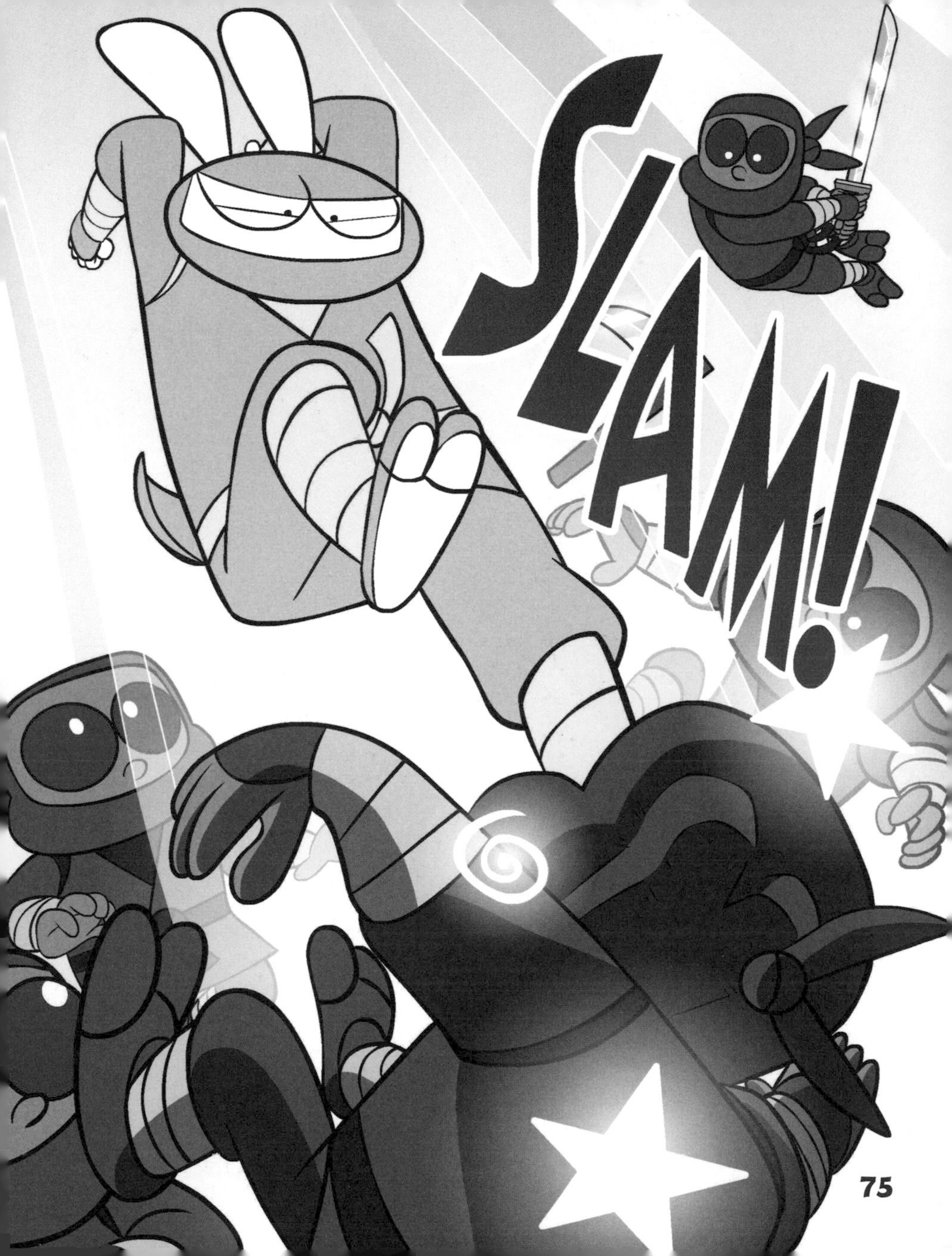
SLAM!

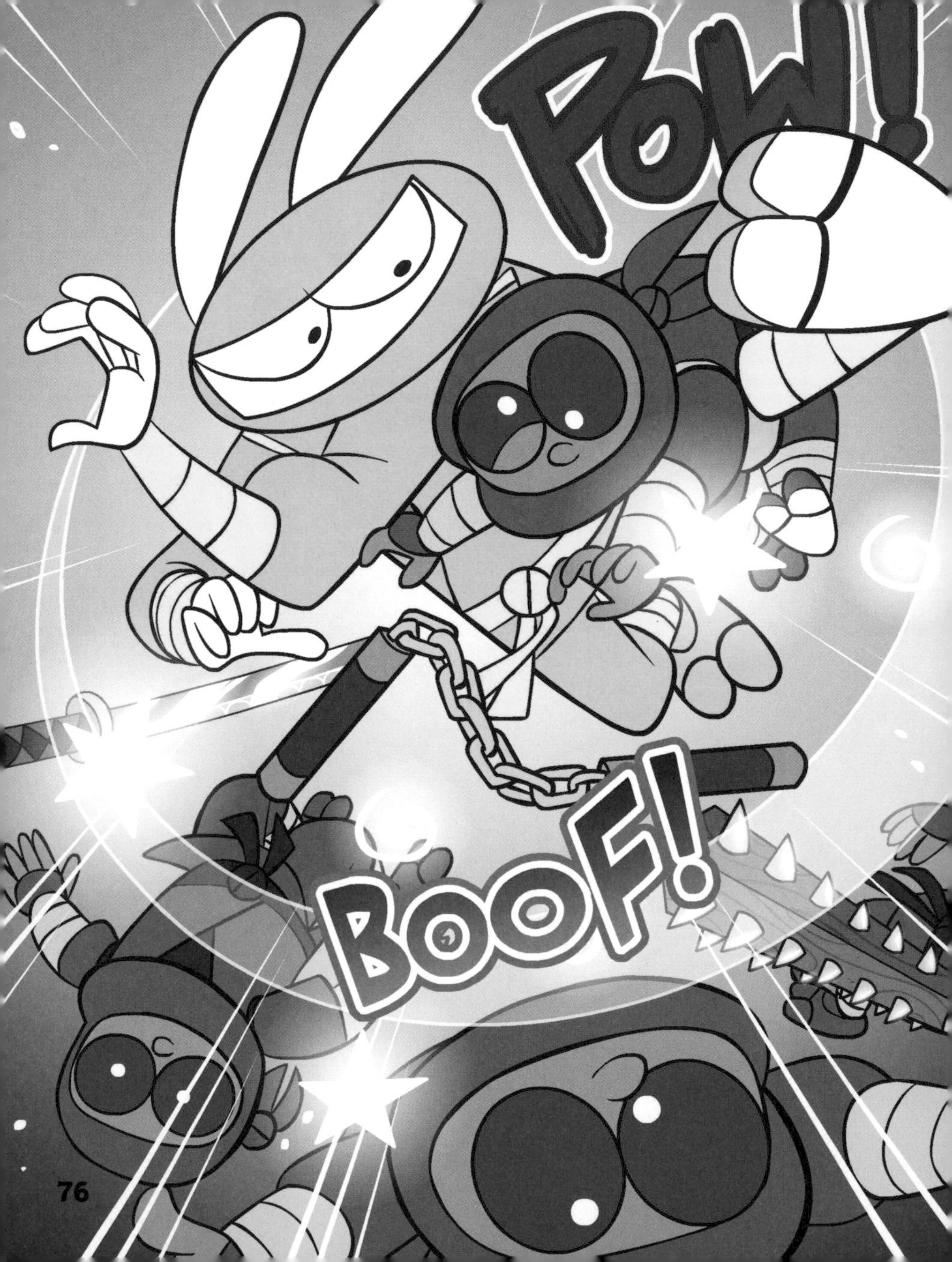
POW!
BOOF!

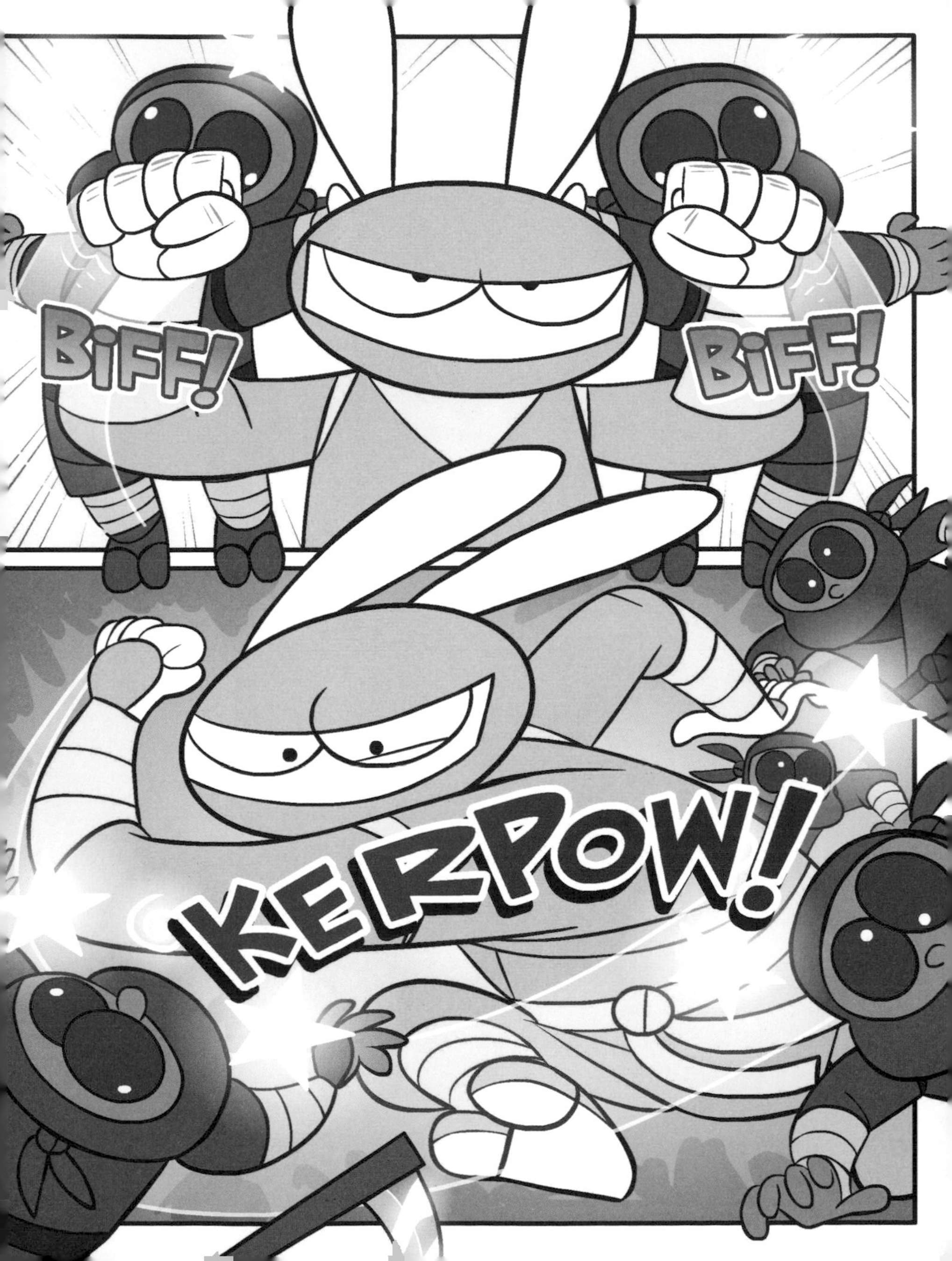
BIFF!
BIFF!
KERPOW!

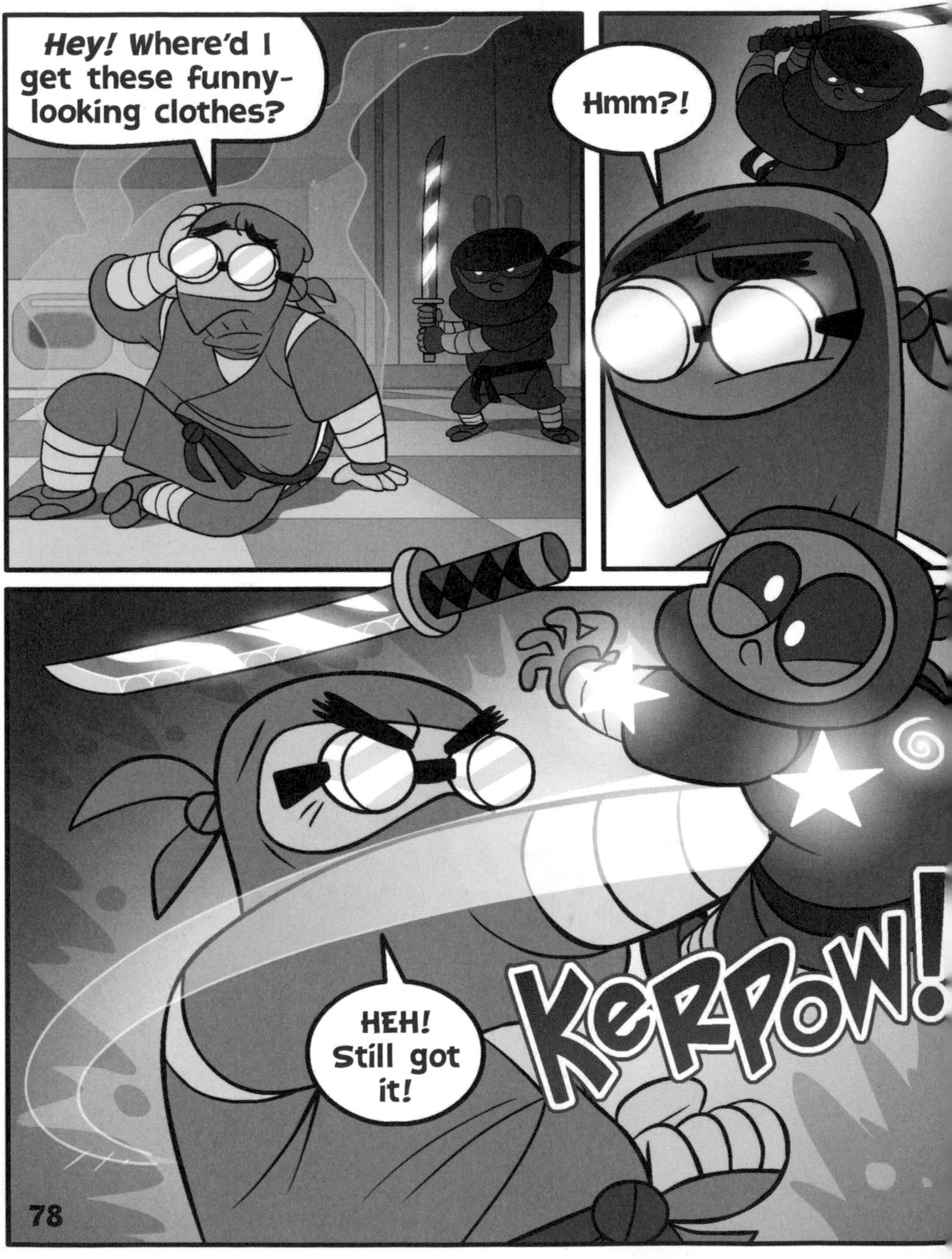
Hey! Where'd I get these funny-looking clothes?
Hmm?!
HEH! Still got it!
KERPOW!

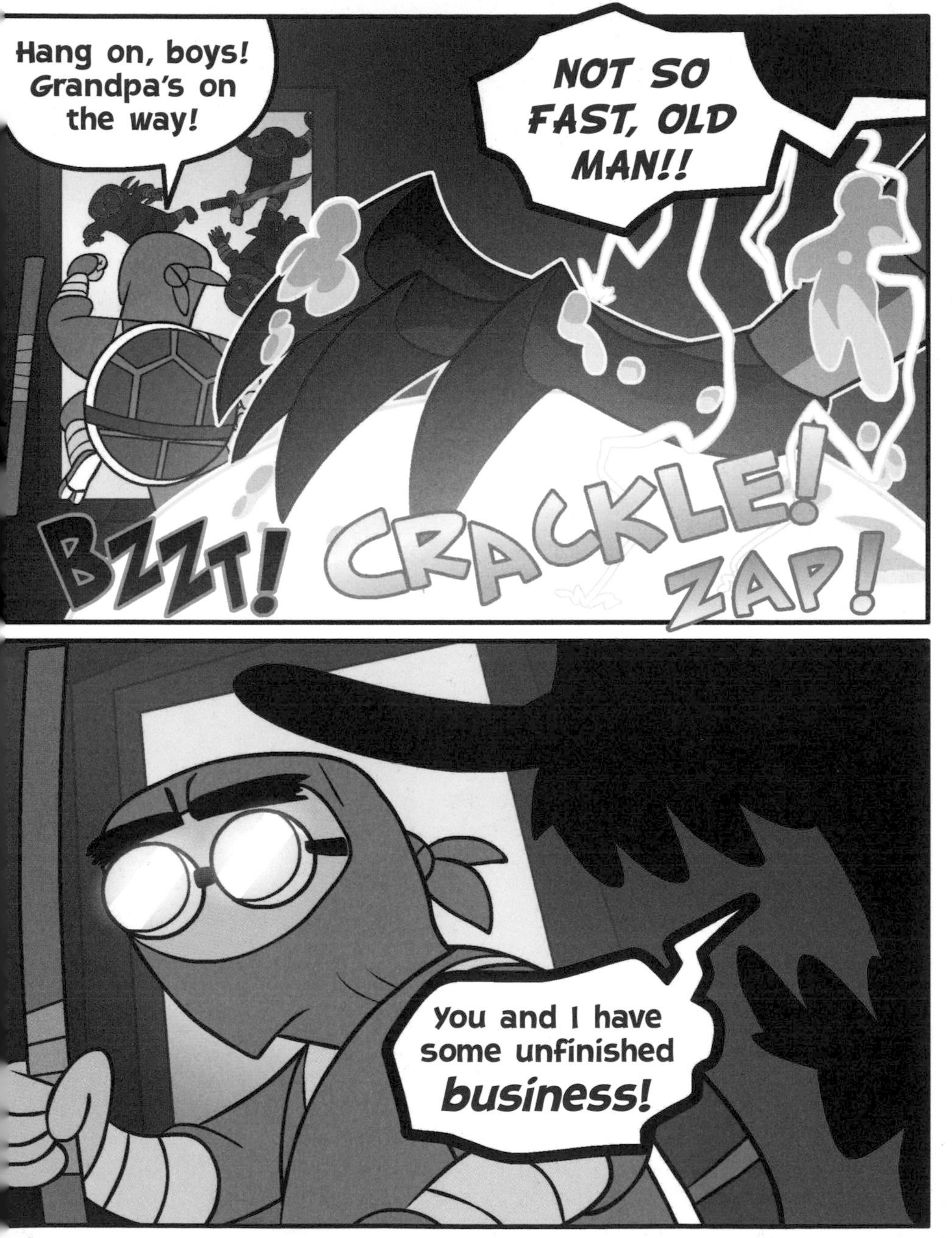
Hang on, boys! Grandpa's on the way!
NOT SO FAST, OLD MAN!!
BZZT!
CRACKLE!
ZAP!
You and I have some unfinished *business*!

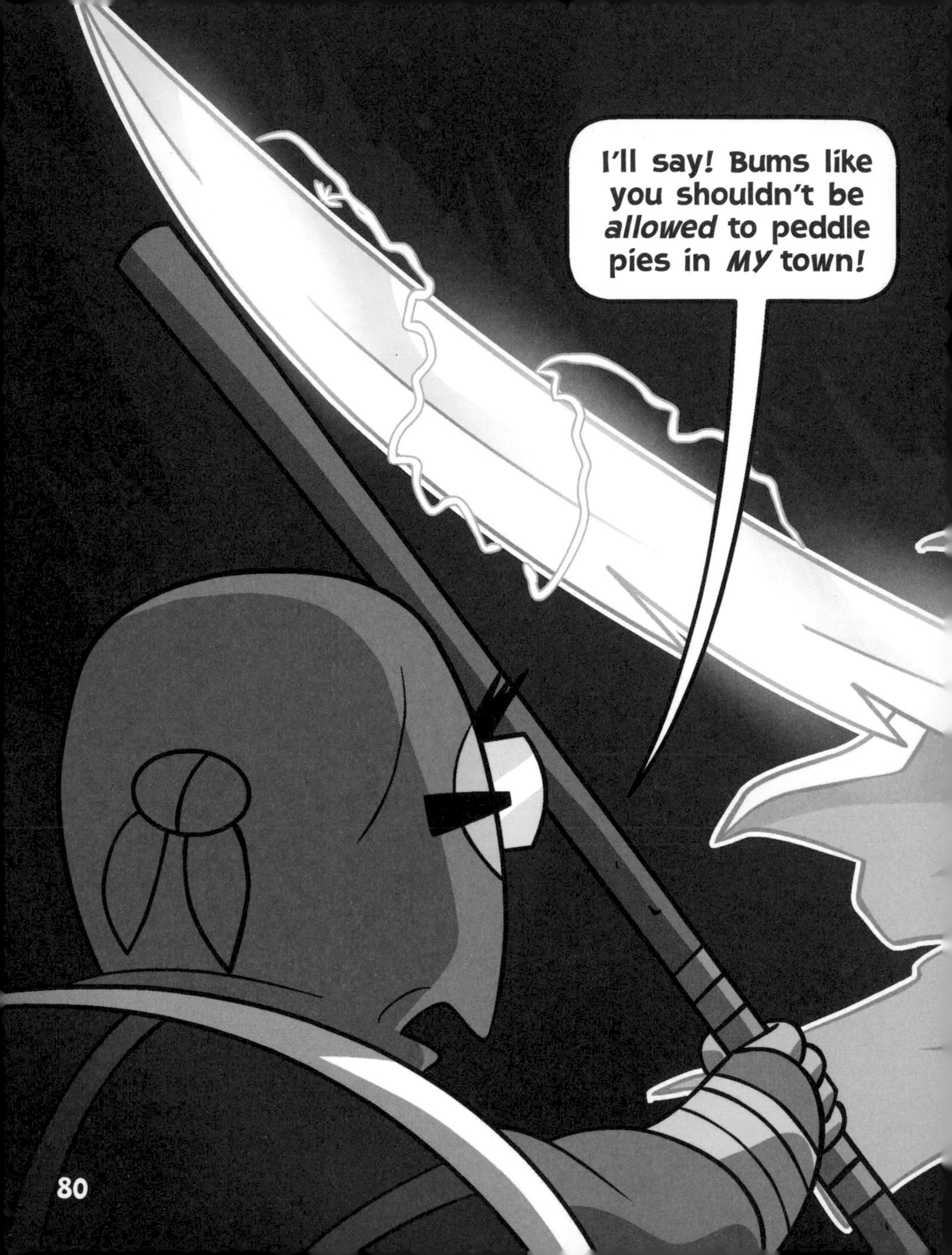
I'll say! Bums like you shouldn't be *allowed* to peddle pies in *MY* town!

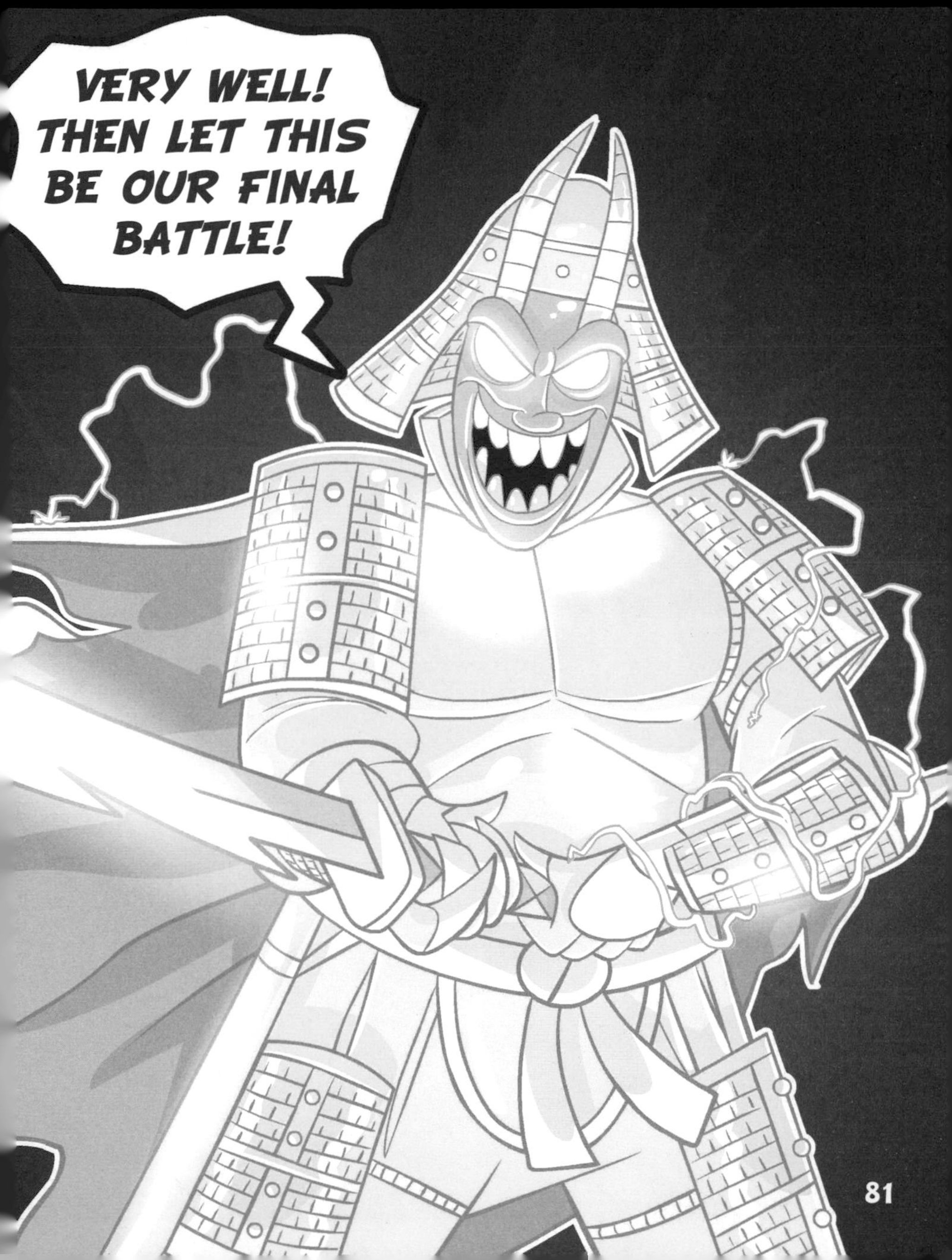
VERY WELL! THEN LET THIS BE OUR FINAL BATTLE!

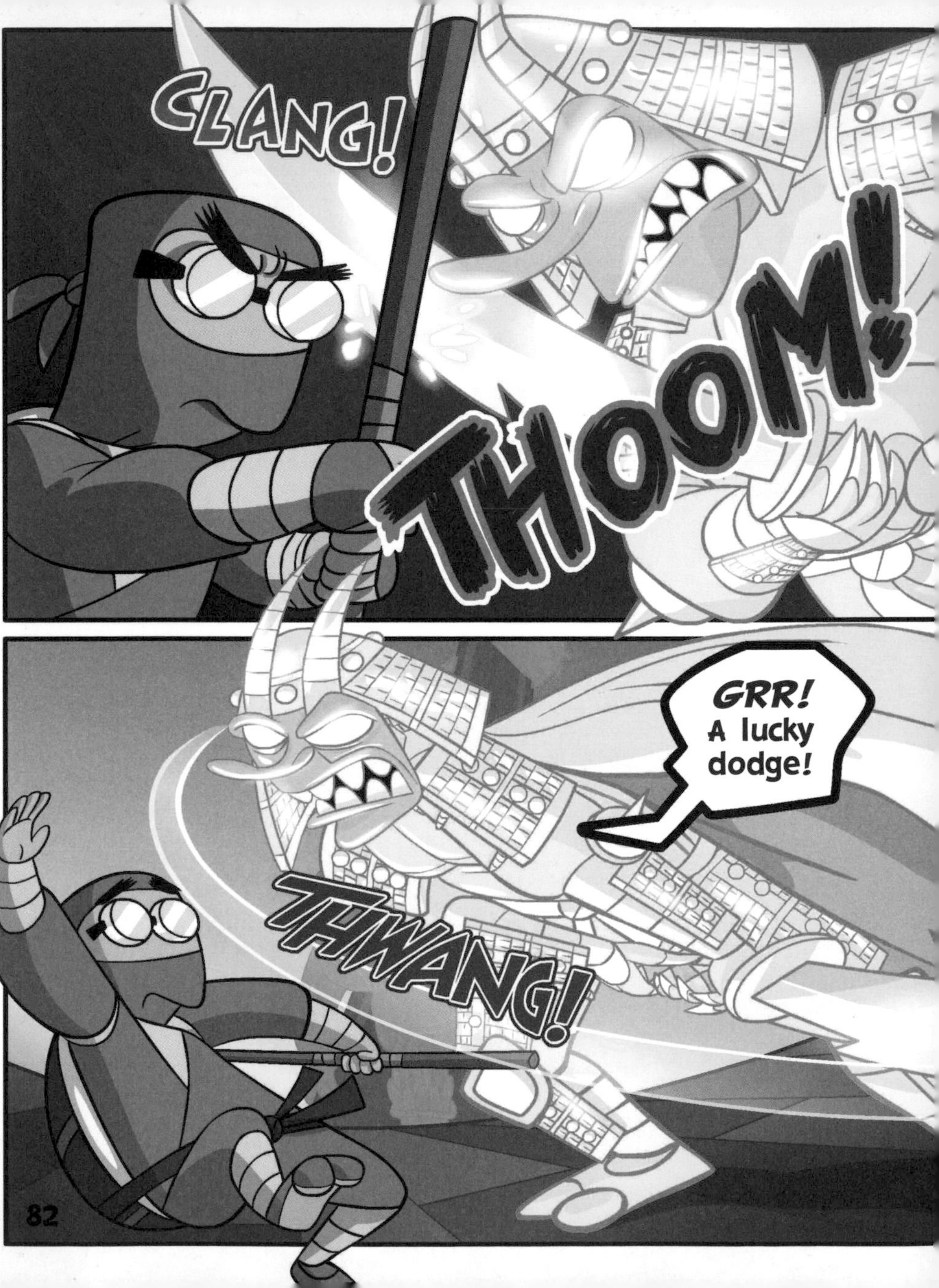
CLANG!
THOOM!
GRR! A lucky dodge!
THWANG!

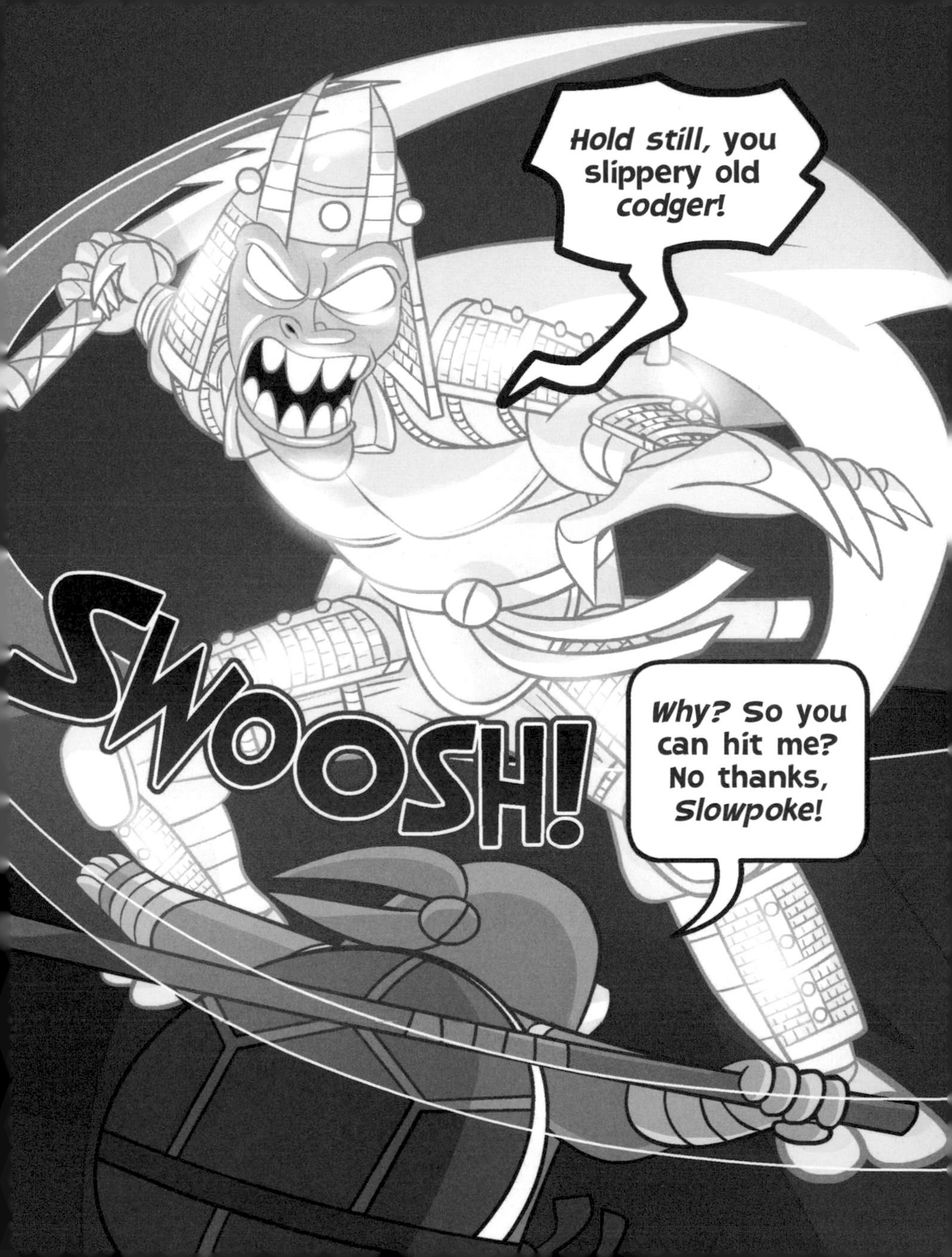
Hold still, you slippery old codger!
SWOOSH!
Why? So you can hit me? No thanks, Slowpoke!

You're almost as slow as that old delivery boy of mine! And, BOY, was he SLOW!
I'm stronger and faster than you could ever hope to be, Grandpa!
SWOOP!
Heh! Like beans you are!

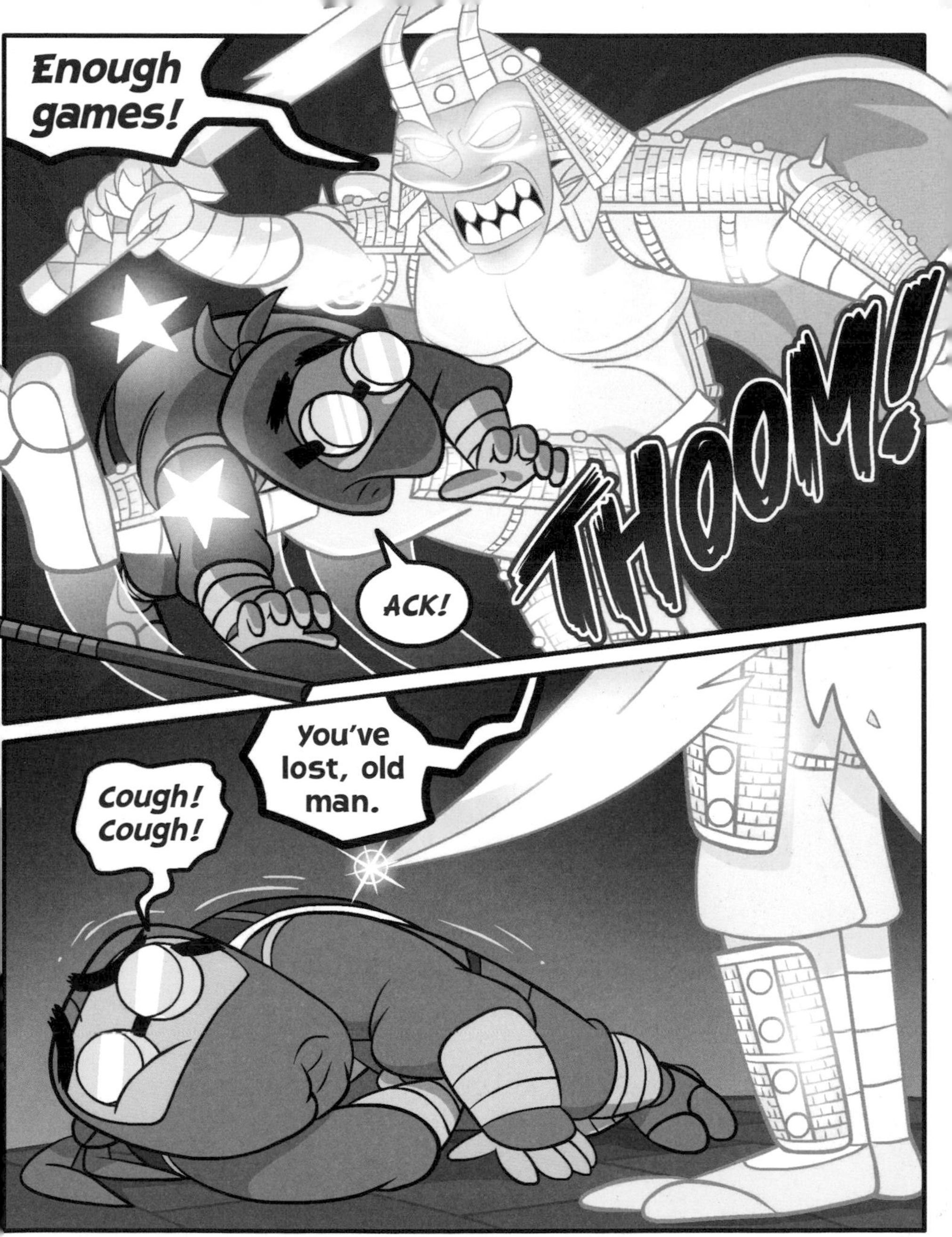
Enough games!
ACK!
THOOM!!
You've lost, old man.
Cough! Cough!

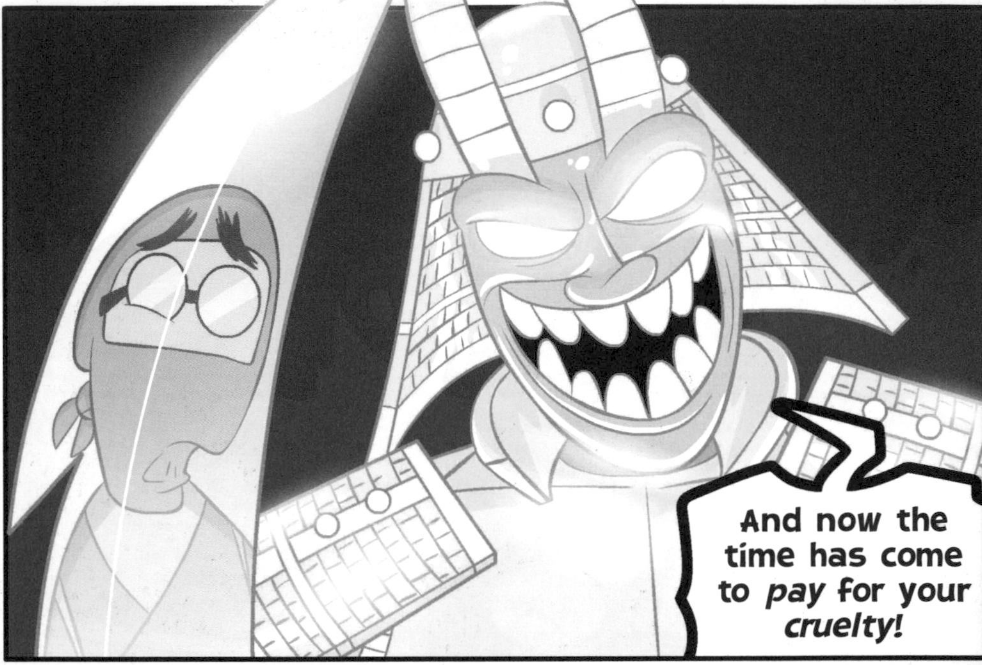
And now the time has come to *pay* for your *cruelty!*

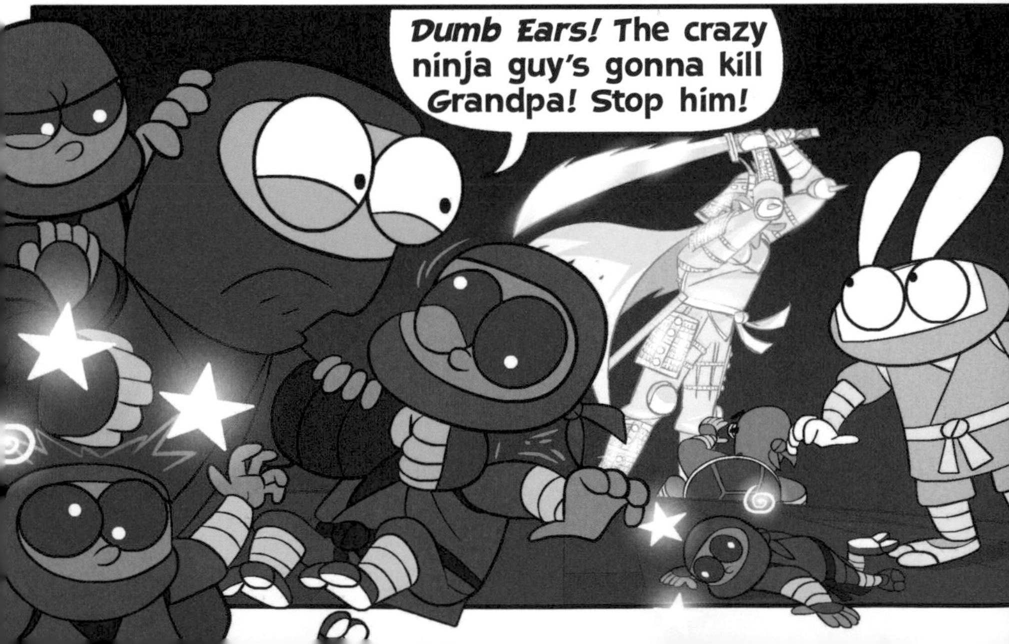
Dumb Ears! The crazy ninja guy's gonna kill Grandpa! Stop him!

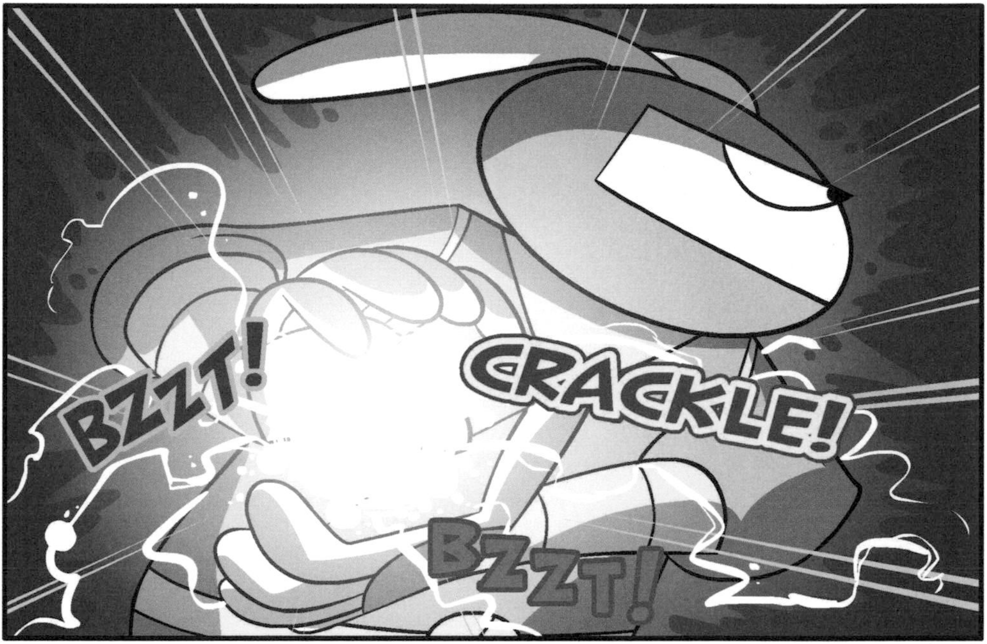
BZZT!
CRACKLE!
BZZT!

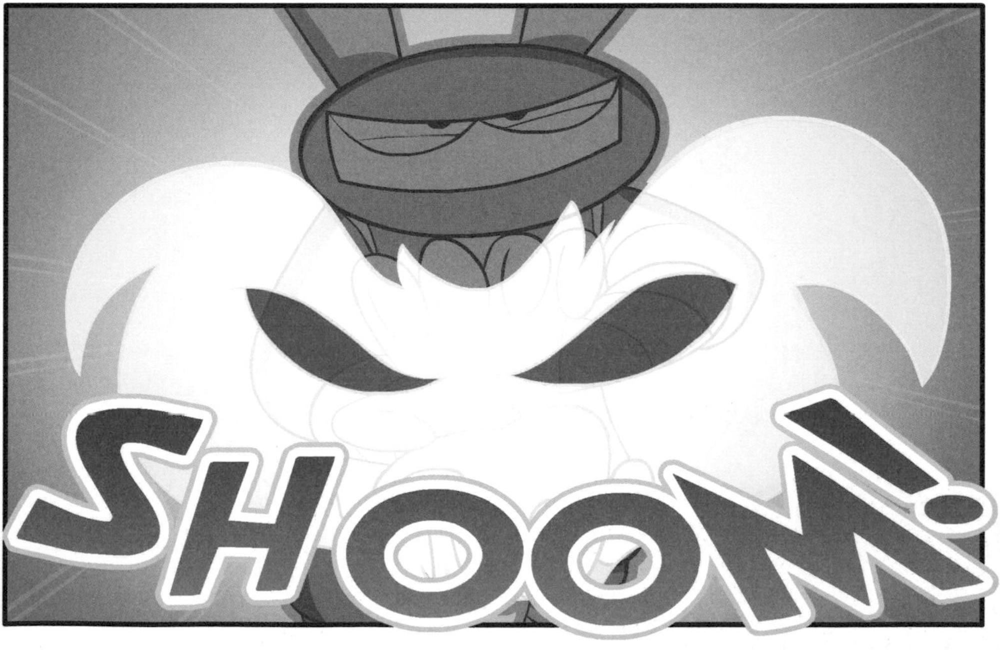
SHOOM!

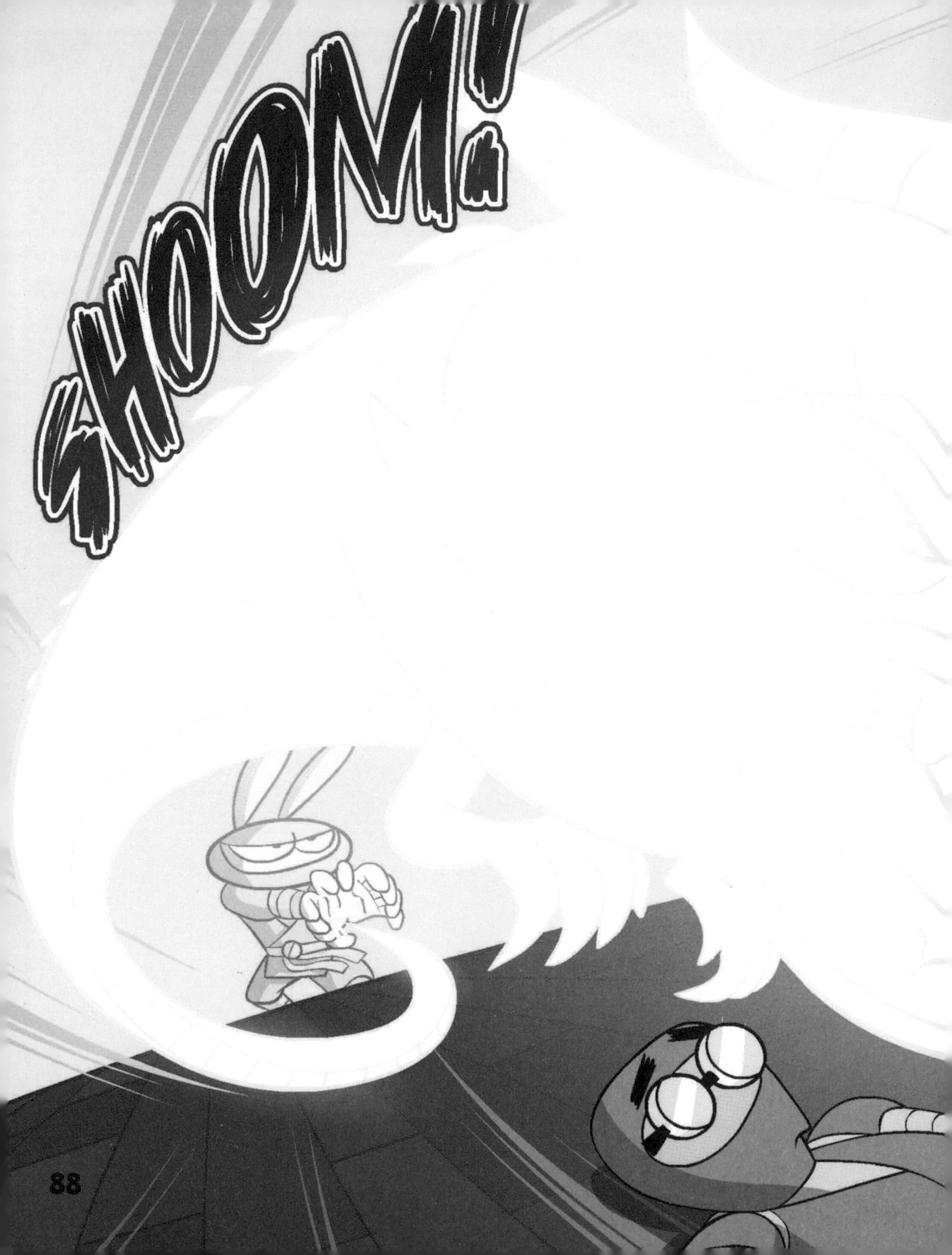
SHOOM!

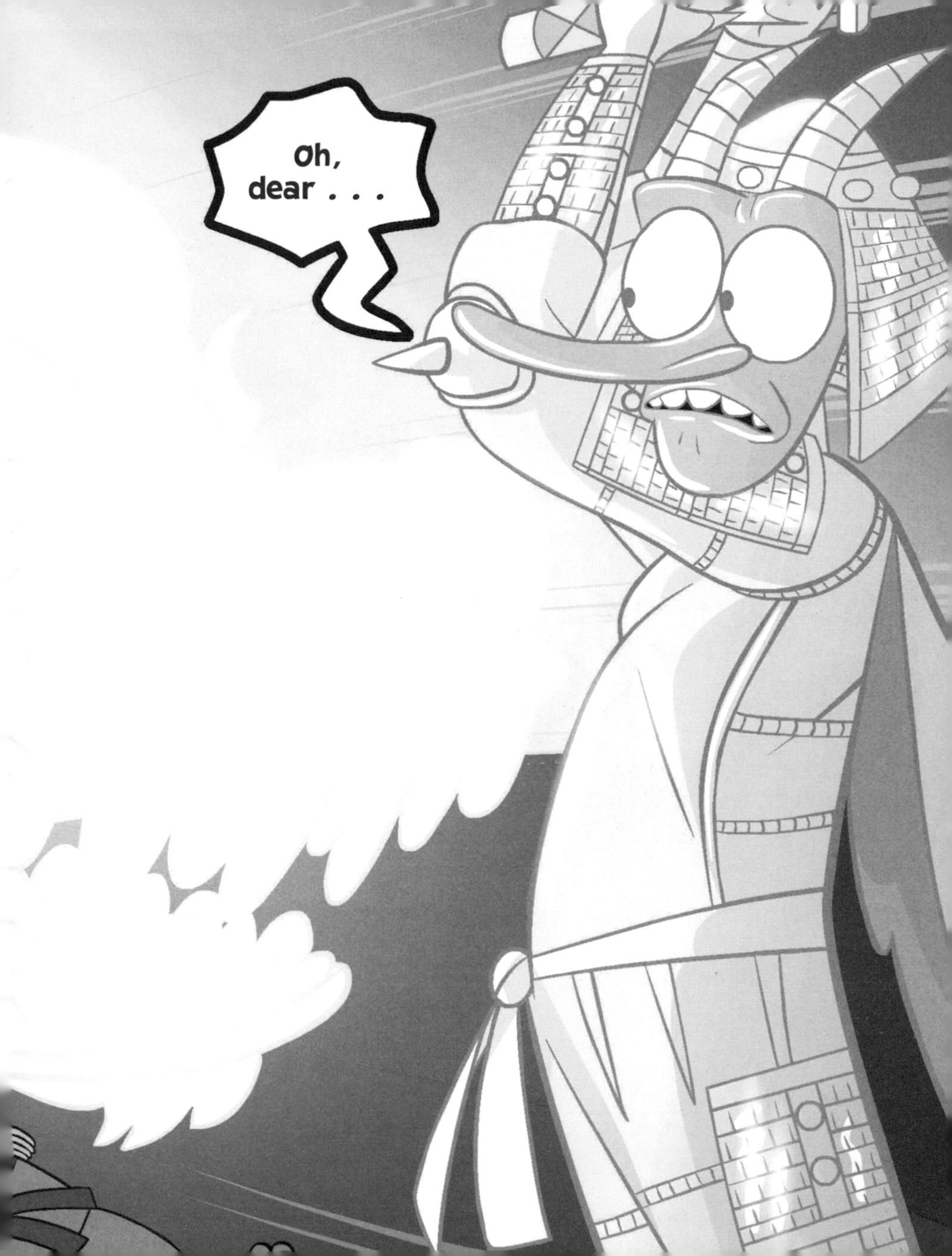
Oh, dear . . .

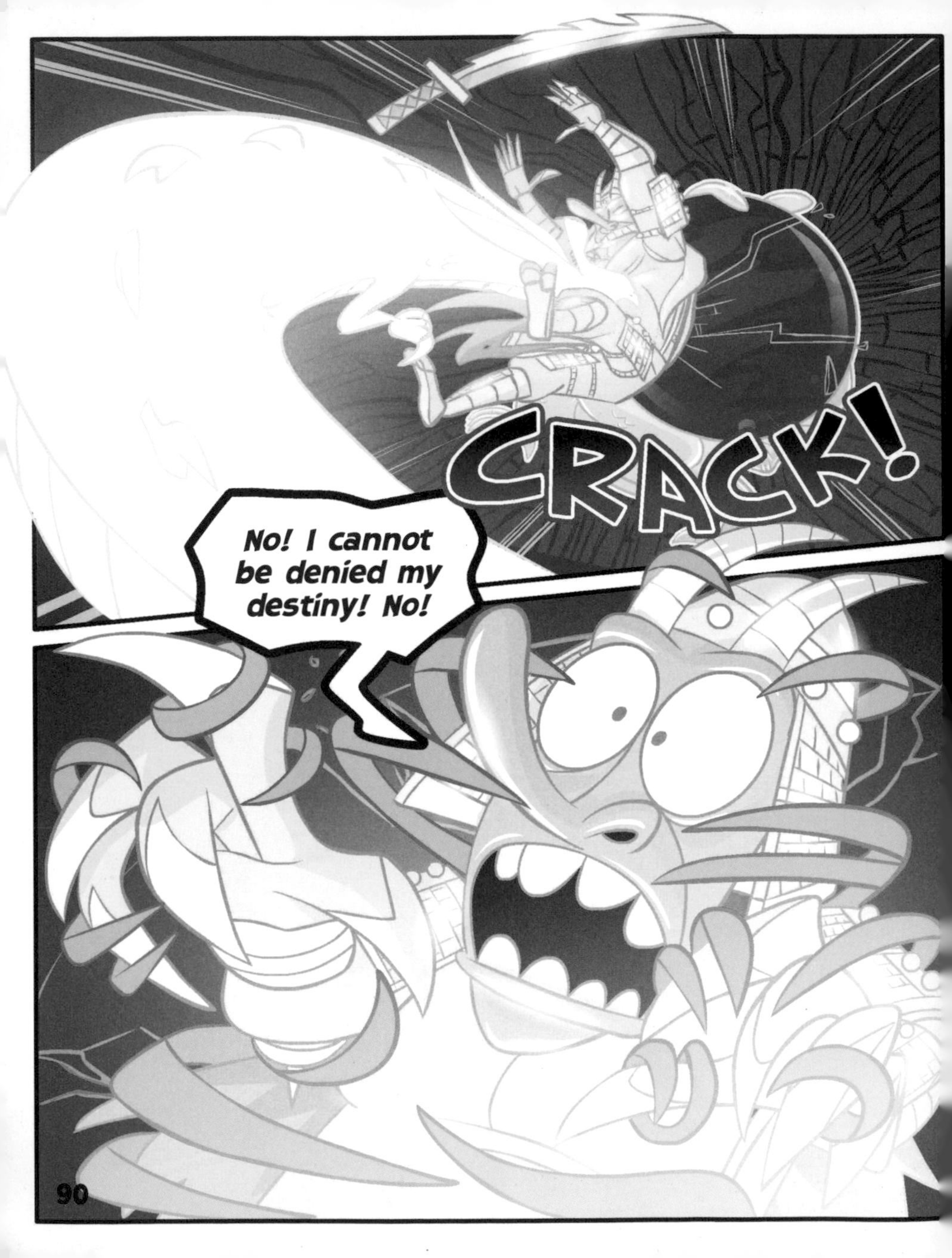
CRACK!
No! I cannot be denied my destiny! No!

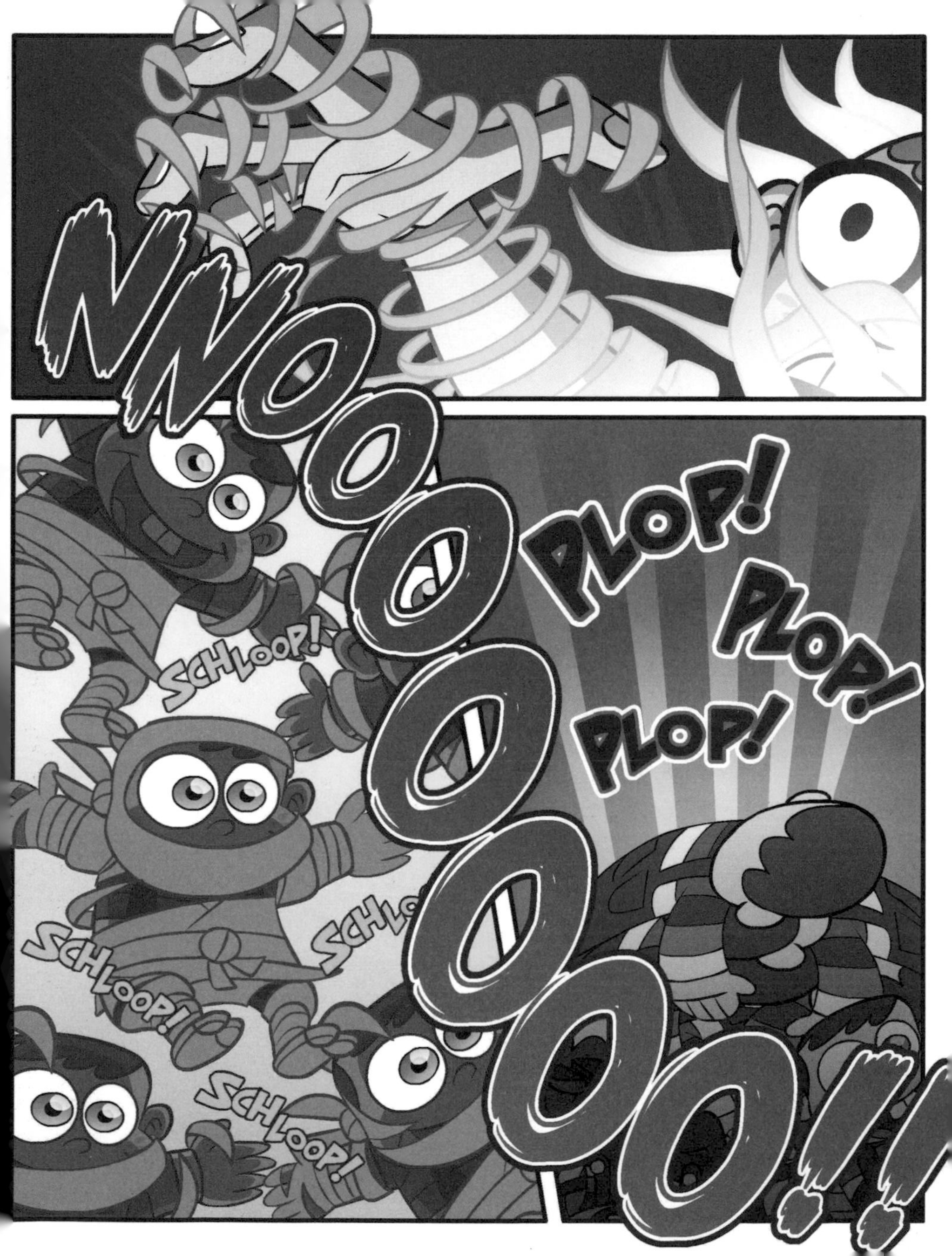
NNOOOOOOOOOOO!!!
PLOP!
PLOP!
PLOP!
SCHLOOP!
SCHLO
SCHLOOP!
SCHLOOP!

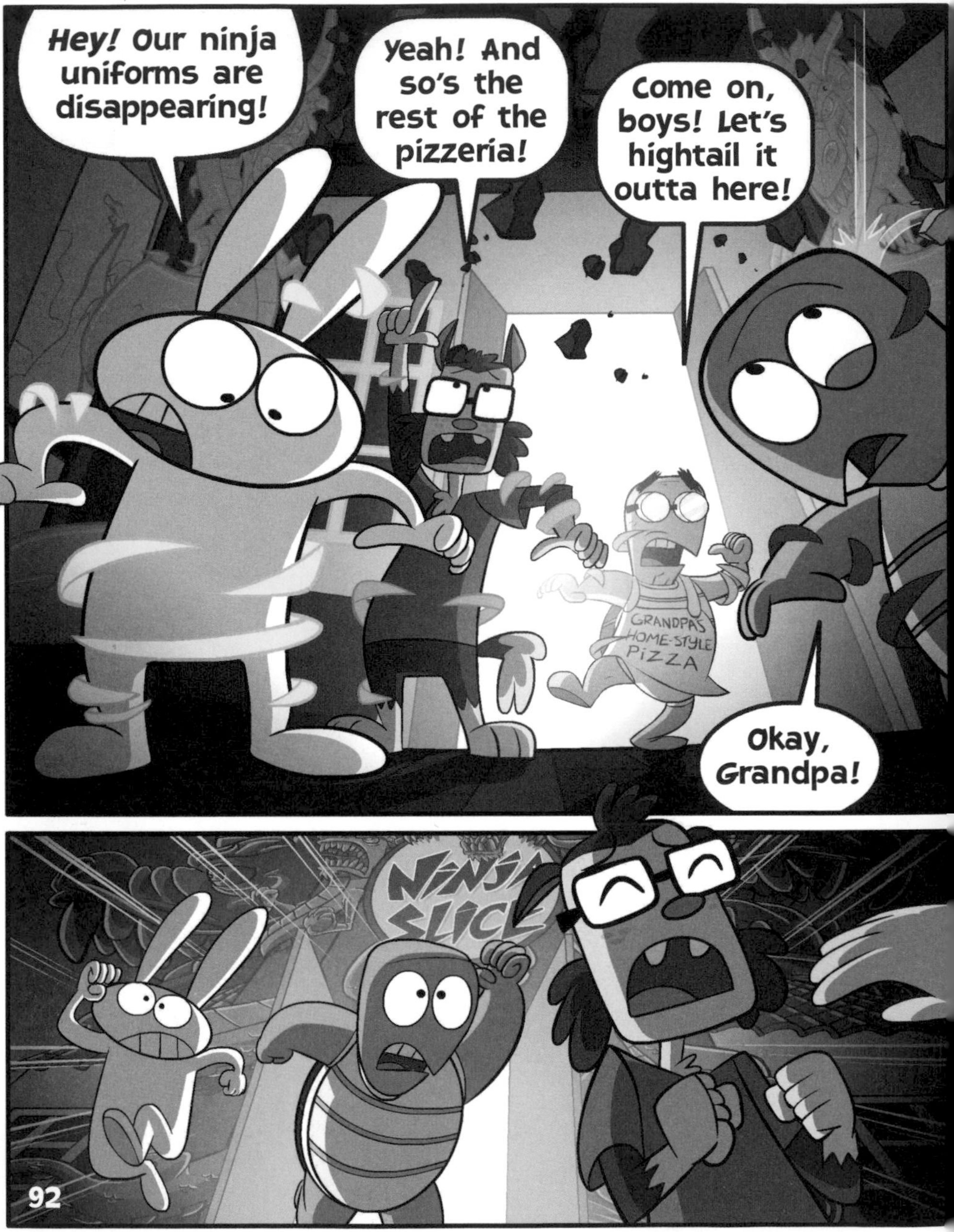
Hey! Our ninja uniforms are disappearing!
Yeah! And so's the rest of the pizzeria!
Come on, boys! Let's hightail it outta here!
GRANDPA'S HOME-STYLE PIZZA
Okay, Grandpa!
NINJA SLICE

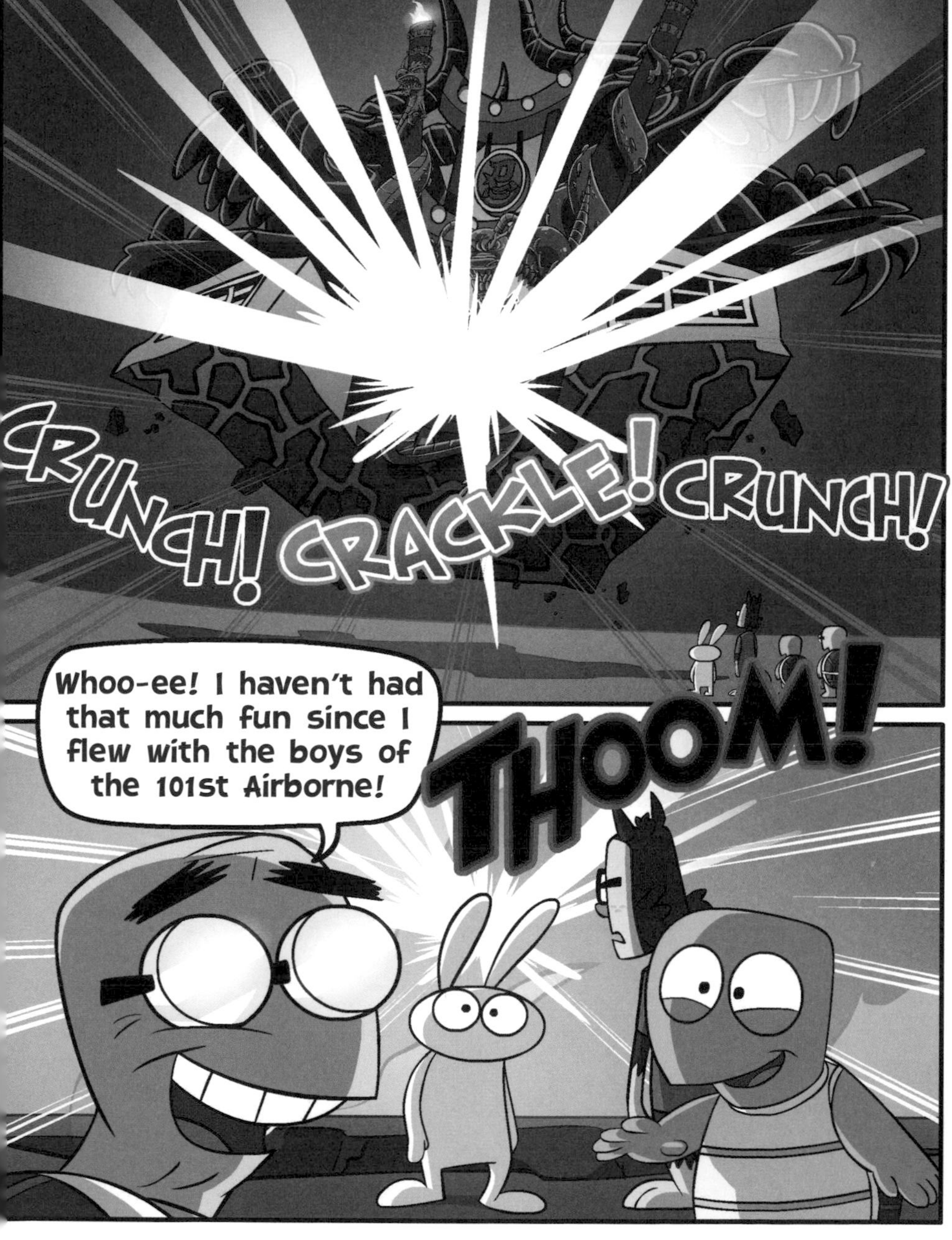
CRUNCH! CRACKLE! CRUNCH!
Whoo-ee! I haven't had that much fun since I flew with the boys of the 101st Airborne!
THOOM!

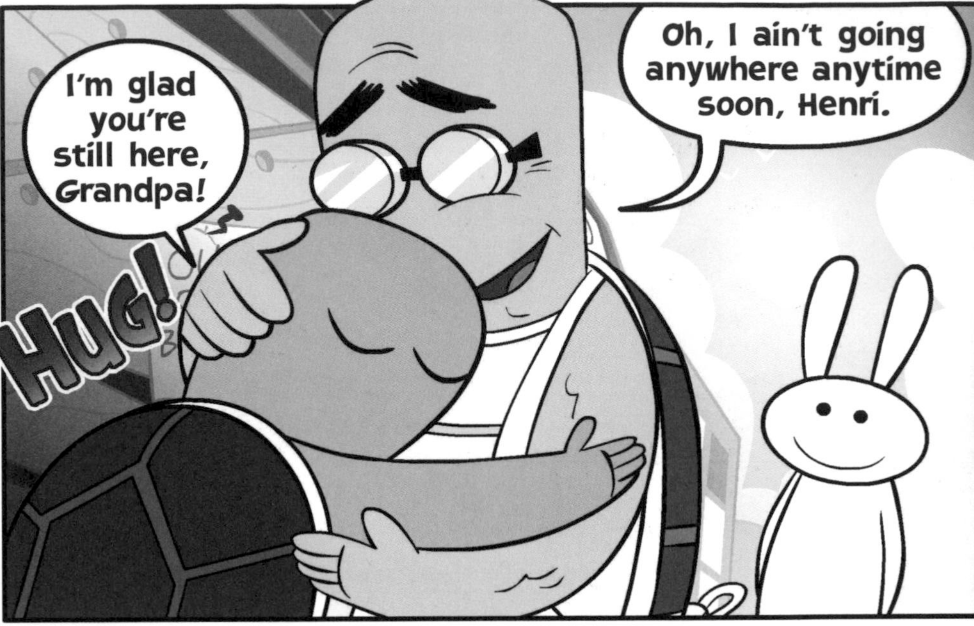
I'm glad you're still here, Grandpa!
Oh, I ain't going anywhere anytime soon, Henri.
HUG!

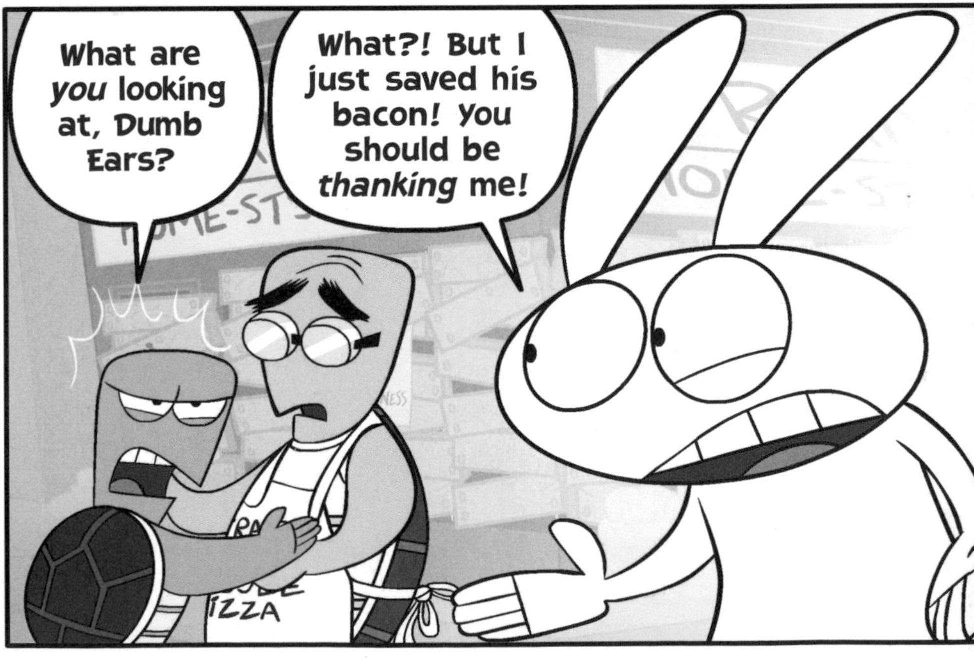
What are *you* looking at, Dumb Ears?
What?! But I just saved his bacon! You should be *thanking* me!

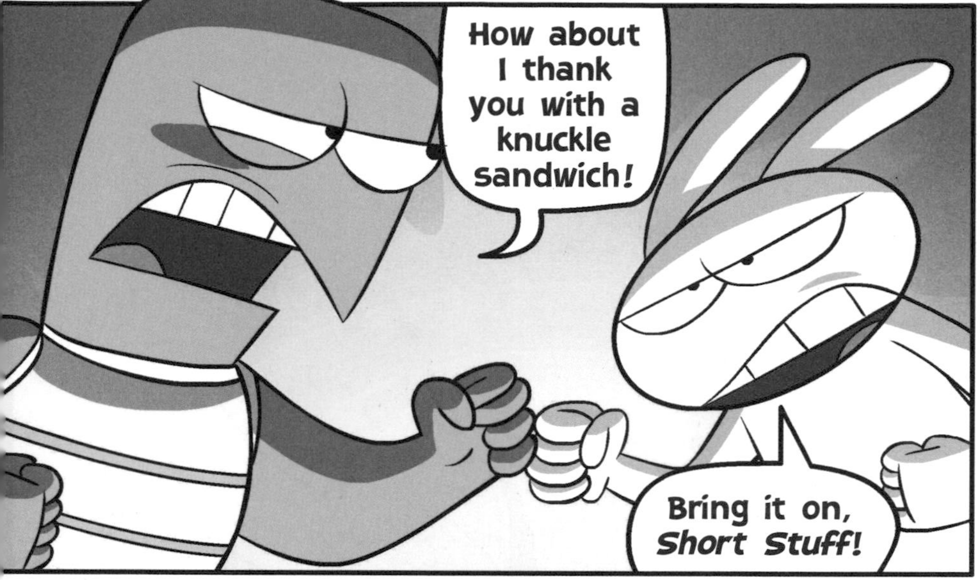
How about I thank you with a knuckle sandwich!
Bring it on, *Short Stuff*!

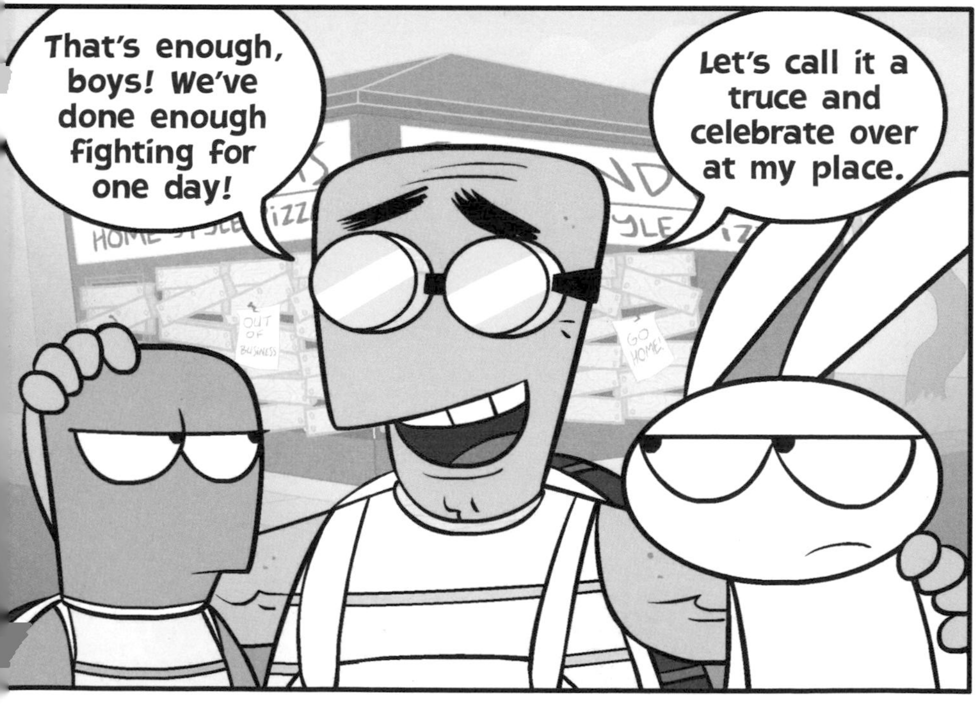
That's enough, boys! We've done enough fighting for one day!
Let's call it a truce and celebrate over at my place.
OUT OF BUSINESS
GO HOME!

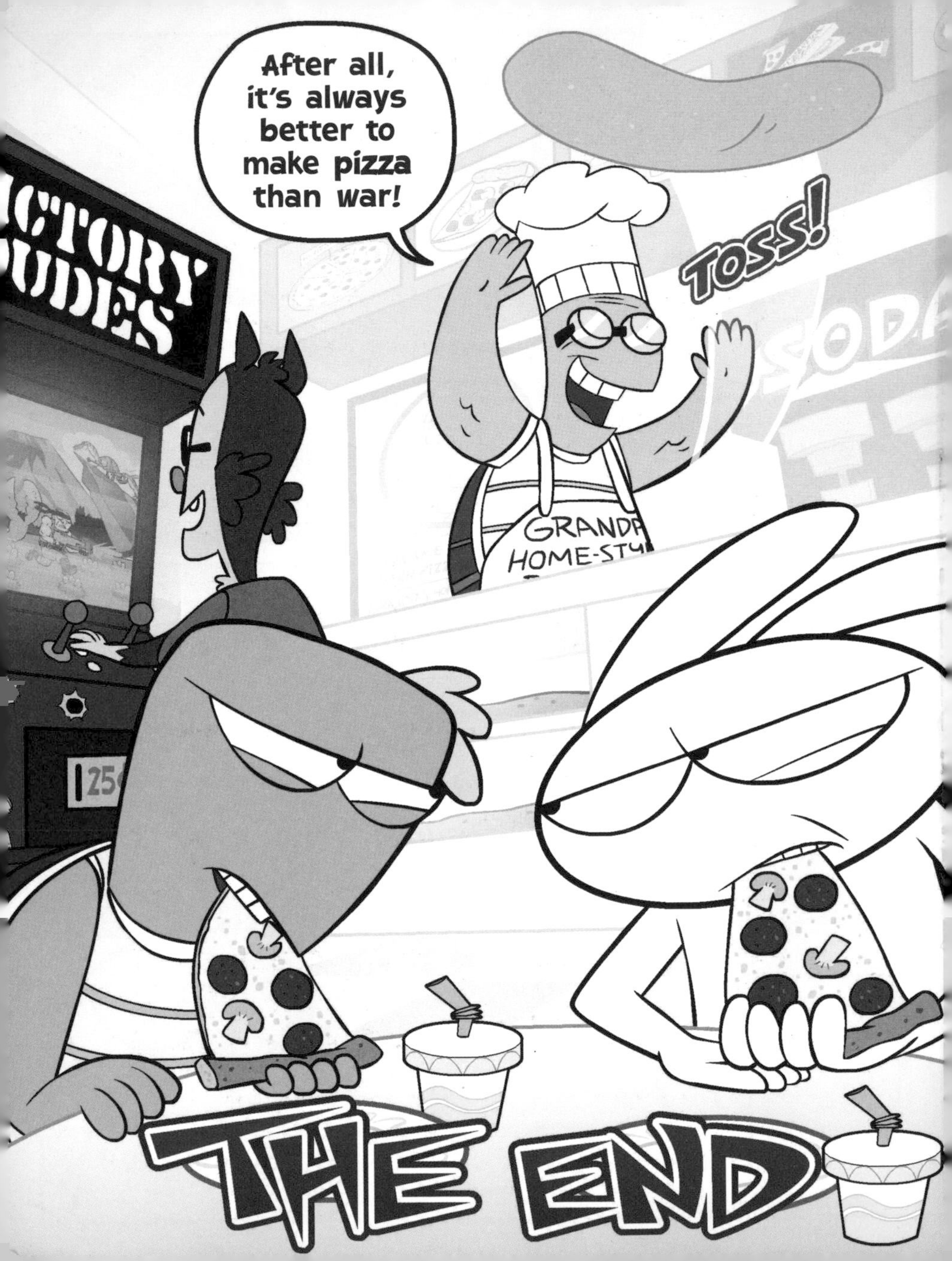
After all, it's always better to make pizza than war!
TOSS!
CTORY
UDES
GRAND
HOME-STY
SODA
THE END